Trigger

David Swinson

MULHOLLAND
BOOKS
HODDER

First published in Great Britain in 2019 by Mulholland Books
An imprint of Hodder & Stoughton
An Hachette UK company

2

A CIP catalogue record for this title is available from the British Library

Trade Paperback ISBN 978 1 473 61822 0
eBook ISBN 978 1 473 61823 7

Printed and bound in Great Britain by Clays Ltd, Elcograf S.p.A.

Hodder & Stoughton policy is to use papers that are natural, renewable
and recyclable products and made from wood grown in sustainable
forests. The logging and manufacturing processes are expected to
conform to the environmental regulations of the country of origin.

Hodder & Stoughton Ltd
Carmelite House
50 Victoria Embankment
London EC4Y 0DZ

www.hodder.co.uk

For my mother and father

To love means loving the unlovable. To forgive means pardoning the unpardonable. Faith means believing the unbelievable. Hope means hoping when everything seems hopeless.

—*G. K. Chesterton*

Fear is a man's best friend.

—*John Cale*

Trigger

ONE

I never count the days. Why would I want to know how long it's been since I quit? It's only a reminder of what it is I'm trying to let go of. I loved the fucking lifestyle. I loved cocaine. Didn't want to let it go. I still have cravings. Pops in my head like it's a good thing, visit from an old friend, but all I got to do is remind myself of why it is I quit—because of all the people I hurt, even got killed. And yes, it is something I did for me, too, but not for the reasons you might think.

Sometimes what gets me through the day is doing what I'm best at.

It still gives me a rush, even more so without the cocaine high. You realize how reckless it is. Just how dangerous.

I slip on my tactical gloves, grab my suit jacket from the front seat, step out of the car. I put the suit jacket on, reach back in to take my backpack. I shoulder it and lock the car door.

The house I'm going to is up the street, second from the corner, an unattached, paint-peeled, light-blue two-story with a large patio.

I ring the doorbell. Wait. Ring again. Open the storm door and knock on the door a few times.

When enough time passes so I feel comfortable, I take the tactical pry bar out of my backpack, wedge it in between the door and the frame, about half an inch below the dead bolt. I smack the heavy flattop of the handle hard with the palm of my hand, and with one solid push inward, I pry the door open, bending the dead bolt out with the door.

I scan the area, slip the pry bar back in my pack, and enter. Once inside I stand and listen, then secure the backpack over my shoulders and quietly shut the door. There's a fold-up chair leaning against the wall beside a filthy sofa. I take the chair and prop it against the door to keep it closed.

My stun gun is clipped to my belt at the small of my back. My Glock 19 is in a holster on my right side, but I don't want to have to use it unless I find myself facing another gun. I'd figure out a good story after. That's why the stun gun is preferable. Saves me having to think up a good story.

I've known about the occupants of this house since I was a detective working narcotics. It's low-level. Detective Al Luna, my former partner at Narcotics Branch, and I hit it a couple of times. Sent a CI in to make a buy, then drafted an affidavit in support of a search warrant and rammed the door in the next day. A good quick hit, and we always got enough to make us look good when other work was slow. Luna's still on the job. Me? Well, that's another story.

Nothing has changed with how the boys in this house operate, except a couple of new faces that replaced the two who are doing a bit of time. They're working the same park area a couple blocks north of here, where some of the local drunks and junkies still hang, but not near as many as back in the day. Gentrification has seen to that, pretty much cleaned everything up. Lot of the dealers had to change up their game. These guys didn't have enough sense to. From what I've been able to learn, they haven't been hit by the police in a while. That can be good for me.

What has changed is who the boys cater to and all the homes in this neighborhood, once vacant shells, now worth a million bucks. They're dealing mostly to young clean-cut men and women who drive nice cars with Virginia tags and consider themselves social users, pulling up and making their deals without stepping out of the cars. Times change. Old street junkies die or go to jail for getting caught up in something bad. The boys gotta move up if they wanna make a living.

My cell phone vibrates inside my blazer's inner pocket. Nearly sends me through the roof. I don't pull it out. Instead I just let it go to voice mail.

This house is messy and still has that bad-breath-after-a-night-of-hard-drinking smell. A few of those empty Moet bottles on the floor and empty beer cans stuffed with cigarette butts have probably been there since Luna and I were here last. Gets me to wondering if they still keep their stash and money in the same spot.

I walk up the stairs to the room and that old spot.

Fuck. Sure enough they do. In the inner pockets of a couple of winter jackets hanging in the bedroom closet. I pull out baggies containing a good amount of zips with heroin, crack, and what looks like meth. All dimes and quarters, and a few larger. Fortunately, no cocaine. That'd be too much of a temptation. But that's why I targeted this spot. I was pretty sure they weren't selling that shit. I go through a couple more jacket pockets, and then, *oh fuck,* a baggie with about an ounce of powder. The wrong side of my brain starts to work me, and I say to myself, *Take it. Recreational purposes only. I can control it.*

Who am I kidding? I put it with the rest of the drugs. My cell vibrates again. I let it go to voice mail again. I'm not going to jinx this shit by pulling it out.

I find a wad of money in another coat pocket. Doesn't look like more than a couple thousand. Small bills, rolled up and secured with one rubber band. I stuff it into my empty left pants pocket. Nice bulk there.

I search the rest of the room and find a little more cash, a couple boxes of 9mm ammo, cheap rounds, only good for the range. I leave them and open the nightstand drawer. There's an older-model 9mm Taurus sitting on top of some other loose rounds.

I pick it up, drop the mag, let it land on the floor, then lock the slide back. A chambered round flips out, but I catch it, put it on the nightstand. I pull out the barrel and take the spring out. Pocket it, grab the mag, and put the gun back together. I leave the live round on the table and slip the gun in my pack.

I do a quick search of the rest of the house, but don't find shit.

I take the narcotics to the upstairs bathroom, break the baggies open, and drop the contents into the toilet, along with all the little zips. I flush, wait for the reserve tank to fill. Flush again. Wait a bit longer to make sure nothing pops up, then flush one more time. I grab the baggie of coke and quickly pour the lovely white powder into the toilet, too. Damn, that's hard, but I passed the test. Again. How many more tests before I don't have to worry about failing?

This is what I do.

Two

C louds are high, moving over the city slow. Smells like snow.
    On the way to the car, I toss the Taurus spring into a gutter drain, try to be discreet when I pull the gun out of my pack, drop it at my feet, and kick it into the drain.

After I start the car, I check the phone, see who called.

Leslie.

Damn.

Haven't talked to her in more than a year. Don't wanna think about that morning we last talked. I was so fucked up. I fucked up. I can't even remember most of what was said. She kicked me out of her house after, so it must have been bad. One of the worst days of my life. Losing her was. It's the hardest thing I've ever had to go through, even tougher than giving up blow. That shit was the reason I lost her to begin with. After I got myself four months clean, I called her and confessed and asked for forgiveness. Didn't matter. I think it made it worse 'cause I lied for all those years, even about why I had to retire from the police department—pissing dirty. According to her, I'd even jeopardized her law practice. So that was that.

What does she want now, after all this time?

She left a message on the second call. I hesitate to listen, but tap the screen, put the phone to my ear.

"I'm calling on behalf of Al Luna. It's important, so please call me back."

That's it.

On behalf of Al?

What kinda message is that, unless he's in trouble or sick? Al's still one of my closest friends, but I haven't talked to him in a few weeks. I was caught up in this bullshit domestic-violence, cheating-husband case that was resolved just yesterday. In fact, Al's busier than me, working that same Narcotics Branch assignment from when we were partnered and I went down, forced into early retirement.

Best thing to do is drive home, catch my damn breath, and call her from there.

Three

Once inside, I lock the door behind me, hang up my jacket, and go to the kitchen to pour myself a Jameson on ice. It's still early, but for me it's never too early.

In the laundry room I slide open the secret wall panel on the side of the washer and place the wad of money from the house I hit on a shelf beside several stacks of ones, fives, tens, and twenties that're bound tight with red rubber bands. I always pocket the hundreds that I find. I'll count this wad later. Need to call Leslie back first.

Back in my armchair I consider lighting a cigarette but decide against it. Too much of a trigger. Always makes me want. I'm stronger, but weakness is always trying to find a way in.

I swear I stare at the cell phone for more than ten minutes before I decide to return Leslie's call. Then—

"Leslie Costello's office," a receptionist answers. Not the voice I remember for the woman who used to work for Leslie. And damn, Leslie didn't even call from her direct line. I go straight to the receptionist.

"Frank Marr returning Leslie's call," I advise her.

"One moment please."

I take a breath.

"Hello, Frank." She answers evenly—professionally.

Aside from the tone, she sounds like the same person, but lacking a certain once-shared familiarity. May as well have answered with "Hello, Mr. Marr."

"Hi, Leslie. Sorry it took so long. I was working something."

No response.

"I didn't want to call you," she begins matter-of-factly. "It was Al's decision."

"What's going on? Is he okay?"

"He's in some trouble—"

"What kind of trouble?"

"He was involved in a shooting. Doesn't look good."

"What the—did he get hurt?"

"No. He's on administrative leave, though. Just listen for a second. You know the police shooting—a sixteen-year-old kid in Northwest, near Howard?"

"No. I don't watch the news anymore. But damn..." Because I know what's going to come next.

"He was the cop who shot the kid."

"Fuck."

"The department determined that it was a bad shooting. No gun on the kid, but Luna swears there was. He said the kid pointed it right at him. That's why he wants you."

"Of course. Anything. So you're representing him, then?"

"Yes, and you're not my first choice for investigator."

"You sorta made that clear, Leslie. I got it a long time ago. So why didn't Luna call me himself?"

"That's something you'll have to ask him."

"Is he home?"

"I believe so. There's a lot of media attention on this, but the department has managed to keep his name out of it for now. But that won't last. We both know how it goes."

"I'm going over there now."

"I'll meet you there."

"What, I need a babysitter?"

"Yes," she says a little too firmly.

Four

Luna lives in Northeast DC, near Catholic University, an older home on a small one-way street off Michigan Ave. It has a large front porch. We used to sit there on rickety old rattan chairs after a hard day's work, smoking cigars and drinking good scotch. Luna liked the good stuff. Still does.

Lot of families living in his neighborhood now. Not like when he bought it in the early nineties. There were a couple of good families then, long since passed, though. It used to be a rough area, but that's why he could afford it on a cop's salary. Hell, that's why I could afford my house on 12th Street, in Northwest. We still got our problems in both neighborhoods. That's the price you gotta pay if you want to live in DC.

The shades in his front window are pulled down. The patio light is on, even though it's daytime. Can't tell if he has any lights on inside, and I don't see his car, but then he's had a take-home vehicle for as long as I can remember. I'm sure the department took that back along with his badge and gun.

When I'm about to hit the steps that lead to his front door, I notice a cab pull to the curb.

Leslie steps out, carrying an expensive-looking teal-colored briefcase and sporting a gray three-button overcoat.

Damn, she looks nice.

I wait for her by the steps. "Hello, Leslie. You look good."

"Fuck you."

I shoot her an uncomfortable smile. *Was that necessary?*

"Is this how it's going to be? 'Cause it's getting awkward, and I'm here for Al. So, can you try to forget what I can't even remember?"

"That's what the problem is. But yes, because I'm here for Al, too. And I got it out of my system with the 'Fuck you,' so that's that."

"Okay, then."

I allow her up the steps first, then follow.

She rings the doorbell. After a few seconds, she rings again.

"You sure he's home?" I ask.

"No, but like I said, I know he's been keeping a low profile. I don't know where else he could be."

I open the glass security door, knock a few times on the front door.

"Al, it's Frank and Leslie! Open up!"

A moment later I hear footsteps on a creaking wooden floor approach the front door. Then we hear the dead bolt unlock.

Door opens.

Al's wearing baggy jeans and a T-shirt it looks like he's been sleeping in for a few days. His face is a week's worth of scruff.

"Come in," he says, his voice throaty. He backs away from the door to give us room. "Good to see you, Frank."

He manages a slight smile. I can smell the alcohol on his breath. Something peaty, probably his go-to, Laphroaig.

"You too, my friend."

We enter. He closes the door. Dead-bolts it.

I notice a blanket and pillow on the sofa. Been sleeping there. Probably his comfort spot, trick the mind into thinking it's a nap and you fall asleep faster. I also spot the nearly empty bottle of Laphroaig on the end table at the pillow side of the sofa, an empty tumbler beside the bottle as well.

"Sorry about the mess," he says, tries to straighten up the sofa.

"Don't worry about that, Al," Leslie says.

He scoots the blanket in a pile by the pillow and sits beside it. I take the recliner, and Leslie sits on the cleared-off side of the sofa, next to him.

Like I said, it's an older house. It smells like an old house. Not a terrible smell. Old wood. Your grandmother's place maybe.

He starts to get up again, says, "Oh, can I get you anything? I can make coffee."

"No. Sit down," Leslie tells him, like a polite order.

He obeys.

Damn, he's looking frail. Probably hasn't been eating, just drinking. I wanna say something, but I don't.

"Well, Frank," he says, turning to me. "You want I should tell you the story?"

FIVE

Al lifts the bottle of Laphroaig toward us like an offering.

"No thank you, Al," Leslie says.

It's early. Still, I wouldn't mind. But doesn't look like there's enough in that bottle to go around so—

"Me either, but thanks."

He looks at the bottle, then at me, and says, "I got another bottle," as if reading my mind.

I consider it, but don't want to piss Leslie off. This is a job.

"No thanks, bro."

He pours what remains in the bottle into the tumbler, nearly fills it to the edge.

Takes a careful sip.

"The kid had a fucking gun, Frank." He tells me direct.

"Talk to me."

A hefty sip this time, and a pause after, because he's either savoring it as it goes down or trying to figure where to start.

"You fill Frank in about any of this?" he asks Leslie.

"No. Just that it was a kid and it happened near Howard."

"I'm telling ya, I don't know what the hell happened to the gun."

"Tell Frank what happened."

"I was at that spot off Sherman Ave. You know, the place you and I used to meet our CIs at?"

"Yeah."

"Won't be able to use it much longer with all that construction going on. Shit." Sips his scotch. "So, when we're done talking, my CI steps out of the car. I watch the CI walk off. It was a little after sixteen hundred hours. Traffic was already heavy, and I was working evening. No rush. Right? I step out to smoke a cigar. That's when I hear someone walking on the gravel behind me. I turn, see this young kid standing at the back end of a trailer, just looking at me. He was wearing a puffy jacket. When he saw that I saw him, he stepped up like a challenge, pointing what looked like a gun at me. I thought I was about to get robbed. My take-home doesn't look like anything a cop would drive, so I figure that's what this dope is gonna attempt. I step around the car toward the rear to get a better view. That's when I see he's closer and holding a gun in his right hand, stretched out and pointed at me. I draw my weapon, quickly move to a position behind my vehicle where I have better conceal-ment, but I can still see him. He starts walking toward me. I don't think he saw me take my gun out. I yell out, 'I'm the police!' And for him to drop his weapon. I have mine with sights on him at this point. He has to see the gun. He's like twenty-five yards away. I keep repeating for him to stop and drop the weapon. He says some-thing, but I don't understand. He just stands there, fucking aiming at me. I shoot. Don't remember how many times. It was fast, but slow, you know what I mean?"

I nod, 'cause I do.

"He drops to the ground. My slide is locked back. Didn't realize I had fired so many rounds. Empty magazine, so I get down behind the tire, drop and reload, scoot around the rear of the vehicle, and get a bead on him. He's still on the ground. I scan the area. Don't see anybody else. I slowly make my way toward him, still calling out commands for him not to move. I notice that his right hand is under his lower torso. Fell on it. Can't see his gun anywhere. 'Must've been under him,' I thought to myself. I had my weapon right on him."

He pauses, reaches for the tumbler and takes another heavy swig.

Still holding the glass, he looks at me and continues. "I get up over him, nudge him on the shoulder with my shoe. Doesn't move. I didn't want to check his carotid. Too much blood. I move around him, his hand still tucked under his belly. I scan the area. 'My fucking radio,' I thought to myself. 'I forgot my fucking radio in the car.' I get my cell out with my free hand and dial nine one one. I ask for an ambulance, too. I get back behind my car, still keeping an eye on the kid, and wait for the backup."

Couple more sips. He doesn't continue. Goes blank for a moment.

"What next?" I ask him.

"Homicide arrived fast, and so did EMT. EMT called it on the scene. Dead. When they rolled him over, they didn't find his gun. I knew it had to be somewhere, maybe tossed under the trailer or one of the construction trucks. Everyone was searching the perimeter. Never found it."

"Did they identify the suspect?"

"No ID, but couple days later, the homicide detective that was on the scene, she came over to ask if I knew anyone by the name of Arthur Taylor. I said I did not, and then she showed me the death photo, see if he looked familiar. I said only when he was about to shoot me. Other than that, I never seen him before."

I notebook the name and ask, "Any construction surveillance cameras found on or around the lot?"

"Nothing on that lot," Leslie says, "and the ones they were able to locate didn't reveal anything. It was blocked by the trailer."

"Besides, Frank, you know that's why I use that spot for my meets—no surveillance cameras on the lot. Last thing I wanted was to get one of my CIs caught on camera."

"And you said you scanned the area after he was down, didn't see anyone?"

"Didn't see anyone, but that doesn't mean shit."

"When you took cover to reload, how long do you think it was that you lost sight of the suspect?"

"I don't know. Couldn't have been more than a couple of seconds. I was quick."

"But still, you didn't have eyes on him for a bit?"

"No."

"And you didn't hear anything?"

"No, Frank," he tells me like he's getting irritated. "Homicide and then IA asked all the same questions you asked. In fact, that's what I figured—that he had his boys in the area and they scooped the gun up after he went down. Only thing I can think of. You remember when we first came on, Frank, and that happened to an officer in Southeast."

"Yeah, in the middle of a street, and that kid shot back. The officer also saw the boys who ran out after, even shot at the one who picked up the gun and got away with it."

"What are you saying?"

"Don't mean it like that. They had good evidence that it went down the way the officer said it did, including gun residue on the shooter's hand."

"You don't think it went down the way I said it did?"

"I'm not suggesting that. The other shooting shows that it has happened before, and it's why I know you're telling the truth. You could have made that part up—that you saw one of his boys take the gun from the scene. But you didn't."

"Hell no. I wouldn't lie. I honestly thought about it, but then, what if the shooting was caught on some off-sight surveillance camera."

"You did right," I say.

"Yeah, but look where it got me."

Six

It's still a battle. Never meant to suggest that it was ever easy. Some-
times comes to me just like that. No trigger that I can think of.
Unless sitting here interviewing Al is a trigger. Regardless, I do think
about how nice it'd be to go to the bathroom, have a couple of bumps.
Be like waking up. Again. I do want that feeling back. But I look at
Leslie, and I realize the collateral damage. And shit, she's the least of it.

"I assume IA knows why you were there?"

"Of course. Why else would I be there?"

"You talk to your CI since the shooting?"

"No. 'Sides, it has my cell, and I would've gotten a call if sh——it
had seen anything."

We always refer to informants as *it,* even in the write-ups or af-
fidavits. He's been on a drinking binge for who knows how long and
slipped, giving up the gender.

"Can I talk to her?" I ask.

He looks at me sorta hard. "Why? I've been working with this CI
for years. If it had seen or heard anything, I'd get a call. That would
be some good money."

"But still, I think you need to call and make sure."

"He's right, Al. Could be a witness. Internal Affairs probably already has the subpoena ready to bring your CI in."

"Johnny Freudiger at IA said he's gonna have to do that, and I said do what you have to do. CI had walked off and was out of the area by the time it broke. Isn't a witness."

"Johnny's on this?" I ask.

"Yeah."

"At least you know you'll get a fair shake. He's good people."

"He's Internal Affairs," Al tells me. "Don't fucking kid yourself."

"He's good people," I repeat. "Listen, either you're going to call your CI, or you're going to let me or Leslie do it. Gotta rule her out as a potential witness. Also, you don't want them to think you're hiding anything."

Al doesn't call me out for suggesting the CI is female. Doesn't strike me as anything unusual. He's being by the book. Don't know why he won't call her in, though.

"I ain't hiding shit. Just trying to protect the identity of my CI. Been involved in some big cases. Last thing I want to do is fuck my CI up with all this *high-profile* shit."

"We know that," I say. "I wouldn't want to do that either."

"Fuck it. I'll call her," Al says.

"All we need is a statement. I'll talk to Johnny, get it arranged so we're the only ones that know."

"Fuck that. I talk to her, and maybe you. I ain't gonna reveal a top source to Internal Affairs. That's bullshit."

Leslie looks frustrated now.

"Let's do it your way, then," I say, knowing this is gonna go nowhere. "You hungry, Al?"

"Naw."

"Maybe you should eat something anyway," Leslie advises.

"I'll go to our spot, get you one of those Italian subs," I say.

21

"No, man. I'm good. Don't think my stomach can handle it."

I've been there, but I still forced myself to eat. I don't tell him that, though.

I'll talk to Johnny. Need to see what they've got. Probably won't tell me because Al hasn't been charged yet, and they don't have to give Leslie anything. With any luck, there won't ever be a need to.

I'm worried about Al. I know Leslie is, too. I asked him if he wanted to stay with me. He refused. Knew he would.

"Why don't you give your source a call now?" I ask him.

He nods, looks around like he forgot where he put his cell.

"Behind the bottle," I tell him.

SEVEN

T amie Darling. I sorta figured. Both Luna and I signed her up
  years back. I still work with her on occasion, mostly okeydokes
over a burner cell 'cause she has a helluva sexy voice—doesn't matter
that she's a crackhead and physically nothing more than skin and bone.
Haven't had a reason to use her for a while now, though.

I talked to her for a bit on Al's cell phone. She told me after she
met with Al, she walked down Sherman to head to the McDonald's
on Georgia Ave, when she heard what sounded like gunshots. By
that time she was only a couple of blocks away, but thought the shots
came from the area of Garfield Terrace.

She seemed genuinely concerned for Al. There's nothing odd
about that. She's been his CI for a long time. You get to know them,
even like them. Damn, I even like her, but it's not like I want to hang
with her.

Al's right, though: She's responsible for some major cases, including a couple of mine, both when I was on the job and then off.
It wouldn't be good getting her burned. I agree she has to be kept
out of it. It might not be a bad thing to talk further, when I'm on my

own, and see if she can get her ear to the track with respect to the shooting.

After I hand him his cell back, he returns it to the table and slowly pushes himself off the sofa. He walks to a corner cabinet on the other side of the living room, pulls out another bottle. A bourbon this time.

"You have to take it easy, Al," Leslie says.

"I'm good. I'll sleep it off."

He will at that. Al can throw them down. His tolerance has to be high, maybe even higher than mine. But somehow I doubt that.

He twists the cork out of the bottle and pours a generous amount into the glass, then sets the bottle on the end table beside the empty Laphroaig.

"Can you share what case you were using Tamie for?"

"C'mon, now, Frankie. I love you like a brother and trust you with my life, but you know better than to ask that."

"Yeah, I do, but still…At least tell me if it involves something that's big enough to get a hit out on you."

"You suggesting I'm stupid enough to get burned?"

"You know better than that," I say. "You also know how people talk. Things get around."

"Well, this case involves a low-level crew. I don't know if it'll go RICO or for that matter anything beyond Superior Court. But do I think they followed me to the lot, let Tamie go, and then tried to kill me? Fuck no. Bunch of clueless young corner dopes. Just kids. I think what went down was something like a gang initiation or a robbery. One or more of his boys had to be there somewhere, close enough to grab the gun when I went down to reload. That's the only thing it can be. Fucking gun didn't vanish into thin air."

"What about your partner—Jimmy?"

"What about him?"

"Why wasn't he there with you?"

"He's been on sick leave. Fucked up his shoulder. He'll probably try to stretch that shit out through Christmas. I've been working this one ten-ninety-nine."

Leslie's cell rings. She pulls it out of her briefcase, looks at the display, decides to answer.

"Yes."

Her eyes close, and her head bows. I know that look. Can't be good.

"Thanks for the heads-up, Michael. Okay. Yes. Bye."

Michael?

She disconnects, slips the phone back in, and turns to me.

"That was an associate of mine. He said there's at least a couple hundred protesters in front of police headquarters now. Media, too. Apparently, someone leaked it out that this might be a bad police shooting."

She looks over to Al's TV on an entertainment console across from where we're sitting.

"Don't even think about turning on the television," Al says. "Last thing I want to see."

"I understand," Leslie says.

"Can't keep anything wrapped up in this damn department. Always some fucking idiot...," I say.

"Shit, now I'm gonna find media on my front lawn, banging on my door?"

I stand up, walk to the living room window, open the curtain to peer out.

Nothing.

"Trust me, they'd be out there by now if your name got leaked."

"Just a matter of time," Al says.

I know he's right about that.

"Maybe you should come stay with me," I suggest again as I sit back down.

"Fuck that. I'm comfortable here."

"It may not be safe. You know how it can get," I tell him.

"They may have taken my service weapon, but that doesn't mean I don't have my own personal weapons here."

"What are you talking about? I don't think that's what Frank meant by 'not safe.'" Leslie looks alarmed and then cuts a look at me sideways.

I return the glare, but not as hard.

"Thanks, brother, but I'm staying home."

"I have to get back to the office. It's going to be a shit storm," Leslie says. "You don't go anywhere, Al."

"Does it look like I'm gonna go anywhere?"

"I'll stick around, talk to Al a bit more."

"Maybe you should come, too, meet me there," she says. She doesn't like the idea of leaving me alone with him.

"I'm going to stay."

Her lips tighten just a bit. I know that look, too.

"Stay off that bottle, Al." It's a command.

"Sure thing, Mom."

Al walks her to the door to let her out. Locks up after.

He returns, but before he can sit down, I say, "Maybe I'll have a bit of what you're having."

He smiles.

Sometimes it's best not to drink alone.

EIGHT

The department's going to be pressured into acting fast. That's why Leslie left. It's out there now, and she has to get on damage control. Not good. The media will be all over this one. No witnesses. That we know of. Just Al's word that the kid was armed. And no gun. A young black kid with no gun. That's all they need.

I believe Al. I do.

The only story that makes sense is that one or more of the decedent's boys were there, too, and one of them did snatch up the gun after. The kid was close to a trailer. One or more could have been in hiding but close enough to get to him fast. Like I said, it has been done before. More than once.

Just thinking about it gives me vertigo.

I down what remains of my glass. Al offers me more. I can't refuse. He pours generously. The buzz I get with alcohol is much different these days. It's a bit more of a downer now. I've always preferred the ups, not the downs. But what the fuck. I have to keep my mind from going off on its own. So this is better than nothing.

Al's drinking is getting out of control, but my boy needs to self-medicate. Might do something stupid otherwise. I've known him for almost as long as I've known Leslie. He was and still is my best friend. Maybe my only friend. And I might be his only friend too. Jimmy? Yeah, they're bros, but Jimmy's married and has a life outside the job. I do believe that the job is all Al has ever had, aside from me. That's why I believe him. That the kid had a gun.

Feeling trippy.

"Don't get pissed," I begin, which is never a good way to begin, "but did you have anything to drink before the shooting?"

"That doesn't piss me off. No. But you know how it is with me. There's a nice bottle tucked away in a drawer of my desk. Reserved for the end of the day or after a good hit."

"I remember those days."

"I might indulge a bit too much at home, especially now, but not like that on the job."

Yeah, Al, he sure as hell ain't nothin' like me.

Before I can finish my drink, Al nods off in a sitting-up position on the sofa. I worry for a second, but then he starts to snore, so I know he's still alive.

I nurse my drink, staring at him, or more like through him.

What do I do now? Find a blanket and tuck him in? Shit.

He's got me by ten years, and he's got almost twenty-eight years on the job now. Going for the maximum percentage before he goes out.

My old boy sitting there, slouched over, like a scarecrow that's lost all the straw in its belly, is the man who taught me most everything. He's the reason I was one of the best narcotics investigators in the department. I owe him. I often wonder if he knows why I retired early, that I was forced into early retirement. Quietly. Would he have kept it to himself if he knew I was using coke while on the job? I'd like to think he'd come to me first. Kick my ass maybe. Or at least try. I'd probably let him, too.

I stand up, reach over him to grab the bottle and pour myself a couple ounces. After I set the bottle down, I look around his living room. It's bigger than mine. The dining room is bigger, too, and opens into the kitchen, a kitchen that needs a remodel and newer appliances. Don't know how he can cook on that ancient stove.

I decide to pick up the empty bottle of Laphroaig and trash it. I walk to the kitchen, open the cabinets beneath the sink, but can't find a recycle bin, so I drop it in the regular trash next to the counter.

The kitchen's a fucking mess. I'm a good friend but not nice enough to clean this shit up. I head back to the living room.

He's snoring louder, brief pauses between, like he's lost his breath. Apnea?

I sit on the chair where Leslie was sitting, notice the slightly open end-table drawer beside the sofa where the bourbon is set. Looks like a pack of cigarettes in the drawer. Newports maybe. I open the drawer. It is a pack of Newports, and it's open. More than half the smokes gone. We used to carry those around with us on the job to offer a suspect when we were interviewing them. Doesn't smell like cigarette smoke in here, but then my nasal passages are pretty fucked up. There's an ashtray in the drawer, too, wiped clean, with just a bit of old ash sticking to the clear glass bottom where the cigarettes have been snuffed out. I pull out the ashtray and set it on the end table. I grab one of my own smokes and light it up.

A couple more sips of bourbon, and then I flick the ash of my smoke into the ashtray. That's when I notice papers in the drawer and what looks like the bottom white edges of old Polaroid photos. I gaze toward Al, 'cause I'm about to go sneaky on him.

I quietly open the drawer, a half smile on my face, like I gotta be careful or my big brother's gonna catch me going through his stuff.

There are three Polaroid pictures.

My mouth nearly drops when I notice the top one. It's Tamie

Darling naked, on top of a bed, legs spread wide, exposing her vagina, and with the index finger of her right hand, she is touching herself like she's masturbating.

It's an old photo. Has to be when we first signed her on 'cause she didn't look as bad then as she does now. She still used crack, but it hadn't been the kind of long-term usage that starts to wear at the skin and age you fast. Her face is rounder, too, maybe nineteen years old.

What the fuck, Al?

Where was this taken? Did she give it to him, or did he take it? I'm hoping the former.

I look at the other two photos. Still Tamie, but different, with equally distasteful poses. I can see the nightstand beside the bed in the last one. Looks like a Glock 17 sitting on it, under a lamp.

Fuck me.

I stand up, take the photos with me, and walk up the stairs to Al's bedroom. Same lamp on the nightstand. After all those years, he still has all the same shit. Should have at least bought a new lamp.

Fucking his CI. Is he still fucking her? Was he at the lot getting a little something on the side?

It's a good thing no one else found these, but he's still gonna catch some shit from me.

NINE

He's fallen back on the sofa now, mouth open, head resting against the wall. Gurgling out snores. I sit back in the armchair, lean forward, and smack him hard on his thigh with the palm of my hand.

Nothing.

I smack him on the cheek this time.

He pops up. I move out of the way just in time, 'cause he's about to swing at me.

"What the fuck, Frankie!"

"What the fuck, Al?" and I drop the photos on his lap.

He doesn't look at them for more than a split second and snatches them up just as quick.

"What the hell you think you're doing searching my stuff?"

"End table drawer was open, so I grabbed the ashtray. Surprise. Surprise."

"Damn, Frankie. This is ancient. I got these at a search warrant years ago."

"What? A search warrant for your own home? Damn, Al, these were taken in your bedroom."

"Now you're searching my bedroom?"

"Stop already. It's disgusting, man. How could you get with her? She was—still is—a crackhead prostitute. But that's the least of it. You fucking jeopardized every case you made with her and whatever cases we made together with her."

And who am I to speak? Hypocrite I am. I jeopardized that and more.

"You know what these photos can do to you?"

"You going to give them over?"

"Hell no. In fact, you're damn lucky I'm the one who found them."

"I didn't even remember they were there, it's been that long."

"Bullshit. Fresh pack of Newport cigarettes. Isn't that what Tamie smokes?"

"I do, too, on occasion."

"Remember who you're talking to. I know you like family."

"Sounds more like an interrogation to me."

"It could've been, if these were found by anyone else."

"You mean like Freudiger? How the hell would he have found them?"

"C'mon, Detective, you forget how to do your job? Lord forbid, but let's say you get charged. You know a good detective's gonna get a search warrant for your house to see if there's anything that might connect you with the decedent. He'd at least get it for gun parapher- nalia 'cause it was a shooting."

"Internal Affairs doesn't go all out like that. It's too much work."

"You don't remember Johnny."

He downs the rest of the bourbon, pours more after.

"You've been off the job too long, Frank."

He tries to put the photos back in the drawer.

I snatch them out of his hand.

"Hey now!"

"I'll take care of these," I snap. "Anything else like this hidden anywhere that I should know about?"

He doesn't respond fast enough.

"No, that's it."

"If there is—Tamie, some corner prostitute, or even some assistant US attorney that you fucked back in the day—get rid of that shit or give it to me and I will."

"Yeah, yeah…"

"Damn you, Al. I never would've dreamed…Fuck, I need a smoke." I light one of my own up. "So, tell me what you were meeting Tamie for."

"Honest to God, Frank. It *was* about a case. I swear."

You swear.

"If they subpoena her and she says otherwise, you're fucked. They'll consider everything you said, whatever statement you wrote, a lie. End of story. End of you."

"It was about an investigation. That's why we met." He stands firm.

"Leslie needs to know about this, just in case."

"Hell no! I don't want her seeing those photos. And just in case what?"

"Just in case it comes back to bite you some other way. This alone is the kinda shit that'll end your career, but you have this shit and a shooting they might come back saying is unjustified."

"It was a good shooting. And Tamie has nothing to do with anything. Destroy the fucking things. I don't give a shit. No one will know, especially Leslie."

"You know more than anyone that you can't trust a CI. They talk to her, who knows what she'll say. I damn well hope you've been keeping her happy."

He smiles briefly, but pulls it back after he realizes.

"Bastard," I say.

Ten

What the hell's he thinking? I wouldn't even cross that line, and trust me, there's a lot of lines I've crossed in my time.

I made Al go to his room and sleep it off. Good parent/friend I am. I lock up and decide to grab a sandwich at this deli/liquor store near my home.

On the drive there I give Leslie a call, but it goes to voice mail.

"I left Al. He's in bed sleeping it off. Call me when you can." I disconnect.

She's probably dealing with a shit storm right now, and I don't think she needs to know about the photos. I might have to tell her about the possibility of Al and Tamie still having some kinda fucked-up relationship, though. She'll need to know that in case it ever comes out. And the only way it'd ever come out is if Al admits it or Tamie gives it up, if or when she is ever interviewed by IA.

Crazy how things have changed, with me, mostly. I don't know. I would have thought giving up blow would have made me sharper, more ready to handle a crisis like this. But look at my hands on the steering wheel. I could fucking vibrate right off the driver's seat.

34

Coke would have been the thing to keep me right on these rails. Now that I'm straight, I'm a rusty ticking bomb. Luna's a trigger. Leslie's a trigger. A sandwich might do me some good. It's always been my comfort food.

I park on Columbia Road, about a block away from my spot. Been a while since I've been here for a sandwich. The old man who owns the place does have a good scotch and bourbon selection, but there's another liquor store closer to my house that I go to because I usually drink the cheaper stuff.

The top of the door hits a little bell when I step inside. It jingles, and the old man behind the counter turns. I give him a wave. He looks the same kinda old that he's always been, and I've been coming here off and on for more than twenty years. Doesn't seem to age. Never smiles, either, just a slight wave of the hand, like he's shooting from the hip.

The deli counter is across from the shelves of spirits and a few low-end wines. A young man's working the deli, his medium-length dreadlocks covered with a mesh skullcap. The glass counter is stocked with cheeses, slaws, potato salads, and deli meats. There's a whiteboard with a handwritten menu on the wall above a couple of slicers. Even though I already know what I'm gonna order, I check it out. The young man turns.

Fuck!

It hits me like a wave of heat that folds over my body. I go flush. Wanna sit down.

I know him. I mean, how could you ever forget the face of the young man you left for dead at the river?

Calvin. That's his name, but they called him Playboy.

He looks at me the same way, except he's holding a butcher knife and I can see his knuckles whiten as he tightens his grip around the handle. He looks afraid, but not the same look I remember he had when it was the fear of death at the river. Now it's something

35

more like seeing a ghost. The large counter separates us, but it doesn't ease my tension. I can easily pull my weapon before he comes around, if that's what he's fucking thinking. I'm thinking he's just as stunned as I am. And it's like a standoff. Who's going to do or say something first.

"Turkey club on wheat. No mayo," I tell him.

Playboy scrunches his face, like, *What the fuck?*

He stands there looking that way for a couple of seconds, then a side glance toward the old man behind the counter, and then back to me again.

Does he wanna call for help, tell the old man to call 911? Maybe just jump over the counter and slice my throat?

With a look and a slight shake of his head, like he's snapping out of a daydream, he simply sidesteps toward the slicer, but hesitates before setting the butcher knife down. He does, but keeps it close, with his eyes still on me. What the fuck am I supposed to say? Sorry? Hell no. He deserved worse than what he got.

He does his job. Looks pretty good at it. How long has he been here? He turn his life around 'cause I scared the fuck out of him? That wouldn't be so bad. Or maybe he's got something going here, dealing a little something on the sly. Behind the counter, slipping whatever it is he's selling in a sandwich. I hope turkey club simply means *turkey club* and I won't find a little zip containing crack between the turkey and the cheese.

I watch him carefully as he makes the sandwich, make sure he doesn't spit on it or drop something bad inside. Who knows what. He places the sandwich on a square of deli paper, cuts it in quarters like he means business, and wraps. A little tape, writes "TC" on the paper with a black felt-tip. He picks up the butcher knife. I grip my sidearm. He picks up the wrapped sandwich with his free hand and slides it over the counter to me. Waits for me to grab it.

Butcher knife through my good hand if I do?

I decide to grab it with the hand that's already damaged, so I can keep my hand on the gun.

I do.

For a second he looks like he's going to do it. I can see it in his eyes. Burning red. Even tearing a bit.

I look at him a bit hard. What do I do? Hell, what do I think he's going to do, stab my hand or call the police after I leave? He won't call the police. Something that happened more than three years ago, something I'm sure he doesn't even want the police to know about? Fuck, he was the driver of a car used in a drive-by, one that got a cop killed. Almost killed me, too. The shooter, they called him Little Monster, just took advantage of the officer being there at the same time. Two birds with one—fuck, you know what I mean. Hell, now this?

I was so fucked up back then, I can't remember why I didn't turn Playboy in. Decided to take matters into my own hands, but I couldn't finish the job, so I left him on the filthy bank of the Anacostia River. Actually believed in my head that the river would suck him back in, like an angel of God. Do the job I couldn't do. No, he ain't gonna call the police. They don't have his real name, but I'm sure they still know him as Playboy.

I gotta know what the fuck he's doing here.

I take the sandwich, walk over to the old man at the counter, and pay him. Exit.

I see him through the window as I walk, still standing there holding the butcher knife, watching me as I pass.

I'm still surprised. Still rattled. Cocaine pops into my head, not like an image or a word, but a summons. I close the door on it. No way to lock it down, though. That shit has a key to every door in my head. I turn around, make sure Playboy's not peeping out to catch where I go. I walk past my car to the next block, cross the street, and walk around the block.

A disheveled bum, with layers of clothing on, is at the corner digging through the trash. Slate-gray clouds overhead. Looks and smells like snow. I drop the bag with the sandwich in the trash, hitting the bum on the hands. He turns to give me a look.

"That's for you," I tell him. "Figured you'd rather take it outta there than from my hand."

A different kinda look this time. Maybe he agrees.

He grabs the bag and opens it. I don't stick around to see if he likes what's inside. All I know is I don't have the stomach to eat it anymore. I know Playboy didn't do anything with it, but he made it with his hands and that's enough.

I look down the street toward the storefront. When it looks clear, I hop in my vehicle.

On the way home I drive by 17th and Euclid, where it all happened. Block's empty. Couple of regular-looking folks strolling by.

The row house looks the same. Probably still a brothel. A brothel/gambling house between two well-maintained million-dollar homes. That shit'll always be here. You only need to know where to look. There was a time, before I was a cop, that I was clueless. Maybe not as clueless as the young couple I just passed, because I did have a certain edge, but still naive enough to never give a place like that row house a second glance.

I want to hit it or maybe some other stash house. It's too dangerous, though. Not for fear of being caught but of doing something stupid. The hope of finding a wonderful stash and going off on a binge.

Last thing I ever imagined was running into an animal like Playboy.

I crack the window, fire up a joint. *Get calm, Frank. Get calm.*

ELEVEN

W hen I get home, I put the photos of Tamie in a pocket of my shoulder pack. They might come in useful, but not when I talk to Tamie. That's a delicate matter, 'cause I don't want to piss her off. Last thing we need is her working against us.

I pour myself a bit of Jameson, sit on the sofa. It's not time for the local news on TV, so I go to the Fox 5 app on my iPhone. My left hand starts to shake. The result of nerve damage, getting stabbed through the palm of my hand. I massage it, but it doesn't help much. I can deal with the slight pain, but not the shaking. Makes me feel like an invalid. I hold the phone in my right hand, wait for the shakes to stop, then take a sip of my drink and check out the top stories. Of course, the shooting is the top story.

According to the reporter, at least a couple hundred people gathered in front of 300 Indiana Avenue in protest.

There is police presence, but no one in riot gear. DC police are smart enough not to incite a riot, but they sure as hell know how to handle one if it breaks.

No chief out there, though. Fucking Wightman was the deputy

chief, and now he's the man. The one with the sword over my head. He was doing his job, and him pushing me out was better than the alternative. But fuck Wightman anyway 'cause he's all about politics and catering to what that crowd is chanting out there. He sure as hell ain't gonna back up Al. It's only a matter of time before he finds out I'm the investigator working for the defense. Gonna have to watch myself on this one.

This one is close to home. Something like this hasn't happened in DC for a while. Now it involves someone I care about. I don't doubt Luna that the kid had a gun, 'cause I know Al wouldn't lie to me, but maybe he just thought the kid had a gun. How the hell am I going to work this thing? I'm gonna have to call Tamie Darling. But first I want to get with Freudiger at IA.

My cell rings.

Leslie.

"I was just going to call you," I answer.

"It's a clusterfuck, and it's all going to turn on Al real fast."

"Are you saying he might get indicted?"

"Frank, this isn't Baltimore. I'm not saying the US attorney's office isn't getting pressured by the mayor and probably the chief, but things like this don't move that fast here. It could take months, but it can happen. Especially with all the attention it's getting now."

"So now what?"

"I need to prepare Al for the worst. He'll be on admin leave for a while. His name will eventually leak."

"But you don't think they're going to get a grand jury on this right away?"

"Anything can happen, Frank, but I seriously doubt the US attorney's office will move that fast. They will move, though. Where are you?"

"At home, but I was going to call you because I should get with Johnny Freudiger, see what he can share. Al's CI, too."

"IA doesn't have to share anything with you. But you need to be careful what you say to Freudiger."

That pisses me off, but I try not to sound like it does.

"I know how to talk to Internal Affairs, and I go back with Freudiger. He'll probably give me what he can."

"If or when they indict him, I'll get a discovery package from the AUSA, so I think it's best that you stay away from him. They don't know any more than we know."

"I don't want to stir anything up with you, Leslie, but I think it'd be in Al's best interest, probably yours, too, if I just work for Al. I don't mean keep you out of the loop, just not be on your books for this one."

"What? No! You report to me. The last thing I want is you going off on some rogue investigation. This is by the book."

Rogue investigation. That's funny, and a bit dramatic, but not altogether untrue. She did catch me, after all. Or rather, from what I remember of that night, I stumbled into her house at, like, four in the morning with bloodied clothes and a backpack full of narcotics. Blacked out after. You might say I gave myself up on that one. She kicked me out of her house and her life. I'm sure, even though I later confessed, that it was something she already figured out for herself. She's no dummy. Point is, I don't use now. But I do, on occasion, break the rules.

"I don't work that way anymore," I lie.

"Track down his CI for me. She needs to be interviewed before they get to her," she orders, like she refuses to acknowledge what I said.

"I'll keep you informed with everything. Don't worry," I try to reassure her.

"By the book, Frank." She disconnects, I think 'cause she wants to get in the last word.

I search my phone contacts. I still have a cell for Johnny, but I don't know if it's good anymore. It's from when he worked Major Crimes out of headquarters. That was a few years back. Most detectives stick with the same number, especially if it was their personal phone.

I tap it.

Couple of rings and "Freudiger," he answers.

Twelve

Johnny agrees to meet me, but on the street a couple of blocks from their office.

"I'll be in a dark-gray Chevy parked on the west side. Park ahead of me at the fire hydrant. I won't give you a ticket."

He's probably already there, eating lunch outta his car.

Lunch-hour traffic. Always a bitch, and where we're meeting is through downtown.

I get there, see his vehicle on the right, pull up to it, and roll down the front passenger window. When he sees it's me, he rolls his down.

"Frank."

"How's it going, Johnny?"

"Park in front of me."

I nod, roll the window back up, pull my car ahead and back into the space, careful not to tap his bumper.

I step out and lock the door, walk to the passenger side of his vehicle, open the door, and slide in.

We shake hands.

"Been a while," he says.

"Yeah. Wish we were meeting under different circumstances."

"Me too."

His olive-green suit jacket is folded neatly on the back seat, along with an overcoat. I think he's around my age, but I've never asked. He keeps his hair tight and his face clean-shaven. Not like it was back in his District Vice days. Still married, I think, but don't ask, and with three kids. I believe all girls.

"Why so clandestine? Is this like a *back-channel* kinda meet?" I ask.

"You might call it something like that. Only reason I agreed to meet with you is because of our history. A courtesy of sorts."

"Didn't know our history was all that good," I joke.

"We had a few good times, back when I was allowed to have a good time."

"Buffalo Billiards?"

"Damn, that place still around?"

"For the life of me I don't know. They had the best turkey burgers in town, though."

"Yeah, and waitresses. You still living on Twelfth?"

"Yep."

Maybe not married anymore.

"Place has to be worth something now, right?" he asks.

"A lot more than I paid when it was nothin' but a broke-down shell."

"Damn. Wish I had the vision you had. Would have invested in all those shells off Seventh, near the convention center."

"Coulda retired early if you did that. Me too, for that matter."

"You did retire early."

"Yeah, but just saying. With a lot more money."

Nods and sips expensive water out of a plastic bottle. Sets it back in the pocket of the center console.

"Heard rumors about your early retirement."

Oh fuck.

"Rumors? What kind of rumors?" I'm afraid to ask.

"Everything from you weren't really MPD. You were an under-cover fed."

I belch out a laugh.

"Yeah…to something about you fucking one of the lieutenants at NSID and she went psycho on you."

"Now, that one's ridiculous. And even if we were, why would that make me wanna retire?"

"So, then, you were a fed?"

"You're too smart to fall for that shit, Johnny, so quit busting my balls."

"Ha! You still working for Leslie, though, right?" he asks.

"No, not anymore. I'm just helping out a friend on this one. She's the one who called me, though. I've been outta the loop, so I didn't even know about it."

"I don't know Al like you do, but he has a good record."

"That gonna help at all?"

"Fuck no."

At least he's being honest.

"So I take it you're getting a lot of pressure on this one."

He doesn't answer, but sort of shrugs. I'll take that as a yes.

"Anything you can tell me about the decedent?"

"Come on, Frank."

"I thought you knew that's why we're meeting?"

"Yes, but doesn't mean I'm going to tell you shit."

"Arthur Taylor, right? He got a record, part of a crew? Give me something, man."

"He's not spic-and-span, if that's what you're after."

"Gun charges?"

Shrugs.

"You think it's at all possible that someone was with him and snatched up the gun after he got shot?"

"Anything's possible, but there's no evidence to show that, so I work with what I have."

"Are you going to *work* on it or just go with what you have?"

He shoots me a look. "You know me better than that, Frank. Last thing I want to do is fuck up his life."

"But there's no leads, anything that might work in his favor?"

"Unless there's something you can tell me, no."

I'd give up the CI if I knew she was a good witness. Why doesn't he ask me about her?

"I've worked dozens of officer-related shootings, Frank. Almost all of them are found to be justified. A few not so much, just plain stupidity. Others, fucking criminal, officers that never should have gotten in the department. As far as the public's concerned, they don't give a fuck that almost all the shootings are justified."

I don't want to go there, into all that shit, so I say, "Al's not stupid. Nor is he a criminal."

"There are others, and I'm not saying Al is one, where they really think the person had a weapon. It was nothing more than a cell phone, a wallet, or a shadow. Kid wasn't holding anything and nothing dropped near him, so..."

"I can't believe that. He's a good cop. Well trained. Been involved in more close calls than you can imagine. Never had to shoot. Force, that's a different matter."

"There's no evidence."

"His blood come back clean?"

"I can give you that. Yes."

No alcohol. Now, that's a fucking miracle.

"How fast is this going to move?" I ask.

"Like every other police shooting."

"So he'll be on admin leave for a while?"

"I can't say one way or the other, Frank. I will say that I'm not the one pressuring the US attorney's office. And from my experience, they won't kowtow to it anyway."

"I know it's not worth shit, but I believe him."

"Yeah, well, I wish that meant more, too."

He's holding something back.

"How much time does he have? The truth. Please."

He looks at me, shakes his head 'cause he knows I saw right through him after what he said last.

"I know how the US attorney's office works, too, Johnny. I also know it doesn't have to go GJO, and MPDC doesn't always listen to the AUSA. You just admitted there's pressure. A detective gonna try to walk a warrant through? Arrest him that way? Something quick to pacify the mayor's office?"

His lack of an immediate response confirms it.

"That's what's going to happen, right?" I say.

"You only have a few days. I can't say much more than that."

"Fuck you guys, Johnny. You know a grand jury investigation is the right way to go, not cave in to the fucking pressure, make a big mistake with a man's life."

"It's a different climate nowadays. You know that."

"Yeah, it is, but that doesn't make it right. So, about how much time?"

"A few days."

"A few days like three? A week? What?"

"A few days, Frank. Listen, it's not up to me. It could be a week. It could be more. That's it."

"Will you at least give me a heads-up so I can be there for him?"

"You know better—"

"That's all I ask, brother."

A nod is all he gives.

"Why'd you hold this from me?"

"'Cause I can be an asshole. Part of my job."

"Who's the homicide detective that caught the case?"

"Lori Rattan."

"Who the fuck is that?"

"She's a rookie detective, but she's good."

"Can you give me her cell?"

"Dammit, Frank, you're asking too much of me."

"I can do a bit of digging and get it myself. It's just easier if you give it to me."

"This didn't come from me. You had to dig for it, all right?"

"Of course."

First thing I do when I get to the car is call Leslie. She needs to know about the pending warrant. I also have to convince her to keep it between us. Al hears about that, it might be enough to put him over the edge. Better to let it be a surprise or, if Johnny still has a heart, he'll give me a heads-up before they come knocking at the door so I can be there.

Thirteen

After I make dinner I turn on the local news. Finally mounted a new TV on the wall. It took me a while after my house was burglarized and most everything, including the television, was stolen. There was a time when the thought of having one there would be a constant reminder that I was a victim of a crime, so it took me a while to replace it. I don't usually watch the news, but I feel compelled to now. Sometimes these guys come up with witnesses before the police do.

After the local weather and a few commercials, they cut to Paul Wagner on the scene of an accident. Apparently, a uniformed officer who was working traffic on Wisconsin Avenue in Georgetown was struck by a vehicle. Hit-and-run, according to Wagner. Vehicle was identified only as a four-door black sedan, occupied two times, last seen heading east on P Street. Uncertain if the officer was intentionally targeted. The officer was hospitalized and is in critical condition. Damn.

After that, the latest on the government. I watch until the end. Nothing on the shooting. Too many other things going on locally and in this fucked-up world today. I turn the TV off and get on my cell to call Tim Millhoff, a buddy of mine at Homicide, see if I know the officer who was injured.

"Millhoff," he answers.

"What's up, brother?"

"Same, same. Stack of open cases piling up on my desk, that's all. What's going on with you?"

"Just saw the news and wanted to know if you have the name of the officer in the Georgetown hit-and-run."

"Yeah, Devon Jones. Probably no one you know. He came on after you retired."

"How is he?"

"Stable."

"Good to hear. Appreciate the info."

"You talk to Luna?" he asks.

"Yeah. I'm helping him out on this one."

"Shit. Good luck. Seems cut-and-dry to me."

"He said there was a gun and then there wasn't a gun. You know Detective Rattan?"

"Of course."

"She working it for witnesses or any other leads?"

"Just like every other case. Unfortunately, I don't know how much more can be done on this one. Like I said—"

"Yeah, I know what you said," I interrupt. "I was going to give her a call later. You mind giving her a heads-up that I'm okay, so she'll be more inclined to talk to me?"

"Fuck, who says you're okay?"

"Fuck you."

"Yeah, I'll tell her."

"Thanks, bro. I'll keep that officer in my prayers."

"Yeah, and I hope it works out for Luna. He's a decent guy."

"I hope so, too. Talk later."

"Yeah." He disconnects.

Good to hear that the officer is stable. Not so good to hear that the general feeling with respect to the shooting is the case being closed. I'm beginning to question whether there was a gun. Not whether Al thought there was one, though. I've been in a couple of shootings. I know how fast it happens, but also how the time slows down. But this wasn't your average shooting. Al was not being shot at. He merely reacted to what he said was a threat.

Tamie is the obvious next step. Still, where will that lead if she didn't see anything?

It's not an image I want to have just before bedtime, but I can't get the Polaroid of her outta my head. And then, out of nowhere, Playboy pops in.

He's like a monster leaping out of my closet.

I down a Klonopin with a shot of Jameson, with the hope it'll ease my racing mind and erase these unwanted images. One good thing is I do get tired earlier now, for obvious reasons, not to mention fall asleep faster.

I hit the sack with that last thought in my head. Sleep.

It's still dark when I wake up, a vivid memory of a dream with me.

I'm in my small front yard, stretched out across the green grass. On my stomach, I scour between the blades of grass, like it's an indoor carpet, searching for tiny bits of fallen cocaine, and I'm hopelessly picking between the blades with my fingers.

I don't check the time because I'm afraid to know.

Fourteen

I manage a couple more hours of sleep. The dream stays with me. After I shower, I hit the floor for three sets of push-ups and crunches.

Coffee doesn't work, but I have it anyway, along with grapefruit, which I still order by the crate from a Florida farm. A lot of acid going into the stomach, so I pop a Pepcid after.

About an hour later I get to Al's house. Curtains still drawn, with no sign of light inside. It's still morning, but not so early that I'm worried about waking him up. He's always been an early riser, but he's been hitting the bottle hard, so that might make a difference.

A couple of hard raps on the door and I hear footsteps, like his feet are dragging along the wooden floor.

Door opens.

Looks like he's wearing the same clothes. He stands inside, a couple feet away, but I can still smell his foul breath.

"Dude, you gotta brush your teeth," I say.

He slams the door in my face. Should've said hello first. Didn't hear the dead bolt, so I turn the knob and it opens.

When I enter, Al's dragging his feet, walking toward the sofa, plops himself down over the crumpled blanket and drops his head on a queen-size pillow. A half-empty bottle of Jameson is on the end table, along with an empty tumbler.

I sit in the armchair to the side of the sofa where his feet rest, his left leg now over the cushion and dangling above the floor.

"Fuck, man" is all I can think to say.

I can honestly say I've been there. Not fun. Not something I want to say to him. He doesn't need to hear how bad it feels. He already knows.

"I talked to Freudiger."

His eyes roll toward me. "How fucked am I?"

What do I tell him?

"The investigation's going to take time, so you'll be on admin leave for a while."

"When they taking it to grand jury?"

"Couldn't say. At least you're on leave with pay, right?"

"Honestly, Frank, you think you're going to find a gun that'll have that kid's prints on it, or maybe get one of his boys to admit he took the gun? All it boils down to in the end is my word, so I'm fucked."

I wanna yell at him to get his ass up, 'cause I know he isn't like me and his body and mind can take only so much of the self-medication and suffering. That won't do any good. I know him well enough that he'll only tell me to fuck off. I have to just pray that his heart is strong and he can take this self-abuse and pull himself out of it sooner rather than later.

"I'm gonna call Tamie today, see about meeting up with her."

That gets him to a sitting position.

"What good is that going to do?" he asks me with more than a bit of hostility. "I told you she's not a witness to shit."

"What are you worried about, Al? I know her as well as you do—" *Well, maybe not as well...* "Unless you're still fucking her—"

"Shut the hell up with that!"

"Unless your relationship with her has anything to do with the shooting, why be so bothered that I need to talk to her?"

"There isn't anything more there. I just want to keep IA away from her."

"They're going to subpoena her."

"They have to find her to do that."

"Damn, Al, all they have to do is get the file you keep on her at NSID."

"They have to find that, too."

"Aww fuck, man, what did you do? You have that file hidden in your house somewhere?"

"Give me a break, Frankie. It's an old file. They get misplaced."

"That's gonna be hard to explain, especially since you recently had a meet with her and paid her for it. Had to document that for the file."

"Paid her out of my own pocket."

"Off the books? I'm your friend, Al. You're my best friend. Tell me what's going on."

He pours himself a half glass of whiskey, downs almost the whole thing. Coughs, probably because he's not used to the cheap shit.

"Damn, that burns."

"You get used to it. Talk to me."

"There was a gun in that kid's hand. Tamie has nothing to do with the shooting. She isn't a witness. Yes, we're fucking around, and I don't want that getting out. Plain and simple."

"Where's her CI file?"

Hesitates.

"Buried under some old tools in my shed."

"How did you manage to get it after you got into the shooting?"

"Said I had some personal stuff to clear out of my locker. I did. The file was one of them."

"You kept the file in your locker."

"I was updating it. Didn't have a chance to turn it back in to the LT before he left, and I don't have the combo to the filing cabinet where they keep them."

"I'm taking it. For safekeeping."

"Fuck no."

"If they don't find it at the branch, they'll come looking here. I'm taking it. You tell them that when you couldn't get the file back to the LT, you slipped it in your desk drawer. That's the last place you saw it. Understood, bro?"

"Yeah."

"I can understand that you want to keep her identity safe, and I don't wanna hear shit about anything other than that."

He nods, knowing I'm referring to their fucked-up relationship. He is going to have to eventually give up the file and her name. It'll look bad otherwise, like he's hiding something, which he is, but it's not related to the shooting.

"You need me to get some food for you? Anything at the store?"

"I'm almost out of booze. And don't preach to me."

"Preach? Who the fuck you think I am?" I smile. "What else do you need?"

"I got leftover takeout. I'm good. Thanks."

"I'll stop back later this afternoon."

He nods.

Looks so pitiful.

FIFTEEN

O n my second attempt to call Tamie, she answers. We agree to meet, but not at the usual spot.

"Eleventh and Kenyon, across the street from Wonderland, around the middle of the block where the murals are. I'll pick you up."

"See you there, hon," she says.

There was a time when I would not have even thought about meeting at that spot. But it's a trendy location now, and no one there to worry about. The elementary school takes up the long block.

When I pull out from near Al's, I notice through my side-view mirror another vehicle pulling out a couple seconds after. Normally, I wouldn't think twice about it, except that it's a four-door black SUV, the kind cops and reporters drive, so it piques my interest. I take a right at the next block, heading west. When I'm about half a block over, I notice the SUV making the right and staying just far enough behind that it's not suspicious. I can't tell how many times it's occupied. I do notice a waft of smoke push through the driver's window.

Cigar or weed? Maybe simply cigarette smoke made thicker when it hits the cold air.

It's still with me after a couple of blocks, so I decide to take the next right, head north, and go around the block. If the car is stupid enough to follow me all the way around the block, then I'd say I have a tail and more than likely not a cop or a fed. They'll usually have another vehicle pick me up if it looks like I made them, or if they're alone, they'll break away and hope they're lucky enough to catch up to me again.

I make the turn to go around the block and hit the same street I was on. Sure enough, the SUV stays with me, still about half a block behind. I stay the course. Instead of making a right to head north on 11th, toward Kenyon, I stop at the intersection. The driver is so fucking obvious, though, because the vehicle slows down, trying to let me take the turn so it doesn't have to pull up right behind me. That's my intention, and since it's a one-way street, the driver has to make a choice—try to find a parking spot, hit the narrow alley a little farther ahead, or pull up behind me.

The dope stops, still waiting for me to turn. But another vehicle comes up behind it, eventually honks because the street is too narrow to pass, so the SUV pulls up and takes the south entrance into the alley. When I don't see it, I make a right to head north, but I'm still not comfortable enough to head Tamie's way so I continue north to Lamont Street, where I make a left. I find a parking spot toward the corner. A couple of cars pass me by, but not the SUV. The vehicles that pass either continue across Sherman or make the turn to go north or south on Sherman. I watch them until they disappear. SUV was probably just some reporter, but they usually don't care that you know they're following. So who the fuck knows. With any luck, I'll see the car again.

I'm thinking I should give Al a call, let him know, but I don't want to worry him—or worse, get him riled up so he does something stupid, like sit on the front porch to see if the SUV returns. If it ever does return.

When I feel it's safe, I make a U-turn at Sherman to head back on Lamont toward 11th.

I can see Tamie on the left side, leaning against the mural and smoking a cigarette. For a second I don't think it's Tamie, because she doesn't look so sickly thin and she's wearing nice jeans and a clean white puffy winter coat. I slow down to pull toward her, look around to make sure it's clear, and then signal her to enter the back because the rear windows have heavier tint.

She flicks the cigarette and enters.

"Hi, sweetie. It's been a while."

"Hey, Tamie. You're looking healthy."

I can see her through the rearview mirror as she smiles, shuts the door, and scoots across the seat to the right side, where she's not directly behind me. I don't feel so disgusted with Al anymore. She doesn't seem...dirty.

"Let me go around the block, see if I can find a spot to park on Irving."

"I'm here for *you,* Frankie."

I hang a left at the next street and then another left on Irving. School's not out for Christmas break yet, but it's too cold for the kids to be playing outside. I find a parking space on the north side, along the tall cast-iron fence that surrounds the rear of the school.

I turn to look at Tamie. Damn, she has changed. She looks almost like a normal person, like she's off crack. Maybe.

I slide down the window a bit, light up a smoke. Tamie does the same.

"Damn, Tamie. I almost don't recognize you."

"Been living healthy nowadays."

"Except for the smoking."

"Can't give it all up at once, Frankie."

I sure as hell know that.

"So, you're clean?"

"Almost a year now."

Fuck, just like me. Something must be going around.

"Congratulations! That's damn good."

"How come you never call anymore?"

"Haven't been working a case where I'd need your wonderful voice."

"So that's all I'm good for." She smiles.

Damn, she coming on to me now?

"How's Al?" she asks without hesitation and before I can answer her.

"He's been better. I'm helping him out on this one, so you can be straight with me."

"How you mean?"

"Just that you can talk to me—what you been working for him, shit like that."

"He can tell you better what it is he's been having me do."

I can take that one of two ways, but I won't tell her.

"And he has, but you know he said it was okay to talk to me, right?"

She takes a short drag from the cigarette.

"So, you said you did hear the shots?"

"Yeah. I didn't know it was where we were parked. Coulda been anywhere."

"When you were walking, did you see anyone heading to or already in the lot where you two were?"

Shakes her head. Thinking. "Just a couple of girls that looked like college kids is all."

"See any car parking near there?"

"Didn't pay much attention to that, hon."

I've known Tamie for a long time. Like I said, Al and I signed her up, and I've used her for a few things here and there as a PI. I'm going to have to be straight with her.

"You got something going with Al, something more than being his CI?"

"Why don't you come out and be a bit more direct, Frankie?"

Shit. Getting off crack made her tougher.

"Okay, are you and Al fucking?"

Sixteen

Y ou know how much trouble that could get him into, right?
You, too."

"Me? How could I get in trouble?"

I don't answer because I really don't know.

I hesitate to ask this because I don't want to know, but I have to. "Did Al coerce you in any way into having sex with him, even offer you anything in exchange?"

"Baby, you are so off. I coerced him."

Didn't expect that.

"How long has this been going on between you two?"

"A lot of years, Frank. I don't know."

Al is over. They will find her.

"You know, detectives investigating the shooting are gonna try to find you for questioning."

"Why me? I told him I ain't seen anything."

"Unfortunately, he told them he was getting with you, his CI, and that's why he was there. He didn't give up your name, though. Would have been better if he had just lied. Said he was there to take a fucking nap or some shit like that. But it's done. They'll more than likely get to you. So, what will you tell them? I mean, the reason you were there?"

She's taking too long to think about this.

"Fuck, Tamie. Just tell them you were there 'cause he needed you for an okeydoke or something. Don't think about it too long, and if they ask about the case, tell them you don't know anything about what he was working, just that you were going to make a call."

"I got it, hon. You don't have to worry."

"Do yourself a favor and stay away from him, at least until all this blows over."

This ain't gonna blow over.

She flicks her cigarette out the window, looks at me between the front bucket seats.

"Yes, Frankie."

"Thanks. You are looking real good, Tamie. Healthy. I'm happy for you."

She smiles, sort of a crooked smile.

"And I'm not hitting on ya, either."

"Well, that's too bad, Frankie."

"You need me to give you a ride somewhere?"

"No. I enjoy the walk."

I have some twenty-dollar bills folded up in my front pocket. I pull out three and hand them to her. She accepts, then opens the rear door.

"Call if you need anything," she says.

"I will," and wonder what she meant by *need.*

She struts away, heading toward 11th, where she makes her way south.

I wait for her to disappear before I pull out.

I drive back toward Al's, to a liquor store a few blocks from his house.

Seventeen

After I drop off a bottle of Jameson for Al, I tell him about the meet I had with Tamie.

"You know we won't be able to prevent IA from talking to her 'cause it'll look like you're hiding something bad if you do."

"Fuck that," he responds.

"Not kidding around, Al. You're going to have to give them her contact info soon. Tamie knows when that time comes to only say you were meeting because you were going to talk about using her for an okeydoke. She's not going to give up anything else. She's not going to fuck it up for herself. Got that?"

He seems reluctant, but says, "Yeah. And what do you mean, 'fuck it up for herself'?"

"I don't want to know all the details about what you two have going, but you're still a source of income for her. You need to return to that business relationship, give up the other. And quit feeling sorry for yourself. You'll get through this."

Based on the look he gives me, maybe I was too hard on him. Should've left out the *feeling sorry for yourself* part.

I want to share some of that liquor with him, but it'll just make me tired and encourage Al to drink even more. I decide to leave.

On my way out I shoot him my best stab at a reassuring smile.

He simply nods.

When I get to the car, I hit the ignition to slide down my window a bit, then turn it off. Cold breeze through the window feels good. I adjust the rearview so I get a better view of the street behind me. I want to sit here for a bit, see if that SUV shows.

It's hard seeing Al like this, falling apart, self-medicating with alcohol, who knows what else. *He ain't me.* He's always been tough. Was always there for me, too, when I was going through my own shit storm, a suspect in the murder of my own cousin. That didn't look good for me, either, but it worked out at the end. Not so much, though, for a couple of other good men, and my young cousin. That took a toll on me. That, and losing Leslie. I do miss her. It was a tough couple of months after, but I managed to quit cocaine. Of course, Al never knew that part of my life. I was good at hiding it. Leslie, on the other hand—well, shit.

I give it about an hour and don't see anything out of the ordinary.

A thought comes to me, and then I find myself driving to the little deli on Columbia Road.

I occasionally cut through an alley or go around a block, make sure I'm not being followed. Again, not really worried about it. If it was a reporter, that means Al's name was leaked and it'll be on the evening news.

There's a voice in the back of my head calling me a fool and telling me to stop. That voice used to be under control or easily muted. Nowadays not so much. I just ignore it, because I can't get running into Playboy outta my head. Need to put it to rest—somehow. Haven't thought it all the way through yet.

The storefront has a large glass window adorned with beer and liquor advertisements and sales. Lots of pedestrians on this part of

Columbia Road, so it's difficult to raise the binos and try to take a peek. I wait for the right moment, quickly lift them and focus, and return them to my lap, wait again, and take a quick look through. Can barely see the old man, lifting bottles out of a case and setting them on a shelf. Can't make out the deli. Couple of customers inside, but they're browsing the liquor section.

After about twenty minutes, I decide to walk by, take a look through the window as I pass.

I step out of the car, slow my stroll as I approach. Look inside. Doesn't look like anyone is working the deli. Might be in the back or bent down behind the deli counter. I walk by and stop at the corner. I think about it and figure the best thing to do is return to the car and sit on the store until the deli closes. That's at 5:00 p.m. The liquor store side of it stays open later. I do love surveillance, so I return to the car. If I see him exit, I'll follow him. With any luck, he'll take me to where he lives. After that, who the fuck knows.

Eighteen

I give it till six o'clock, and he still doesn't exit.

"Fuck it," I say to myself.

I walk back to the store, look through the glass front door, and enter.

Bell above the door alerts the old man.

He's sitting on a stool behind the cash register at the counter and stands. Before I walk over, I turn toward the deli counter. No one there, so I walk up to the old man.

"Stopped by for a sandwich, but looks like no one's working the deli."

"Temporarily closed until I hire some new help."

"You don't know how to make a sandwich, then?" I smile.

"Trust me, you don't want that."

"What happened to the young man? Made a good sandwich."

"I don't know. Just didn't show up for work. Was a good worker, too, but those boys come and go. Thought he'd be here to stay, though."

"How long he been working for you?"

The old man gives me a look, like, *Why so many questions?*

"I'm actually a retired police detective, and I knew the kid once. Even tried to help him out myself." Which is not altogether untrue. I did decide not to shoot him, and pulled him out of the Anacostia River before he sank. Even cut him free of the zip ties that bound him. "I know he's from the area of Seventeenth and Euclid."

"He get himself in any trouble that I should know about?"

"No, sir. No. Like I said, I'm retired. Don't know if you remember, but I used to come here years ago with my partner, and off and on after. Was in here the other day for a sandwich. Best sandwiches in the area. Damn nice scotch selection, too. Thought I'd stop by for another one."

"Well, I don't know what happened to Calvin—"

It's him.

"But—but it seems like his cell phone is out of service, too, so I hope he didn't get himself in trouble. He's a good young man."

"I can look into it if you want. Like I said, I knew him when he was younger and he hung out at Seventeenth and Euclid."

"Well, it is payday. Maybe he'll come around for that."

"You want me to go to his home, see if he's okay?"

He gives me another funny look.

"No. Like I said, they come and go. Isn't my responsibility. He wants what I owe him, he can stop by for it."

I'm not going to push this. It'll start looking too weird.

"All right, then. I hope you find a replacement soon."

"I will."

I smile and walk to the bourbon section, find a bottle of Woodford Reserve, grab it, and return to the cash register.

"May as well pick up a bottle while I'm here."

Old man rings it up. I pay with cash.

After he gives me my change, I say, "You take care."

"You too, sir."

I exit to walk back to the car.

Damn.

It's obvious why he skipped. Sees me a few years later—what else is he gonna do? Here's something about it…I don't like the idea of him being out there. Me not knowing. Seeing him all these years later with him knowing what he knows. I do know he wouldn't get the police involved, but it's still unsettling. Maybe he will come back for that money. And I now have a bottle of nice sipping bourbon.

I return to the car, start it, and roll down the window a bit so the windshield won't fog up. I uncork the bottle of bourbon, carefully pour some into an empty water bottle, cork it back up, and put it back in the bag. I take a nice swig, another for good measure.

Nineteen

I fell asleep in the car, with the car running. Half a bottle of bourbon gone.

Not like the past, when I could do this sort of thing 'cause I had the help of that fine white powdery substance to keep it all in balance.

Go away.

I check the rear for my overcoat and backpack. Everything still there. It would've been a perfect opportunity for a theft from auto. Too many pedestrians around, though. Lucky me.

Lights are on in the store. I fucked up. Playboy probably showed up for his money and left. Dammit! I look at my phone display. Leslie called me a couple of times. Didn't even hear it ring. One voice message. I listen to it.

"Call me back, please."

So businesslike, lack of any feeling that was once there.

I light a smoke, clear my throat, and call her back.

She answers, but before I can say hello, she goes off with, "I had to hear it from Al about your meeting with his CI. I thought you said you'd keep me in the loop."

"Sorry. I meant to, but got caught up." I know *caught up* is going to worry her, so, "Actually, I took a nap. I'm a bit worn out these days."

"Did his CI have anything to offer?"

"Only that she heard gunshots in the area and was a couple of blocks away. Didn't see or hear anything else. Basically, no help at all."

I flick the ash out the window, and that's when I see Playboy walking into the liquor store.

"Fuck!"

"What's the matter?" Leslie asks.

"Just dropped a cigarette on my lap and I'm driving. Gotta call you back" is the only thing I can come up with.

"I thought you were taking a nap?"

"Gotta go!" I disconnect before she can respond.

I flick the cigarette out of the car to ready myself for a follow.

Peering through my binos, I can see Playboy and the old man talking. Old man probably asking why he didn't show up for work. I set the binos on the passenger seat.

He exits a couple of minutes later, looks both ways before walking, like he's worried, maybe about me. He favors his right leg. Looks like he's trying to hide a limp. He folds up something, probably the check, and slips it in his pants pocket. He walks east on Columbia Road. I let him walk a bit before I pull the car out to slowly follow.

He crosses 18th, stays on the north side of the block. I hit a red light on 18th, but I can still see him walking. When the light turns green and I catch up to him, he's passing Safeway. I slow down like I'm trying to find parking. Car behind me honks 'cause it's only one lane, but it passes when it's clear.

I'm thinking he's heading toward 17th and Euclid, but he's not crossing to the south side of the street where he can make that right on 17th. A lot of traffic, so it's hard to maintain this slow speed. I take a chance and pass him as he crosses Ontario Road. I pull to the curb and stop, blocking half the crosswalk. He strolls by, on the other side of the street, a walking man. *Where the fuck is he going?*

It's a long block. He crosses a narrow street just before 16th and cuts north through a little park area. I speed up to the light at 16th because I lose sight of him. He's either going to hit Mount Pleasant or 16th.

By the time the light turns green and I can make the turn, staying in the left lane, I see him walking on the west side of Mount Pleasant. I have to take a quick left and an immediate right to get there. Cars traveling south on 16th honk at me because I cut them off. I pull to the corner curb at Harvard and Mount Pleasant.

He walks left onto a narrow one-way street, Hobart. Thankfully, I can follow.

I decide to park along the curb at a crosswalk. Hobart ends on Mount Pleasant, and it's a long block, so I can watch him through the binos until there's enough distance that I can safely make the turn.

Phone vibrates in its cup holder. I hate Bluetooth, so the car doesn't pick it up. I can see the display. Leslie again.

I answer so she doesn't worry and keep hounding me.

"Sorry I didn't call back, but I'm on my way home now."

"Can you call me when you get home?"

"Yes."

He's getting farther away.

"Talk to you later," she says, and disconnects.

I'm sure she's thinking I'm avoiding her, because I am. I set the phone back in the cup holder, turn onto Hobart, and double-park to look through the binos. He walks up a flight of cement steps to the front porch of an old brown-brick attached two-story. I can make him out on the porch. It's obvious he is unlocking the front door.

Enters. I wait for a minute, until another car comes up behind and barely squeezes by, the driver glaring as he passes. I follow behind the car to get the address of the place Playboy walked into.

Is he renting a room, or is it a family home?

It's maintained well, but it's still more of a dump than most of the other homes around it. Is it one of Cordell Holm's spots? That's how I met Playboy, investigating a missing teenage girl. That led to a brothel at 17th and Euclid, run by Holm and his fucking lost-boy crew. Playboy was deep in it, especially the recruiting side, with his round face, big eyes, and tough, boyish charm. He clearly didn't take my advice, which was never to return. Can't let that go.

Damn, what to do? What to do?

I have this odd sense of urgency. My heart's skittering. What is fucking driving me right now? Guess I don't like certain things in the past catching up to me like this, especially when it's something that I shoulda let the river swallow. Now it's been spit out and is here to haunt me.

I find a parking spot, sit on the house for more than an hour, decide I can't let this rest, so I have more bourbon straight out of the bottle and step out of the car.

Twenty

A couple of older red metal outdoor chairs with a round white metal table between are on the patio to the right side of the door. No debris, empty forties, or cigarette butts on the table or the cement floor, which I would have expected.

I hear a man, not Playboy, yelling inside. He's close to the front door and sounds angry.

"Damn well better be soon, Calvin!"

Playboy responds, but all I can make out from him is something having to do with a "job."

"That was one of our conditions! Main one, anyway!"

I hear shuffling closer to the door. I hustle back down the steps to the sidewalk. Right when I hit the curb to cross the street, I hear the door open, but I don't turn around. I walk across the street at an angle, back toward my car, take a chance and turn.

A man, looks to be in his fifties, clean-shaven, wearing dark-blue maintenance pants and a black winter coat, walks down the stairs. He's putting on thick gloves. Seems like a decent sort. A working man? Looks mad. Is it Playboy's dad?

He sees me and waves like he knows me. More than likely he thinks I'm a neighbor. I smile and wave back, look away, and walk past my car. I look over my shoulder when I pass, see him walking the other way, toward Mount Pleasant Street.

Shit, that was without a doubt playing it by ear.

I have my best friend who needs my help right now, and here I am trying to do I don't even know what.

Fate decides to intervene, give me a helping hand, because I see Playboy exiting the front door.

I hop in the car. It's a narrow one-way street, so I can't turn, and I'll lose him if I try to go around this long block. I wedge my way out and back up at a good speed. I don't depend on the rear camera projecting on the dash screen. I look over my shoulder. He turns when I get closer to him, but he doesn't seem to worry and continues walking. I pass him and stop, open the front passenger window.

When he passes, I call out to him, "Playboy!"

He stops in his tracks, eyeballs me, and takes off running, this time with an obvious limp.

"Shit."

What did I expect?

Fuck if I'm going to chase him. I step out of the car, turn around. He's hoofing it toward Mount Pleasant.

"I know where you live, Calvin!" I yell.

He slows to a walk, stops and turns toward me. He's about a quarter of a block back. He's rubbing his right knee like it's bothering him.

"I just want to talk."

A car turns on Hobart from Mount Pleasant.

He's going to take off. Disappear.

The car gets closer. The driver, a woman, taps the horn, a couple of polite honks and a smile.

74

I pull out my wallet to show her my retirement badge. Now she looks worried, like she's thinking about backing up.

"Nothing to worry about," I call out to her, but mostly for Playboy to hear. "I'm going to park the car up the street. Meet me at your stoop. I don't want to have to go looking for you."

The driver looks more concerned.

I throw her a wave, and I step back into the car. I drive back to the parking spot, turn the left signal on so the lady behind me knows I'm trying to park. I look over my shoulder, notice Playboy still standing there. The lady passes. I exit the car and turn. He's still there. Looks frozen where he stands, and I don't mean because of the weather. He's far enough away that he could run, get away if he wants to.

Let me have this one, brother fate.

I shut the door, use the key fob to lock it. Horn chirps. I cross the street and walk toward his home.

He doesn't move.

I walk up the steps to his front porch, sit on the red chair closest to the door, pull out my pack of smokes and tap one out. The metal seat is cold against my ass. I slip the pack back in my outer coat pocket and light up the cig.

He's walking toward the house now with that bit of a limp. Then I remember. His knee was the size of a softball when I pulled him out of the river. Must have fucked it up when I rolled him, hands and feet zip-tied together, down the steep bank to the water's edge.

When he gets to the bottom of the cement steps, he looks up and says, "What the fuck you want with me?"

"I don't know, Playboy. Musta been fate."

"What? What the fuck you talkin' about? You a fag? And I ain't Playboy. You got me confused."

"Okay, Calvin."

"I don't know who you talkin' about."

"Why did you run then, never show back up to the deli where you work?"

"'Cause I think you're fucking crazy. Scare the hell outta me is why."

"You do remember, then?"

He reaches into his coat pocket. I stand, pull my coat back, grab the grip of my gun.

"Cell phone, man. Cell phone." He pulls it out slowly to show me. "I ain't got no weapon, so don't shoot me. Gonna call the police, though. You fucking crazy."

I sit back down. Feel like I'm in some kinda Western and I'm the new sheriff in town.

"I wouldn't suggest that. After all, you were the driver of the car. Remember? For Little Monster. If Cordell or anyone in his crew didn't already give you up, I will. I'm sure your boys would love to see you about now. Might even think you're a snitch 'cause you were never arrested with them."

"They ain't my boys. And if that true, why I never get picked up by the police?"

That makes me smile.

"Because all they got is your nickname. Like I said, me being a witness, almost a victim, could get you locked up for a long time. That your old man who lives here?"

"Naw, and it ain't none of your business, either."

"Seems like a good man. And it is my business. You disappear, I'll have my boy at Homicide visit your old man, get your information, and you'll be done. Sounded like he was pissed at you anyway."

No response.

"Tell you the truth, Calvin, I don't know why the hell I'm here."

"Go on, then."

"Yeah," I agree.

I must be nuts.

I stand.

He takes a few steps to the side.

"Don't have to run," I tell him. "I think I'll check up on you, though, make sure you're not up to no good again, 'cause that was *our* original deal. Remember?"

"My uncle ain't know nothin' about all that. You just leave him alone."

"Huh."

I take my time walking down the stairs. When I hit the sidewalk, he takes a few more steps to the side, keeping a good distance between us.

I look at him direct. He looks different. Not so thuggish. "Go back to making sandwiches or something."

I walk to my car. Don't even look over my shoulder.

"Fucking good sandwich," I say loud enough so he can hear.

Twenty-One

I keep the curtains at home open during the daytime. Not like before, when I was using. Paranoid. Fucking peeking out the curtains, shit like that.

I sit on the sofa, look out the window. Light snowfall, but not enough to coat the ground. Melts right when it hits. It'll be a nice day.

I peel and eat a whole grapefruit and call Leslie's cell after I'm done. It goes to voice mail.

"I'm checking into a couple of things," I say, "trying to follow up on the decedent, Arthur Taylor. I'll call later."

I do want to follow up on him, but Al was the only one in the department I could call to run names, tags, or other info. There's his partner, Jimmy, but he's out on sick leave. I'm sure he would find a way to help, though.

I give him a call.

"Yeah," Jimmy answers.

"What's up, Jimmy?"

"Just trying to heal."

"What I hear is you're looking for a long Christmas break."

A chuckle, then says, "No. It's for real. Even got a nice prescription for Percocet."

I've got a few of those, too, sort of.

"By the way, I tried to call Al a little while ago, but he didn't answer. You talk to him?"

"Saw him yesterday," I say. "You know Leslie is representing him?"

"Yeah."

"I'm helping out however I can. In fact, that's why I called. I need your help with something."

"I can try, but I am limited. Being at home and all."

"The decedent's name is Arthur Taylor. Sixteen years old. Need to get an address for him."

"Fuck, man. I don't know how to get that without setting off an alarm. I don't need Internal Affairs coming after me for that shit."

"He's your partner. Find a way. You gotta have someone you trust."

"Not a matter of trust. I'd do it myself if that shit weren't monitored. You know that."

"C'mon, you know no one pays attention to that shit."

"Maybe back in the day. Fuck, man. Everything nowadays is monitored."

"It's for your partner, our friend. Get me what you can on him, Jimmy."

"I'll see what I can do."

"Today, if you can, brother."

"Talk later."

"Thanks."

I set the phone on the end table.

My vinyl collection is sitting across the living room, collecting dust. I get an urge to listen, but nothing depressing or anything that might set off a trigger. Certain music will do that.

I walk across the room, get on my knees and leaf through the records, land on *Going Out in Style*. Bought the album when it was first released. I place it on the turntable, set the stylus on the record, and turn up the volume. Gotta listen to these guys loud.

I sit back on the sofa, light another smoke, and try to figure out the next step. Funny how a smoke can focus you, pull down one deep groove of thought. The gun's got to be found, or the story that leads to it.

I'll have to drop by the scene. Even though I know the location well, it still helps to see where it happened. I'm also going to trust that Jimmy is gonna get me what I need on Arthur Taylor. I'll just be walking over the detective's tracks on that one, so I have to be careful not to step on her toes. I'll give her a call soon.

Dropkick Murphys get me going. Hard not to. Thanks to them I have me a nice shot of Jameson. Just one, 'cause I gotta roll. After side one plays itself through, I grab my backpack and head out.

Flurries stopped. A light cold wind is pushing the clouds through. That's probably about all this city will see. Every year the winters here are milder. We need a hard-hitting snowstorm. It'd be good for the city. Paralyze it.

TWENTY-TWO

I pull into the lot. Three cargo trailers are lined up on the other side near a chain-link fence that surrounds the area. There's enough room to park a couple of cars between them. Al would have parked between the second and third one with the first one about thirty feet from Sherman Avenue. Good concealment if you're meeting with a CI or a source. I met here several times with Tamie Darling both back in the day with Al and as a PI.

There's no crime scene tape. Looks like a crew of people have been working the area, though. The gravel's kicked up around the trailers, probably EMT and the detectives on the scene. I park my car between the two trailers where Al would have parked when he was here. I step out, slip on my overcoat, and walk to the rear of my vehicle, look around the second trailer to the third one on the other side. The end of that trailer sticks out about ten feet beyond the other two. The kid he encountered that day could have easily concealed himself on the other side of the trailer and then moved out to the back where he would have a good angle on the rear of Al's car, and on him. But still, it's about twenty yards. That's a tough dis-

81

tance to hit a target. I'm not surprised Al emptied a magazine with only a couple rounds hitting the other.

I walk to the area where the body would have fallen. The fire department or Crime Scene cleaned up well. What appears to be dried blood is only on bits of soil and rock.

I hear tires over gravel and turn toward the entrance to see what looks like a detective cruiser. It has a little antenna sticking up from the rear trunk and a front tag that looks like it is from the DC government.

One person driving. The car pulls up to the far side of me, but still a good distance because I'm sure the driver doesn't know who the fuck I am. When it parks, I can see through the front passenger window that it's a female and that she's on the mic, probably running the tag of my car through the dispatcher.

I turn to face her direction with my hands to my sides and a smile on my face. A moment later I can hear the muffled voice of the dispatcher filtered through the car. The driver mouths something like "copy," turns my way, then exits her vehicle.

She walks toward the front end, her detective badge hanging around her neck. She's wearing slim-cut suit-type black pants, with a short-cut black blazer that matches the pants. I can make out her Glock 17 holstered at her right hip and the magazine pouch on her left, housing two mags. She is attractive, looks to be in her early thirties, keeps her hair pulled back tight in a ponytail.

"I'm assuming you're Detective Rattan?" I ask.

"I don't know you," she says. "You with DC police?"

Her assumption makes me feel good. I still have the look, maybe because I'm not so disheveled anymore. Must be the suit.

"Retired detective. Frank Marr."

"I've heard of you."

"Don't know if I like the way that sounded."

"Mostly good. Some bad."

She moves around her car toward the passenger side, walks toward me.

"Detectives Millhoff and Caine have talked about your escapades."

"Escapades? I don't know how to take that, either."

When she's in front of me, I extend my hand to shake. She accepts. Firm grip. Soft hands.

"What are you doing here?" she asks.

"I'm a PI now. Al Luna is a good friend of mine and my former partner when I was on the job at NSID."

"You don't look old enough to be retired."

"I took an early out."

I should ask what she's doing here because you'd think they finished up with this scene and there shouldn't be anything left to follow up on.

"So, you're working for Luna?"

"Helping, 'cause I believe him."

She's smart enough not to respond to that.

"I'm checking out the scene. I know you all canvassed for surveillance cameras, but I wouldn't be doing my job if I didn't do the same. And it doesn't look like a secured crime scene anymore."

"It's not."

"Something you missed here, then? That's why you're back?"

A bit of a hard half smile because she knows I'm fishing.

"No. I was at the Fourth District picking up a report and thought I'd drive by here on my way back to the office. Saw you, thought you might be a cop and wondered why you were here."

"Driving by the scene. That's good. Still in your head, then."

She looks at me like she's wondering why I'd say that.

"I mean most of the detectives I know, except for Millhoff and Caine, would have already closed the case with what they have. Let

Internal Affairs run with it. I'm sure Luna would appreciate that you're still working it."

"I'm just doing my job."

Wow, she's such a rookie. I wanna ask how much time she has on, but I know she'd take it as an insult. Probably already getting razzed for being assigned to Homicide because she doesn't have that much time on as a detective. *Who'd she have to fuck to get here?* is what her coworkers might be wondering.

She reaches into her right front pants pocket, pulls out a card and offers it to me. I take it.

It reads: DETECTIVE LORI RATTAN, HOMICIDE UNIT. Her cell and office numbers are on the bottom.

"If you come up with something."

I slip it into my shirt pocket.

"I'll be sure to call. Appreciate it."

She turns and walks back to her car, drives out, taking a left onto Sherman.

Older-model cars that look abandoned are parked against the back fence at the 9th Street side. I walk there and peer into the vehicles one at a time. Ignition is popped out of one, but none looks like some homeless person is making it a home.

Couple cars drive north on 9th, passing the firehouse on the other side of the big building on my right. The second car is an old hooptie, music thumping from within. It slows as it passes me. I can't make out how many times it's occupied or even what the driver looks like. The tint is heavy. It speeds up after it passes, skidding tires on pavement. Fucking mopes.

I walk around the inside perimeter of the lot. I don't know what I expect to find except maybe a little motivation.

All the construction going on and not one surveillance camera to catch even a glimpse of the scene.

I hear feet shuffling on the gravel at the other side of the trailer to my right, near Sherman Ave. I walk to the rear of my vehicle and look toward the trailer that pokes out farther than the others.

Nothing.

I stand there. Traffic along Sherman is busy.

Then again. Someone is walking on the other side of the trailer. And two young boys, looking like fucking mopes, appear. They're wearing puffy winter coats and red tactical-type shemaghs that conceal most of their faces. I flick my cigarette to the ground. They stand there looking at me, and the taller boy standing to the right of the other raises his right hand, directed toward me and gesturing like it's a gun, and his index finger pulls the trigger. They're baiting me. Want me to chase them.

"Fuck the poleece," the tall one says.

I grip my 19, ready to draw. They both raise their hands, like the protesters do, turn and walk toward the gate and then left along the sidewalk at Sherman.

I pull my weapon, keep it tucked to my side, rush to my car, and start it, back out, my rear tires spitting gravel out as I skid and turn toward the gate.

Cars going each direction, so I can't make the turn, but I'm poking out far enough to see down the sidewalk.

Gone. They must've hoofed it. All those construction barricades along the road to prevent parking, so I'm sure they ran up to Barry Place. Fuckin' balls, man. Gotta have fucking balls to pull some shit like that thinking I'm the police. Damn, they had to be smoking dippers or some shit.

I never doubted you, Al, but now I got confidence.

Twenty-Three

I manage my way out, turning left on Sherman. When I get to Barry Place, I make a left. It's nearing lunchtime, but still a lot of construction workers around. The whole north side of the block is fenced in, but a couple of workers are leaning against the chain-link fence on the outside perimeter, one of them smoking. I pull to the curb across from them, slide down my window.

"You guys see a couple of dudes running this way?"

They look at each other, back to me, I'm sure wondering who this guy in a Volvo is.

"I saw them snatch something from the bed of a work truck, looked like a Sawzall. Just being neighborly."

"Shit. They ran up there and down 9th," says the smoking man. "Didn't see them carrying anything with them, though."

"They might have dropped it back there when they saw me. I'll see what I can do. Thanks."

I speed away, take a right on 9th. I'm sure they're long gone, and I'm wondering if it was those mopes in the hooptie that drove by the lot. Maybe they looped around, parked down here somewhere. Damn, wish I'd gotten the tag.

That's the way it is nowadays for the police. Morons who aren't afraid of them anymore 'cause they know most of the cops are scared to act. And the kinda scared I'm talking about is the fear that if you act, justified or not, you're gonna get hung out to dry. Most of the guys and gals in the department have families to think about and who they want to go home to. There have been some shootings in this area, up around Garfield Terrace, which is near where I live. A few armed robberies, too. DC is getting loose again.

I feel like those two were baiting me, trying to get me to draw on them and get in a foot pursuit. Fucking felt like a setup. It was the tall guy's hand plain as day, though. No gun that I could see. I don't believe Al would have pulled his gun out in that kind of situation either. He damn well would've been prepared to, though.

I canvass the area a bit longer, then drive to Al's house.

I notice Al peeking out the curtain to see who it is. I shoot him a wave. He opens the door. He's cleaned up. Looks like he showered and shaved, and he's out of the clothes he's probably been wearing for a few days.

"You're looking better."

"Tired of moping around, feeling sorry for myself. Come in."

He locks the door behind me.

The bottle I bought him is on the end table and is more than half empty.

"You want a drink?"

"Yeah, I suppose," I say, even though I shouldn't. Feels like I'm encouraging him in the wrong direction.

He walks to the dining room, returns with a clean tumbler.

"Neat, right?"

"Yeah, just a couple fingers."

He pours more than that, hands it to me. I sit on the armchair. He sits on the sofa. The blanket that was spread out on the sofa is now neatly folded and resting over the back.

"You see the news?" Al asks.

"Yeah, all those fucking protesters at headquarters."

"No, I mean the morning news."

"No. What's up?"

"An officer from 4D got ambushed. Midnight shift. Shot in his car."

"Fuck."

"They're trying to determine whether it was terrorism."

"Is he dead?"

"Yeah. Pronounced at MedStar."

"You got a name?"

"Weibe, young officer. Not even five years on."

"Damn. I'm sorry to hear that."

"That's how it is out there now. Fucking war zone."

"It is, brother. Where did it happen?"

"Georgia Avenue. I think near the corner of Otis. He was parked in his car. Probably a drive-by 'cause they recovered ejected casings scattered in the street."

"Damn."

Al raises his glass. "Here's to officer Sam Weibe."

We clink glasses together and take sips.

"I need to know what you were investigating, Al."

"I thought we went over that already."

"Not in detail."

"Like I told you, a few low-level mutts. Officials aren't giving us the time we need to investigate anything long-term, so we're doing quick hits like these guys, not more than a week. I was getting ready to send a special employee into their house to make a buy. Heroin, but nothing like major players."

I don't want to know the exact location because it'll be too tempting for me, so I ask, "What area? No address. Just the area."

"Fuck. I'll give you the address. Not like anyone's gonna hit it now."

Shit.

He gives me the address.

"That is a spot Cordell Holm used to control. Did you know that?"

"Fuck no. Like I said, we don't get the time to look into things the way we used to."

"When were you going to hit it?"

"Was going to draft an affidavit for a search warrant right after I sent the SE in, which would've been the day I got into the shooting."

"Was Darling working this one for you?"

"Fuck no. You seen her. Cleaned up. No one's going to sell to her. I use her mostly for phone calls. You don't think this has anything to do with those corner dopes, do you? They're not smart enough and they don't got the balls for something like that."

"A week-long investigation and you know them like that?"

"I still got my Spidey sense, Frankie."

"I don't doubt that. You identify any of their vehicles?"

"No. Just the info on the house—when they re-up and how they work, which is mostly outta the back door into the alley. What are you thinking here?"

"Just ruling things out is all. I'll go sit on the house for a bit, maybe later today."

"I think it's a waste of time, but do what you have to."

I decide not to tell him about the hooptie or the two boys at the lot, 'cause that'll get him worked up. If I ever do see those two again, I'll fucking get one of them identified, and that'll be the one that's still conscious.

Twenty-Four

Damn, this block hasn't changed. Still rollin' like it did when I was working. Couple dudes looking like clowns, riding up and down the street on 50cc mini bikes. About four others hanging at the stoop and on the front steps of the house Al identified. He was right. They don't look like high rollers, more like orphans. I'm parked a block back, but I have a good view. None of them wearing anything that looks like the ISIS wannabes that fucked with me at the lot. I scan the block with my binos, checking out all the vehicles. More than a couple of hoopties, but none of them match the description of the one that drove by on 9th Street.

The longer I hang, the more I want to hit that house. But I can't if it's busy like this all the time. Maybe if they go out at night. Damn. The way I think.

Another boy exits the house.

Fuck if it isn't Playboy! Sonofabitch.

What's he doing there, unless he's back in the game? And after I warned him what would happen if he ever chose that path again. What else would he be doing there? Fucking idiot.

He knocks knuckles with a couple of the boys on his way down the steps and walks west, my direction.

He's on the sidewalk on the other side of the street. I slump down, try to stay out of his sight. After he walks by, I start the car and pull out, make the first right so I can go around the block before he gets to the next corner.

When I get to the corner around the block, I can see him crossing. If he continues west on that road, he'll hit 16th, and then it's only about four blocks to his house. I hate following walkers, especially on these narrow roads. No place to turn in and park, and you always have to maintain a decent distance and depend on your binos.

Fuck this.

I drive up, make the next left onto the road he's walking, and pass him. He doesn't look my way. He's smoking a blunt. I drive about twenty yards ahead of him and double-park so that the front passenger door will open between the front and the rear of two cars parked along the curb.

I wait until he's a couple of cars behind me, then step out and close the door. I look the other way while I walk around the front of my car toward the sidewalk, try to keep him from seeing my face. I walk a car's length ahead of him and cut in front of a parked car. Just as he's getting ready to pass, I step to the sidewalk and snatch him up by the left arm. He drops his blunt to the sidewalk. Smells good. Strong.

"Wha—fuck!" is all he gets out.

I swing him around, grab his wrist for control, twist it until he yelps, and then body-slam him against the hood of a parked car.

A well-dressed man is walking on the sidewalk on the other side of the street. Looks our way, but only for a split second. He continues. Nothing new here.

"I ain't do nothin'," he yelps, like he thinks I'm the police. Guess he doesn't recognize me. "My knee! I got a bad knee!"

I pull out the handcuffs I keep at the small of my back, secured by my belt.

He struggles, but I have too much height and weight on him, so it doesn't take much. Fucking *click, click,* and that's that. I pat him down, find keys, a cell phone, a little roll of money, and a baggie of weed is all. Not even a wallet.

I turn him around by the arm so he can see me.

"Oh no! Shit!"

"Yeah. Shit," I say.

Twenty-Five

I have him in the passenger seat of my car, hands cuffed behind him and the seat belt on for safety. I'm still double-parked, but there's enough room for what few cars drive through this block to get by.

"Not again, man. C'mon...No way. What're you gonna do?"

"What did I tell you, Playboy?"

"I don't go by Playboy no more. For real. I don't wanna get kilt, man."

"I'm gonna take you to the police, tell them you're the one I saw driving the car three years ago when Little Monster opened up on me and killed that officer. You remember him? Officer Tommy."

"I liked Officer Tommy. I had nothin' to do with that shit."

"Keep talkin', fool. You were the driver, so you're just as responsible."

Bows his head.

"And you're the one that got away when the cops hit that house on University Place, climbing that fence and running across the alley in your boxers. You remember all that, right? The trunk of my old car? I sent you into the goddamn river, you piece of shit."

"C'mon, now."

A couple more pedestrians walk by. Not even two blocks from where the boys are slinging and riding their mini bikes, and here are regular-looking citizens ambling by, talking on their cells. I drive. Fucking don't know where, because I'm not going to take him to the police. That's a bluff. If I did, it'd raise too many questions I don't know that I'd be able to lie my way out of.

"I listened to you. I ain't a part of nothing like that no more."

"Just saw you knocking knuckles with your bros on your way out of a dope house, so don't fucking lie to me."

"No, no. I just bought me some weed is all. You got the baggie outta my pocket. I ain't a part of what they be doing. Swear."

"What are they doing?"

"C'mon, I ain't no snitch, and what the fuck you be here for? You ain't no cop. Are you?"

"Let's just say, once a cop, always a cop. And if I ask you something, you better answer. You're in no position to do otherwise, so don't get stupid."

"Let me the fuck go. You got no cause to be doing this to me. I got you the girl back. You almost killed me. Fucked up my knee for life. You got no cause no more."

I find a parking spot a few blocks up, just before 16th, and park.

"What you doing?"

"I got no cause? I told you then if I ever found out you were back to the old shit, I'd kill you. I don't wanna kill you anymore, just turn your ass in to the police, let them deal with this shit."

"That was a long time ago. I didn't even wanna be in that car. Little Monster was fucking crazy. And you found me in the deli making sandwiches, not working whores."

I slap him hard across the face. His head swings to the side, hitting the window.

"Fuck!"

"Those were teenage girls. You turned them into prostitutes. And one of them almost died because of you."

"I swear, I don't do that no more. Cordell and most of his boys be in jail. I don't even know what the fuck be going on around there no more."

"I'm sure Cordell is wondering why you're not in fucking jail with them."

"No. Fuck no. They know I ran. Got away."

"Do they?"

"Yeah, they do. I seen a couple of his boys when I walk home. They know I got away when the house on University got hit."

"I thought you said you don't go around there anymore?"

"I don't. I walk Columbia Road to get home. I see them up there sometime."

"Just the same. Cordell probably misses you. Would love to have you by his side while he's doing hard time."

Shakes his head.

"So, Cordell working his boys from jail?"

"I don't know what they got working. Fuck, I ain't got nothin' no more, so just take me back to the river and finish what you shoulda done. 'Cause I ain't gonna go to jail. My uncle gonna kick me out anyway, 'cause I can't find a job."

Is he bluffing now?

I look at him direct, and believe him. I've gotta start thinking things through better. Stop acting on impulse. Would've thought that'd go away when I stopped using, but it didn't. Might have even made it worse.

So, fucking now what? I don't even want to beat the shit out of him, let alone kill him. And he was working at the old man's place on Columbia when I found him. I'm the one who scared him out of there.

"So you're wasting what little money you have left on weed?"

"Helps me think."

The way he says it, like we're having a normal conversation, I almost chuckle.

"Turn your back toward me," I tell him.

"Why? What you gonna do?"

"If I was going to do something, you think I'd warn you? Turn around."

"I can't. The seat belt got me."

I reach over and unlatch the seat belt. It gets caught up on his shoulder, but it isn't restricting his movement anymore.

He turns. I shut off the ignition and take my keys out. I use the handcuff key to unlock the cuffs.

"Why...?"

"Shut the fuck up. And I have your cell, keys, and weed, so don't go runnin' off."

I drop the cuffs in the center console, start the car again.

"I don't know what the fuck I'm doing, because I should turn your ass in to the police." Before he can say something stupid, I say, "I'll drive you back to your uncle's."

"Naw, man, naw. I can walk."

"I said I'm gonna drive you back. Put your seat belt on."

He obeys, shaking his head back and forth.

"Don't say anything. I might change my mind."

I pull the car out and head toward Hobart.

Twenty-Six

I double-park in front of his house.

"Can I get my shit back?" he asks.

Not going to get a thank-you, I guess, but I don't expect one. I am the one who fucked him up, after all.

"Not yet."

"This is fucked up, man."

I pull out a smoke, offer him one.

"Naw, not me."

I light myself one, slide the window down a bit.

"I don't know what the fuck you expect," he tells me.

"I told you not to say anything that might make me change my mind. I need to think here."

He has a worried expression on his face. I'm sure he's worried about what it is I have to think about. Funny, I don't have to worry about a guy like Calvin calling the police. I could beat the shit out of him again, and he'd take it. Something about that I respect.

When I finish the cigarette, I flick it out the window. He's just sitting there, too scared to say anything, but I know that mind of his is churning, wondering what the hell I'm going to do.

What the hell am I doing?

"Your uncle married?"

He looks at me, almost answers, but then scrunches his face, like, *What the fuck?*

"Is he?"

"No. He never got married."

"He own the house?"

"Yeah. He a hardworkin' man. Already paid that house off and everything. Never even been arrested. Nothin' like that. Why you need to know?"

"You should stay there, then. With him."

Chuckles, looks away, and says, "Might not have much choice in that matter."

"Everyone's got a choice."

He doesn't know what to say to that.

Here's a kid whose life I almost took a few years back but had a change of mind, or heart. *I think I had one back then.* Whatever. And now chance puts him here, and I'm sitting here trying to have a fucking conversation with him. For the life of me, I don't know why.

My cell rings.

Calvin jumps out of his seat.

"Hold on there," I tell him.

Jimmy.

"What's up, Jimmy?"

"I have that info for you when you're ready to copy."

I grab a pen and my notepad from the center console under the cuffs.

"Ready."

Jimmy confirms the name as Arthur "Arty" Taylor, and then his DOB and home address on the 1400 block of Clifton Street.

"Copy that," I say. "Appreciate it."

"Keep me posted."

"I will."

I disconnect, close the notepad and slip it under my ass, put the pen back on the console.

Something comes to me. A flicker of an idea, but a bad idea.

I turn to look at Calvin. Uncomfortable, but he looks back.

"I might have a job opportunity for you," I say.

Twenty-Seven

D o what you got to do, 'cause I told you I ain't no snitch."

"Not asking you to be a snitch," I say. "I'm a PI—"

"Wait. You were a PI looking for that girl back then? She wasn't your niece?" His eyes widen. Pissed red.

"She was my niece," I lie, because it's the smart thing to do. "I was a DC cop, too, but retired."

It's obvious he's having a hard time processing all this. I would, too, if I were in his shoes. I sure as hell wouldn't trust me.

"I don't need a snitch. I'm looking for you to work with me. A part-time gig. Learn a skill. Make more money part-time with me than you were making full-time at the deli."

"That's fucked up."

"How is that fucked up?"

"I ain't sayin' I didn't do nothin' bad way back then—"

"Bad?" I interrupt. "Be fucking thankful I didn't kill you back then. You were more than bad, but so was I."

"I gotta finish. Let me finish. Man, you really fucked me up, and I probably woulda been better off if I just got arrested that day. I ain't been right since. And then you come outta nowhere, surprise the fuck outta me at my work, and all I'm thinkin' is *He found me and is gonna finish the job.* Fuck. For all I know, you some psycho playin' my ass right now just for fun before the kill."

"Only one way to find out," I joke.

He doesn't think it's funny.

"Just keep my shit," he huffs, and opens the door.

"Hold on, now, Calvin. I ain't psycho, so shut the damn door and listen." *Really, I don't know why I'm doing this.* "I don't know why the hell I'm offering this, because I think you're the last person I could ever trust. But it is a legit offer and will keep you here, at your family house with your uncle. And you can learn, maybe even get your PI license and go off on your own, work for some defense attorney or some shit like that."

He closes the door.

"City ain't gonna give someone like me a license."

"You wanted or some shit like that? I mean, aside from what I could turn you in for."

"Naw. I ain't been locked up since I was a kid, and that case got no-papered."

"You're good, then. Even if you did have a juvie record, they couldn't use that."

"This is some crazy shit here."

I hand him his belongings, including the baggie of weed.

"Yeah, I know, but I got a sense about you. 'Sides, you're probably more qualified for something like this than most PIs I know."

"Shiet."

"You do any other drugs, aside from weed?"

"Hell no. I don't even drink much. Why you ask that?"

"Just making sure is all."

"You gonna, like, hunt me down if I say I wanna think about it?"

"No. I'll give you that, but only till the end of the day tomorrow."

"A'right." And he opens the door, steps out.

"Do the right thing for your life. This ain't bullshit."

An upward nod, and he closes the door. I watch him through the rearview as he hits his steps and walks up. Then I drive away. He won't call.

Arthur Taylor lived in a redbrick, multistory apartment building on the south side of the 1400 block of Clifton Street. Another hot spot back in the day, but not as bad as the 1300 block and Clifton Terrace. Those boys were slinging 24/7. Cordell's other home on University Place is around the corner from here. That's the house Calvin managed to escape from when the police hit it with a search warrant. During the chaos Calvin climbed the chain-link fence in the rear and ran up the alley and into my fist. He spent the better part of that day in the trunk of an old car I had after mine got shot up.

It's almost like a blur. All the cocaine I was using, not to mention pills and alcohol. Let's hope that the river doesn't spit anything else out. It's still holding a few secrets for me.

The apartment complex on Clifton has cleaned up a bit. Looks like a newer playground in the fenced area, decent landscaping, but it still has that claustrophobic housing-development ambience. It looks like you gotta buzz to get into the front entrance. I hate having to do a cold interview like this. The police have interviewed whoever lives here on numerous occasions, probably even the neighbors, and who knows if they were provided with anything useful.

What the fuck were you doing at the lot on Sherman, Arthur Taylor? I should've asked Calvin if he knew him, but I have a strong feeling he wouldn't have told me. He's still mostly a knucklehead.

I walk to the front entrance for Taylor's address, and the glass front door is wedged open with a rolled-up Pier 1 catalog. Good for me because I'd rather knock on the door than try to talk my way in through a speaker. Lobby is clean, not like the old days. Not even a scent of weed in the air.

The unit he lived in is on the second floor. I take the stairs.

I find the door and knock.

Sound of someone unlocking a dead bolt, and a heavyset woman wearing a long black dress answers. She looks to be in her early thirties. She has puffy bags under her red eyes.

"How many more times do I have to talk to you people?" she asks.

"What people?"

"The police."

That's nice.

"I'm not with the police, ma'am. I work for the court."

That's not a complete lie. Leslie is a defense lawyer and works for the court.

"So that officer who shot my little boy was arrested?"

"Not yet, but that's why I'm here. I want to double-check everything you spoke to the police about and maybe some things you didn't speak to them about."

"What you mean by that?"

"Shouldn't really talk in the hall like this. Can I come in?"

"You got some identification, something that says who you are?"

I have several IDs. Need to make sure I pull the right one out of my wallet. All of them except for my retired police ID, my HR 218 qualification card, and my PI license are fake. I'm looking for the fake one that states I'm an investigator for the court. When I open my wallet I'm careful not to reveal my badge. I find the ID and show it to her. She examines it carefully.

"Franklin Starr, Court Investigator?"

"Yes, ma'am."

She hands it back to me and opens the door to allow me in.

The living room opens into the kitchen and a small dining area. There are several flower arrangements in vases on the small dining table. Some of the flowers are dried out. There's a hallway at the other end with two or three doors. The home is nicely kept.

Nothing from the dollar store here. It smells like coconut, but not lotion, maybe incense. A leather sectional sofa with a large square coffee table take up most of the living room. A large flat-screen is mounted on the wall.

"You can sit there," she says, directing me to the edge of the sofa that faces a window, not the television. She sits at the other edge, keeping a nonconversational distance. "So, what you need to know?"

Twenty-Eight

I open my pocket notebook, date it at the top of the page, and ask, "Can I get your full name, please?"

"You can get that from the police, can't you?"

"Yes, ma'am, but we try to stay independent from their investigation. I don't work for the police department."

She tilts her head, looks at me with a half smile. "Donna Taylor."

I write it down.

"And Arthur was your son?"

"Yes."

"Where do you work?"

"What does that have to do with my son's death?"

"Just for the record, ma'am. We like to know as much about the family as possible."

"Like I'm gonna get money for his death or something?"

"Well, that's civil, and I'm not on the civil side."

"But I could? I mean, I am gonna sue the police and the city and that officer."

"That's a civil matter. What I need will go to the court if it ever goes to trial. What do you do for a living?"

"I am currently unemployed."

"Anybody else in your family work—husband, someone like that?"

"I'm a single mother—was a mother."

Is she all out of tears?

And who the fuck paid for this expensive shit in her home? A sixteen-year-old boy?

"Arthur went to Cardoza?" I ask.

She hesitates to say.

"He dropped out at tenth grade."

"Unfortunately, a lot of kids have to do that nowadays to help keep food on the table."

"Yeah."

"So, where did he work?"

"I don't know where he worked," she says firmly.

She looks like she's getting agitated with this line of questioning. I'm not going to take it further. Don't want to judge or anything, but I'm pretty sure I know what he did to make money.

"No worries. I know this is hard, but when was the last time you saw Arthur?"

"The day before he got killed by that cop."

"He lived here, though?"

"Yes, but he sixteen and he got friends he stay with sometimes."

"It's important I talk to his friends. Can you give me names?"

"My son got shot. Plain and simple. He didn't have a gun. That officer murdered him. You tell me why all this other stuff is important to the court?"

"If there is a possible witness who saw the officer kill your son, then there's nothing more we need. Case closed. You know how the police can be sometimes. Protect their own. Like I said, I don't work for the police."

"The police said he was alone."

"Maybe his friends ran. I know I would if I saw a cop shoot down my unarmed friend. I'd also be too afraid to go to the police. That's for sure."

"He got a couple of friends he be with all the time."

"The names would be really helpful."

"Ty is one of them. They call him Little T. Another one is Marlon. That's all I know."

"Are they the same age as your son?"

"I think a little older."

"And you don't know where they live?"

"Just that it's one of those buildings on the fourteen hundred block of Fairmont is all."

"Have you talked to any of his friends since the shooting?"

"Not those boys. Just neighbors and friends that bring flowers and show their condolences is all."

I don't want to push this any further.

"I appreciate your time, Ms. Taylor, and I'm sorry for your loss."

"When they gonna lock that man up?"

"That's a matter for the police, not me. Is there anything else you would like to add for the court?"

I'm so full of bullshit.

"My son, Arthur, was a good boy," she begins, and so do the tears. "That cop need to be punished for what he did."

"All right, ma'am," I say while standing.

I fold my notebook and slip it into my back pants pocket and the pen into my shirt pocket. I hand her a card.

"My number is on the card if you need to talk to me about anything else. Thank you for your time."

She looks at the card. The number goes to one of my burners.

"I can show myself out."

"You make sure that officer pays for what he did."

I open the door, walk out, and shut it behind me. Nothing to say about that.

Ty and his boy Marlon shouldn't be hard to track down. That is, if they do hang at the 1400 block of Fairmont. I'll work on that tomorrow and, if anything good comes from it, give Leslie a call. I don't know, but I do have a feeling.

TWENTY-NINE

Al is an experienced detective, a good cop. He's got a lot of time on and has never been under investigation by Internal Affairs. Based on what I know now, though, maybe he should've been. But fucking his CI is not like shooting an unarmed kid. I believe him. That the kid was armed. That there was a gun. It was taken from the scene by one of Arthur's boys. And I need to keep the police in the loop. It's not like before. This time it's one of our own. But how the hell do you prove something like that unless we get a confession or a good witness? Obtaining a confession is highly unlikely.

"Detective Rattan," she answers.

"Frank Marr here, Detective. How's it going?"

"Doing some write-ups. What can I do for you?"

"I want to run a couple of names by you, see if they came up on your radar."

"Okay."

"All I have is first names. First one is Ty, late teens, early twenties. Second one, Marlon, also late teens, early twenties. Known to hang in the area of the fourteen hundred block of Fairmont."

"No. I don't know them. How'd their names come up?"

"Looking into Arthur Taylor's associates."

"Who gave them up as associates?"

Last thing I want to do is tell her I lied my way into the decedent's house to interview the mother.

"The old-fashioned way. Working the street. Taylor would stay with them on occasion, and they were good buddies."

"Yeah, he had friends. So?"

"Maybe one or both of them were on the scene the day of the shooting. Maybe they saw what happened. Maybe they heard something. Or maybe one of them took the gun from the scene. I just can't believe Arthur Taylor was there alone, and why was he there? It's starting not to make sense."

"Lot of reasons why he could have been there."

"Yes. Are you looking into those reasons?"

"Mr. Marr"—*Mister?*—"I know Luna is a good cop, but it's really not looking like a good shooting. We're getting to the point where everything has been exhausted."

"I just gave you two names to look into. Shouldn't be too hard to find them hanging around the fourteen hundred block of Fairmont. Have you even looked into his known associates?"

"We have. We've interviewed several people."

"You sound a little different from when we last spoke."

"Not at all. My squad caught two more cases last night. Listen, last thing I want is to see one of our own go down for something like this. The department doesn't need it. We don't need it. I'll look into the names. I do appreciate you keeping me in the loop."

"I've been known to go rogue, so yes, you should be thankful."

No response.

"That was a joke, Rattan," I lie.

"Okay, then."

"Just so you are aware, I'll be looking into it, too, and will keep you posted."

"Thank you. Don't hurt anyone."

Okay?

"That was a joke, Marr. I know you wouldn't do that."

Okay.

"I'll try not to. Thanks for your time. Be safe."

"Thanks."

It's still early enough that Rebellion shouldn't be crowded, and I might find a good spot at the bar. I park a couple of blocks away.

Few chairs at the bar when I enter, and a bartender I know is working. I notice a man wearing a suit, looks familiar from the side. An open chair is next to him. The tender shoots me a wave, and I hit him with a broad smile. When I get to the bar I recognize the guy as Detective Gary Lustig, from the Third District, which is only a few blocks from here. Before he was a detective he worked Vice, but that was years ago.

"Look at the bums this place caters to now," I say.

He turns, immediately recognizes me.

"Frank Marr."

Gary has worked his way through half a hamburger and a pile of seasoned fries. Nearly empty pint of stout next to his plate and his handheld radio, volume turned low. Dispatcher calls out for a patrol unit, but I can't make out the assignment. My ears aren't tuned in to that frequency anymore. Used to dream hearing the dispatcher's voice at night. Not anymore. Gary will no doubt hear his call sign over the radio, if it comes up, even at that volume. It's something you become accustomed to. He's a couple of years younger than me, early to midforties, but the puffy bags under his eyes make him look older. Also losing some of that black curly hair, balding toward the middle. Typical overworked district detective.

"Chair taken?" I say.

"No. Sit down, bro."

"Don't want to interrupt your meal."

"Welcome company, buddy. Good to see you."

After we shake hands, I sit. The bartender approaches, offers his hand across the bar. He has a firm grip.

"What can I get ya, Frank?"

"Zacapa, one cube, thanks."

"Sure thing."

"So, you on evenings?" I ask Gary.

"Hell no. I'm permanent daywork, but they got us on twelve-hour shifts, thinking that's going to curtail the violence. I'm going to head in after this, but my luck I'll get a call."

"I feel for you, man. Can't say I miss that part of the job."

"The Third District detectives' office is rookie central. Lot of new investigators. Lot of the old-timers retired, had enough of this shit. I'm not far behind." He takes a sip of stout.

Bartender sets my drink on the bar. Nice pour.

"Gonna have something to eat?" the bartender asks.

"I'm good for now."

He slaps the bar with the palm of his hand, moves to the other end of the counter to watch the preshow for the Caps game on the wall-mounted television.

Good aged rum is like coffee. The sugars pick me up instead of the caffeine, and the alcohol warms my belly. Was a time when only one thing could pick me up, but my body and mind have rebooted, almost back to what I think is considered normal, except the fatigue. But the drink helps.

"Anything on the officer that was killed?"

"Which one?"

"The one that was shot."

"They're still working it. Powers that be afraid to call it what it is."

"And what is that?"

"Terrorism."

"That what detectives are saying?"

"Fuck, man. Doesn't take some motherfucker from a sensitive Middle Eastern country screaming *Allahu Akbar* before killing someone for it to be terrorism. Could be some corner boy for all I know. But walking up to a parked patrol unit and opening up on the officer inside is terrorism. Shit, even that hit-and-run. That wasn't an accident."

"They thinking that's related?"

"Not that I know. I'm not working it, but I do know that officer was targeted just like Wiebe was, except with a car. Fucked-up times. You still friends with Al Luna?" He changes the subject. Topic might be churning that juicy hamburger in his stomach into bad gas.

"Yeah. In fact, I'm helping him out best I can."

"No gun. No evidence of a gun. Doesn't look good. Damn. I even hate to say that. He's a good detective. A good guy. Give him my best, okay?"

"I will. Arthur Taylor, the kid he shot, lived in 3D. He ever come up on your radar for anything?"

"No, and he would've been too young when I worked Vice."

"They're never too young."

"True that. Some crazy baby gangstas out there nowadays. Getting younger all the time."

"Do me a favor or, rather, Al a favor. Ask some of the guys working narcotics at 3D if they've heard of Arthur Taylor and two other young ones—Ty, or Little T, and Marlon. Both known associates of Taylor's."

"Hold on," he says, grabbing his pocket notebook. "Ty? T-Y?"

"Yeah. Known as Little T, and the other is Marlon."

He writes the names down.

"They live or hang at the fourteen hundred block of Fairmont."

Writes that down, too, says, "I'll see what I can do. You still have the same cell number?"

"Yes."

"I have it saved in mine. I'll hit you if I find anything."

"Appreciate it, brother."

I down the rest of my drink, signal the bartender for another. I'm gonna need a couple more to get moving.

Thirty

I drive with the window down, north on 18th to Florida, and take a right. Instead of continuing on Florida Ave, I keep straight through the light where it becomes U Street. I want to see the Third on the way home, for no reason other than I want to look at it. I never worked out of that building, but a lot of my friends did. Cars pulling out of the upper and lower garages as other cars make their way in. Shift change.

When I get to 12th, I make a left. My house is a couple of blocks up.

While looking for a place to park, I notice a black SUV, driver's window partially open and thick smoke folding up out the window, like a tongue. I accelerate, taking a look through the corner of my eye as I pass the car. Windows have heavy tint, and the engine seems to be off. No exhaust being pushed out of the rear. I get to the end of the block and make a left on Florida, then a quick left at the narrow alley that is behind my house. I stop a quarter way up the alley, see if they're following.

Doesn't look like it.

I continue to the end of the alley. Thirteenth Street is to the right and 12th to the left. I turn my headlights off and make that left, stop before I hit 12th and slowly creep out enough to get an eyeball on the SUV, still parked on the east side of the street. I get my binos out of the center console and peek. Heavy smoke still being blown out, like a cigar or a large blunt. It sure as hell looks like the SUV that was following me. I'm not about to jump out on them. I've got a good amount of alcohol in my system and'll probably blow high. If they're cops smoking cigars and I surprise them like that, I might get myself shot. If they're fucking thugs, the chances are even higher. Best to sit tight, see what they're up to, if anything. I don't have a good enough angle to make out the tag at the rear of the vehicle. I know the car doesn't belong to any of the homes here, but that doesn't mean they're not visiting a neighbor and are out smoking up the interior of the car instead of their home.

After a few minutes the smoke through the window thins out, becomes less frequent, then stops altogether. No movement. I'm not going to fuck around here. This doesn't feel right, and in my opinion that's a suspicious vehicle. For all I know it's associated with someone like Jasper, a dirty cop I got locked up a while back, or even Playboy, maybe in there with some of his boys, waiting to cap my ass.

I passed the car, though, and if it's the same SUV, why didn't they follow? They didn't recognize my car? But maybe they did and are waiting for me to appear at the front of my house or for a light to turn on because I entered through the back door. Fuck this shit.

"Metropolitan Police Department, Third District, Sergeant Kendall."

I know Kendall. Been on the department since forever. One of the few remaining working sergeants left.

"Sarge, this is Marr. They got you working the station now?"

"Hey there, Marr. Yeah, working the desk for a bit. Had minor surgery. How's that early retirement going?"

"Everything's good. And you?"

"All the parts still working, just a hernia is all. Another week and I'll be out of this chair. Something I can do for you, Frank?"

"Yeah. I didn't want to call three one one. Thought I might get a better response calling 3D direct. I'm still living on the 2200 block of 12th Street, and I noticed a suspicious vehicle parked on the east side of the street across from my house. Was hoping you could have a unit respond to check it out. Probably nothing, but you never know. Lot of robberies going on around here."

"Why do you think it's suspicious?"

"It's been parked there for a while now, window part down, engine off, thick smoke blowing out, like they're smoking weed. Just doesn't feel right."

"I can get a patrol car there. Give it a few, though. They're just getting out of roll call. You have a tag?"

"No. Can't get an eye on it."

"What do you have, then?"

"Older-model four-door, black Ford SUV, heavy tint, parked on the east side of the 2200 block of Twelfth Street, NW, about halfway up the block, near Florida Ave. Don't know how many times it's occupied. Can you advise the responding officers that I'm parked in a silver Volvo at the cut on the west side of the 2200 block, near W, and who I am so they don't think it's another suspicious vehicle."

"Okay. Got it. I'll get a unit out there."

"Appreciate it, Sarge. Hope you hit the street soon, back to your high-rollin', hardworking self."

"Ha! Me too. About to go crazy here."

"Thanks again."

"No worries."

Nothing to do now but sit back, see what happens.

Thirty minutes later, and the SUV is still there. No one in or out. A marked unit is driving north on 12th, crosses W and slows. The driver notices me parked in the alley. I shoot him a wave out the window anyway, hoping he'll notice, and point in the direction of the parked SUV. I can see him. Don't recognize him. A young officer.

They slow to a stop a couple of cars behind the SUV. The SUV's lights come on, like they finally decide now would be a good time to leave. Rear reverse lights come on. It's going to pull out.

The officers put their emergency lights on, and the one behind the wheel hits the driver's window of the SUV with the spotlight.

The officers step out of their vehicle, stream lights beaming through the rear window of the SUV. They use the doors as shields.

"Turn your vehicle off, please," the officer who was driving says.

Nothing. Reverse lights are still on.

"Turn your vehicle off!" the officer repeats.

The secondary officer steps toward the sidewalk and the passenger side of the vehicle, shines his stream light into the vehicle. From my vantage, I can't make out the interior. I do know if they were cops, they would have already identified themselves. I want to step out, but that would distract the officers. I can't just sit here, especially when my Spidey sense is tingling.

"Roll down the driver's window and turn the vehicle off!"

The SUV's rear reverse lights go off, and then the rest of the lights. I can't tell if the window was rolled down, but the engine appears to be off. Primary officer steps away from his open door and moves with caution toward the driver's side of the parked vehicle. His right hand seems to be gripping his holstered weapon. The officer stays close to the vehicle so he's not an easy target. He shines the light in the rear window. Patrol car's spotlight is shining bright in the driver's window. I've been on that side of the spotlight before. If done right, it can be blinding, especially if the light bounces off the rearview mirror.

Someone speaks from inside the car, but it's inaudible to me.

Officers are handling this like a routine traffic stop, but I'm not in their shoes and don't see what they see. Personally, I'd stay behind the open door and have the occupants slowly step out of the vehicle, with hands where I can see them. They might be able to see inside, through the heavy tint. I certainly can't from where I'm sitting.

The secondary officer stays back, light still shining through the rear window. The primary steps closer, shines his stream light directly in the driver's window—

"Gun!" the officer yells.

He backs away, running, drawing his weapon at the same time. Fast as shit! *Pop! Pop! Pop!* Muzzle flash with each round. Primary officer looks like he is thrown backwards.

I jump out of my car, weapon out, and run toward them, my legs pumping before I even realize I'm out on the street. I can see the secondary officer with his weapon out, but before he can get a round off, more shooting, this time from the passenger side. Secondary officer drops. Primary officer manages a couple of shots but seems off-balance.

SUV lights turn on. I hear the engine roar.

Primary officer gets a couple of shots off and then suddenly goes limp and falls where he is. I stop, steady my weapon, and get off several rounds. Pretty sure I smash the driver's-side rear window out. The SUV lunges forward, hitting the parked car in front. Secondary officer is standing again. He fires, but the SUV skids backwards, hitting a rear parked car so hard it slides up onto the curb. "Watch out!" I yell out to the secondary officer. But the parked car hits him solid, knocking him to the hood of another parked car and to the ground.

I run for a better angle on the car, can barely make out the driver when I do. I fire. I can see muzzle flashes from the driver's side but hear only a whizzing sound by my ear. Fuck! I fire again. Don't know how many times. SUV turns out, knocking the parked front vehicle so hard it jumps the curb. The SUV speeds north on 12th.

Seconds. Ten, maybe twenty seconds at most.

Sirens.

I holster my weapon so I don't get shot and run to the primary officer first.

Unconscious, but making deep-throated gurgling sounds. He has what looks like a single gunshot wound to the right cheek. Thick dark blood. Can't see an exit.

Sirens are closer but no lights.

I look back to the secondary officer. He's trying to move. Grunts.

"Talk to me!" I call out to him.

"I think my leg's broken," he struggles.

"Help is almost here. I'm gonna stay with your partner."

"He okay?"

"Yeah," I lie.

I can see lights coming north on 12th, and two more cars turning onto 12th from Florida Ave.

The primary officer doesn't sound good. I open his mouth to check for obstructions. Fuck. It's a bloody mess. He's gonna drown in his own blood.

"Police! Back away from the officer!" I hear behind me.

I immediately put my hands in the air.

"Frank Marr, retired police," I advise. "I'm the one who called Kendall."

"Back away. Now!"

Hands still raised as I stand and back away. "You need to call for two ambulances."

I slowly turn. Two officers have their weapons pointed at me.

I'm surprised as I'm grabbed from behind with force and put to the pavement, face-first. Pretty sure I belt out a grunt when they cuff me. Fucking left hand feels like the nerves are being pinched with tweezers.

I know they have to do this, so I go with it. Shut the fuck up. Let them do their job, explain everything later.

"I got a gun," an officer with his knee on my back says.

"I'm a retired cop. Get my wallet," I wheeze out. I don't think he heard me, or he just doesn't care. I'm dragged on the ground, the face of the fallen officer a couple of feet from me, blood bubbling through his closed lips. Two other officers kneeling beside him. His face seems to shine brighter the farther away I'm pulled.

THIRTY-ONE

T he block is flooded with light: patrol car's emergency lights, two Crime Scene Search spots, media camera lights behind the yellow tape that prevents access from Florida Ave and south at W. I see Chief Wightman. He's talking to several reporters at the corner of 12th and W. Yet another crime scene on this block that I'm involved in.

Both ambulances sped out to MedStar about an hour ago. Crime Scene is collecting spent casings, searching areas where bullets may have hit, including the driver's door of my car. Two bullet holes. Other detectives interview neighbors. Detectives Rattan and Millhoff, along with Sergeant Kendall, are with me. The cuffs are off now. I rub the scar tissue on my left hand. Doesn't help the nerve pain. We're next to my Volvo, away from the cameras. Damn. I should call Leslie, not as a personal attorney. I have no worries there, because I didn't do anything wrong. If it was the same SUV that followed me from Al's place, then she should know. Hell, the police should know.

"Marr," Millhoff says. "You okay?"

"Yeah, yeah. What was it you asked?"

"I noticed you had binos in your car, on the passenger seat. Did you get a look at any of the suspects?"

"No. Tint on their vehicle was too heavy. Don't even know how many were in there. At least two shooters. I know that. Listen, I should tell you—don't know if it's related, don't see how it could be."

"Okay," Millhoff says.

"When I left Al Luna's house the other day, a black SUV was parked across from his house and followed me for a while. I managed to lose it."

"You get a tag?"

"No. They didn't get close enough for that. Pretty sure it was a Ford Explorer, though."

"Was the suspect's vehicle here an Explorer?"

"Couldn't make out the model because it was parked too close to the car behind. Could have been. They both had heavy tint. Did the officer that was conscious say anything?"

"They ran the tag before getting out. We're looking into it," Millhoff says.

"Was it an Explorer?"

"Yes. Why do you think the shooting Al was involved in would be related to this?" Rattan asks.

"I said I didn't think so, really. I'm not sure. Maybe check if IA or some reporter was sitting on Al's house and decided to follow me. If it was, then the similarity is just coincidental."

"Doesn't sound coincidental to me," Kendall says.

"I can check with our department, but I'm not sure I can find out about the media."

"Seems to me you just chanced into a situation where cops were being targeted," Kendall says. "Maybe they were targeting Luna, too, because of the shooting."

"There's a lot of black SUVs out there," Rattan says.

"I'll have an unmarked unit sit on the block. Just to be safe. I'll notify 5D and have them do the same for Al," Kendall says.

"Yeah. That'd be good," I say.

"Cops *are* being ambushed," Millhoff says.

"Did the officers have their bodycams on?" I ask Millhoff.

"We'll know that soon."

"Crime Scene is going to have to search your car, try to locate the bullets that hit the driver's door," Rattan says.

"I got an open bottle of Jameson in the back seat."

"Are you offering?" Kendall asks.

"That would be nice about now, but just thought you should know. Open container, you know."

"I think we can let that slide, Frank," Kendall says.

"Are you drunk?" Rattan asks.

I shoot her a glare. "Fuck no. I had a couple drinks earlier at Rebellion. That bottle was meant for Al." The former is true at least. What nerve, though.

"Any other weapons in the car?" she asks.

"No. You all took the only weapon I had on me. And I expect to get it back soon."

"Standard shit. You know that, Frank," Millhoff says.

"Yeah, I know."

I have a couple other registered weapons in the house, so I can live without the 19 for a while.

"Lori, you want to get Stein to work Marr's vehicle?" Millhoff asks her. "And tell him to leave the bottle in the car." He smiles.

"Yeah, sure."

She walks to the other side of the street, where a Crime Scene tech is taking pictures.

An image of the fallen officer pops into my head. Pool of blood in his open mouth. The sound he was making. Something new and unwelcome that'll stay with me now. That would have been me if I'd decided to take care of it myself. Two shooters, possibly more. I wouldn't have had a chance. There was a time, not so long ago, that I would have tried. Fucking stupid back then. Wightman will have all hands on deck for this one. That's for sure.

"You keep me posted about those officers, okay?" I ask Kendall.

"I will," he says.

"You should stay away from the news, Frank."

"I don't have a problem with that. They don't know who I am, right?"

"We don't give out victim information," Rattan says.

I want to tell her I fucking know that. I just forgot I'm a victim in this, too.

Victim. Shit.

THIRTY-TWO

T he snow passed over, leaving us a couple of inches. That was usually enough to immobilize the city, but they had crews ready, obviously expecting more. The main roads are cleared.

The 1400 block of Fairmont has a nice family park on the north-west side. Neighborhood kids are playing in the snow now. A couple of them are trying to build a snowman with what little they have. I don't remember when the park was built, but it's fairly new. It stretches north to Girard Street, where Cookie lives, a onetime snitch who helped me out with the missing girl case that coinciden-tally led to a house on University Place, where Fairmont ends on the west side.

All these fucking coincidences. I'm starting to think that life is bitch-slapping me. You think you can stay clean? You think you can simply stop paying for your sins? Just watch.

This block has always been busy, but mostly in the area of 14th and Fairmont, near the once-infamous five-story apartment build-ings that take up the north and south corners of Fairmont. I've been out of it for a while, but I do know it's not like it was years ago. Shit still breaks on occasion, but nothing like back then.

I'm parked on University Place, where it ends on Fairmont and faces the park. Fairmont is one way going east. Good spot to hang. Don't want to make it an all-day event, though. Gotta make something happen. Time is creeping up on Al. Protesters still in front of 300 doing their thing, making noise. Like Freudiger said, it won't pressure the US attorney's office much, but it will bring some heat down on the mayor's office and the sparks are sure to hit the chief. And like they say, shit rolls down from there. Always has. Always will.

My cell rings. It's a DC government prefix.

I answer, "Marr."

"Kendall here, Frank."

"What's up, Sarge?"

"Don't know if they're keeping you in the loop at Homicide, but thought you'd want to know that they located the suspect's vehicle late last night."

"That's good news. Where?"

"Not such good news. It was recovered off 295 while it was still on fire. By the time the firemen got the flames out, the car was nothing but a torched-out shell. I don't know what, if anything, they'll be able to recover out of that."

"Damn. Well, I appreciate you keeping me informed. They sure as hell won't tell me anything."

"I'm here for you if you need anything."

When someone like Kendall says they're there for you, that means most anything, even running names. He could give a shit. *Shit, Leslie.* I forgot to call her, but I'm also wondering why I haven't heard from *her* about last night. She has to have seen the news.

I give her a call. The receptionist answers.

"Frank Marr for Leslie Costello."

"Ms. Costello is in court all day, Mr. Marr. Would you like to leave a message?"

"Just tell her I called."

"What's a number where she can reach you?"

"She has my number." I disconnect, sort of pissed that she hasn't called me.

I focus my attention back on the corner.

This is bullshit. It's not like I'm going to jump out on them and get their names. They'll just spit on the ground at my feet, sneer after. Waste of my time.

I drive toward 14th, pass the young boys and take a right. I make my way home, and when I get to 12th from Florida, I notice a Fox 5 News van parked at the corner, a reporter, looks like Paul Wagner, and a cameraman. Interviewing my neighbor. Fucking tenacious son of a gun. The last thing I'm gonna do is park and get caught walking to my house. I keep driving. Maybe I'll go back to Al's, see how he's holding up.

Cell rings.

"Hello?" a familiar voice says.

"Frank Marr. How can I help you?"

"This is Calvin. You said I should give you a call."

I hesitate. I know who it is, but I can't believe he's calling.

"Calvin," he repeats. "You call me...*Playboy*."

"I know who it is. What's up, Calvin?"

"You said I should call before the end of the day about that offer of yours."

It's not even noon, far from the end of the day. With everything that happened, it literally slipped my mind, and it was only yesterday afternoon I met with him.

"Good to hear from you, Calvin."

"Yeah, been doing some thinking about that opportunity of yours."

I find an open spot to park on 10th, a couple blocks from my house. I take it, put the car in park.

"My uncle, he give me one of those ultimatums," he continues. "So I really got no choice. I need work or I gotta get out."

"So you're saying my offer's all you got and you're desperate?"

"I ain't desperate. I'm never desperate."

"Well, you said you have no choice but to take me up on my offer."

"That ain't being desperate. That be responsible."

I don't know if I want to even entertain this, especially after last night. For all I know, he's smarter than I give him credit for and he's playing my ass. Hell, but you know what they say—

"When can we meet?" I ask.

...*And your enemies closer*.

"I'll be at my uncle's house all day. I'm taking a chance here that you ain't gonna try to finish what you got started back then."

"What makes you think I didn't finish?"

"Don't start playin' me with words now."

"I can be there at two o'clock."

"I'll be outside waitin'."

"Okay, then."

For all I know he's setting me up. I'll have to be careful with what I say, maybe even occasionally look over my shoulder.

THIRTY-THREE

I pick up a couple of subs from the Italian spot in Northeast that Al and I love and used to always hit. Thought it might be a good gesture to offer one to Calvin. Or maybe a nice test.

I see him sitting in a chair on the porch as I pull up near his uncle's home. He looks my way but doesn't stand. I find a parking space at the curb a couple houses up from his. It's a tight squeeze between two cars, so I have to work my way in.

I step out. The air's got a nice bite to it, so I grab my jacket and put it over my suit coat, lean back in the car to get the bag with the subs in it. I walk to his house.

He's still sitting there. Do I expect him to wave?

The steps leading to the house have been shoveled and de-iced. I don't have to worry about slipping and breaking my neck. Might be something he'd enjoy seeing.

"Your uncle home?" I ask while walking up.

"Naw. He at work."

"Too bad. Like to meet him."

"Why?"

"Courtesy is all."

I step up to the porch, set the bag on the small table between the chairs.

"I don't know you good enough to show that kinda courtesy."

"I can understand that. Those chairs look cold."

"You get used to it."

"Yeah, I like the cold," I say as I sit.

He eyeballs the bag with the sandwiches. I grab the bag, open it, and pull one of the wrapped sandwiches out.

"I got these at one of the best Italian spots in DC, just off Florida Ave, in Northeast." I offer it to him.

Reluctant, but he accepts. "I ain't really hungry."

"Then save it for later," I tell him. "It'll keep."

I take mine out.

"You rather have this one?" I offer. "They're the same, though."

He unwraps his, lifts the bun up, closely examines the contents.

"I didn't spit in it."

"It ain't spit I'm worried about."

"Oh, you mean poison, some shit like that?"

"Yeah, shit like that."

"Well, if there was, you wouldn't be able to see it."

I unwrap mine. He slips the bun back on top of his and wraps it up.

"It's a good sandwich, Calvin. No poison."

He sets it on the table. "I ain't so hungry right now is all. Keep it for later."

"Suit yourself." I take a bite.

"What's the shit on the driver's side of your car? Look like bullet holes."

I look toward my car. "How do you know I have bullet holes on the driver's side?"

"I seen it when you were backing into that spot there."

131

He could have noticed them when I pulled out at an angle to back into the parking spot.

"Good eyes and observation. So, you seen bullet holes in cars, then?"

Huffs and says, "I seen a few."

"Yeah, those are bullet holes. Fresh, too. You know anything about that?"

He looks at me hard, says, "What the fuck you mean by that? I had somethin' to do with putting them there?"

"I never said that."

"You gonna play me like this, then I just gonna get up and go."

"You see the news about the shooting last night?" I ask.

"I don't watch the news. You got people shooting at you? 'Cause I had enough of that shit."

"Not usually. It was the uniformed cops they wanted, not me. My car just got in the way."

"Shit. Where'd this happen?"

"Too close to home."

"Yeah, well, you lucky, I guess. That it was just your car."

Doesn't ask about the cops.

"The two officers, they weren't so lucky," I say, and take another bite.

"Yeah, and that's why you here? You think I had something to do with that shit?"

"No."

Maybe I do.

"I don't think that," I say. "If I did, I'd be here with more than a fucking sandwich."

"Shiet."

He picks up his sandwich, unwraps it, and takes a manly bite, like he ain't scared. After a couple of chews, his round eyes widen a bit, like, *Damn, that is good.*

"So, how you get caught up in the middle of a shoot-out?"

"I just happened to be there is all. Chance."

"I run into a couple chance shootings myself."

"With cops?"

"Fuck no. Just stupid-ass motherfuckers tryin' to kill their own."

"And what did you do?"

"Found myself a good hidin' spot until it was all over."

"That's smart."

He sets the sandwich down and says while chewing, "Like I said, I got no options anymore, and I don't want to be livin' on the street, so that's why I called you."

"Your uncle's ultimatum?"

"Yeah."

"I was hoping to get more enthusiasm for the work."

Looks at me. "Huh?"

"I'm not here just to throw money your way 'cause I'm your last resort. It can be a tough job, sometimes with long hours of doing nothin' but sitting. There's a lot to learn."

"I know that. Do I get a gun?"

"Fuck no."

He gives a Joker-like grin and takes another bite of the sub.

"I can pay you twenty-five bucks an hour to start. It can get better, depending on the workload—and you."

"Twenty-five an hour? How many hours a day?"

"Anywhere from six to sixteen."

"Sixteen hours?"

"When you gotta roll on something, you gotta roll, and sometimes that means not going home for a while."

"There overtime with that?"

"No overtime. No insurance. Just cash. So take care of your teeth."

"What do I gotta do?"

"At first, listen and learn."

Another manly bite, and a few chews later, "A'right."

We sit in silence, finishing the sandwiches. I have to wonder if I'm doing the right thing here and why the hell I'm doing it. I can't fucking trust this kid. Shit, I can't trust myself.

I crumple up my wrapper, stuff it in the bag I carried the subs in and set the bag on the table. Calvin does the same, grabs the bag and, without a word, walks into the house, returns a minute later without the bag. He stands in front of me, looking down at me where I sit.

Outta nowhere, he punches me square on the left side of my face, throwing my head back, but just a little.

"Fuck," he says after, rubbing his fist. Obviously hurt him more. He backs away after, thinking we're gonna fight.

I don't stand. I rub the side of my face, lean back and look at him.

"I get it," I say. "No worries."

"You get what?"

"Something you had to get outta your system."

"Ain't got nothin' outta my system. We far from even."

"That mean I gotta worry about you now?"

"No more than I gotta worry about you."

"All right, then."

He sits back down, looking ahead, over the patio, like he's surveying the land he owns. "So, when you want me to start?"

"How about right now."

Thirty-Four

I unlock the car doors with the key fob. Calvin opens the passenger door, seems to glide right in. I take off my jacket, careful not
to reveal my sidearm under the suit coat.

"Man, what's it gonna look like, me bein' seen with you, and in
a Volvo?"

"You rather I get something that looks more like a cop car?"

"Hell no."

I start the car, but before I begin to ease my way out, I say, "I
want to talk to you about the case I'm already working, which you'll
be helping with."

"Do you give me some up-front money or somethin' first?"

"Are you kidding? I should pay you at the end of the workweek,
but since you're hurting financially, I can pay at the end of the day."

"Under the table, right?"

"Yeah, under the table. Cash money. You ready to listen?"

Nods. "Where's the button to recline this shit?"

"Bottom side of the seat. Second button."

"Which second button?" he asks. "Oh no, I got it."

He reclines almost all the way back.

Fucking knucklehead.

"I know you said you don't watch the news, but you hear about that police shooting off Sherman Ave?"

"The unarmed boy? Hell yeah. You workin' for the family of that kid?"

"No, the detective who shot him."

"Aww, c'mon now." He groans as he lifts himself up from the seat like he's going to step out of the car.

"Why don't you sit back, relax, and let me finish before you start getting all fucking emotional."

"I ain't getting emotional, but I shoulda figured." He sits back. "Go on, then."

"When and if you go off on your own, you can choose who to work for. Right now I choose and you get paid at the end of the day, so let me talk, and if you want, you can walk after, go pump gas or some shit like that."

No response.

"When you were working at the deli, did you ever make a sandwich for any officers? Because I know some who used to frequent that place."

"Yeah. So?"

"Yeah, because it was your job. Didn't matter if they were cops or whoever, right?" Before he says anything, I add, "You ever spit in their sandwiches?"

"Fuck you. Did I spit in yours?"

"I don't know. Did you?"

"No."

"'Cause you had a good job and wanted to keep it. Also, sometimes things aren't always the way you hear it, especially coming from the street. You got friends you trust, right?"

"Why you ask?"

"I'm trying to make a point here." *And maybe overdoing it.* "Let me ask this—you say your uncle's a good man?"

"Hell ya."

"If he got himself into some big trouble—"

"Never would."

"Let me finish. Then you can talk."

I grab my pack of smokes out of my shirt pocket, offer him one.

"No, man. I told you I don't smoke."

I pull one out, light it. Comforting inhale, then blow the smoke out the partly open car window.

"Let's just say that *if* your uncle did get himself pulled in some bad shit that he had nothing to do with, but people were saying he did, who would you believe, if your uncle promised you he had nothing to do with what they were saying?"

"I'd believe my uncle."

"Same situation here. The detective who is being accused of killing an unarmed young kid is like my brother. And he's telling me that's not how it happened, that the kid had a gun."

"Your friend is the police, and even the police are sayin' the boy had no gun."

"Yes, because they're doing their job. No gun was found on the scene, and there's no evidence of a gun ever being there. That doesn't mean there wasn't one."

"How that possible?"

"Lots of ways. That's what we're here to figure out."

"And if you can't, then you still gonna believe your boy?"

"Hell yeah I'm gonna believe him, but he'll be fucked, probably go to jail."

"I don't know about this helpin'-out-the-police shit."

"He's been relieved of his police powers and suspended, so he's not the police right now."

"Yeah, but I'd be a part of helpin' him be the police again."

"Man, your thinking is fucked up. The lady I work for sometimes is a defense attorney. On occasion, she might pick up a case that the court gives her, maybe someone like Cordell Holm."

"That's the court, man. She got no choice."

He's got a point.

"She does have a choice, but she'd still do her job. Back to your uncle. Let's say we've been working together for a bit and he got himself arrested for a felony. Doesn't matter what, but it's bad, so you want us to work the case, try to prove his innocence. Should I help you? I mean, let's just say I don't know your uncle and, for all I know, he's a fucking thug, like you used to be."

"That's fucked up."

"You understand what I'm trying to get at here? You gotta get out of that old mentality."

I do, too, but I won't tell him that.

"You ain't like that anymore, right?" I ask.

"No, man. I told you I ain't."

"And I believe you."

"It's just that the police always get away with shit like this, and I ain't comfortable being a part of it."

"He's not getting away with anything. If he was, they would have planted a gun there and we wouldn't be having this conversation. And I'm not talking about making shit up to help him, either."

I take a last drag, flick the cigarette out.

"All those people protesting, they have a right to protest. But like I said, sometimes they don't have a clue about what really happened 'cause they weren't there. If the shooting was caught on an iPhone, then that might be something different. But even then, it may not be what it looks like."

"You're full of shit. This whole system is."

"We're not working for the police here, Calvin. I'm working for a good friend. He could be a thug and I'd still be trying to help him. Roll with me or roll out. Enough said. I made my point."

I look at him, but all he's doing is shaking his head.

THIRTY-FIVE

I'm sure Calvin is asking himself what the hell he's doing here with me, just as I keep asking myself what the hell I'm doing by hiring him. It's not like I need the help. When you think about it, it's sort of whacked. Well, not sort of. It's fucking whacked. I'll have to keep a close eye on him. I don't trust him, but I would love to be wrong.

My head is scrambled. I need a drink, but I don't want to drink in front of him. What kind of example would that be? I drive down 14th Street and park at the bus stop at 14th and Rhode Island to use the restroom at the 7-Eleven.

"I gotta hit the head," I say.

"You parked illegal. What do I say if a cop come up?"

"That it was an emergency stop."

I grab my backpack from the floor behind the passenger seat, push on the hazard lights, think about turning the engine off and taking the keys, but don't.

"You want anything?" I ask.

"Naw. I'm good."

I step out and walk in.

"Restroom?" I ask the man behind the counter.

Looks at me briefly, then lifts his head toward the bathroom door.

"Appreciate it."

I walk into the bathroom, lock the door. It's clean but smells like too much ammonia. Places like this can be a trigger. There was a time when I'd have to break away, just like now, but to snort up a couple of hefty lines. This time, I grab the flask out of my backpack, unscrew it, and take three nice swigs, then drop a couple of mints in my mouth. I secure everything, flush the toilet, and head back to the car.

It's still parked there.

"No ticket, huh?"

"No cops. They woulda stopped if they seen me in the passenger seat, though."

I shoot him a glare. That's fucked-up thinking again, but unfortunately, he's probably right.

When I can, I pull out, make the next right and then another one onto 15th.

"Where you going?"

"You know the boys that hang at the fourteen hundred block of Fairmont?"

"This some kinda test?"

"No. This is work."

"I was raised at Clifton Terrace. What do you think?"

"Really? With your mom? Your dad?" Fucking assuming it can be only one or the other.

"My moms." I don't want to get into his life history unless he offers. Probably piss him off if I start asking too many questions. Besides, I don't feel like hearing it right now.

"We need to locate two boys, one that goes by Little T or Ty, and the other one Marlon."

He huffs a laugh.

"Yeah?" I say.

"I knew that what you needed me for."

I'm tired of hearing that shit. I wanna pull to the curb and slap him silly, but I fight the urge and keep driving.

"Work, Calvin. Fucking work. They were known friends of Arthur Taylor, the kid the detective shot. Our job is to check everything, rule shit out, including the possibility that there could have been witnesses, maybe even friends of his. Enough of that snitch shit, all right?"

"I know a couple stoopid skinny-ass young 'uns who go by those names."

"And live at one of those buildings on the fourteen hundred block of Fairmont?"

"Yeah."

"Do they know you?"

"They were nothin' but little wannabe players back when I was doin' that shit. They should still know me, but I sure as hell ain't gonna talk to them, if that's what you're gettin' at."

"No. Just need you to recognize them."

"You're not gonna pull that *in the trunk of your car and take them to the river* shit like you did me, are you? I can't abide that."

"Like I said, I need to talk to them. What do you know about the boy who got shot—Arthur Taylor?"

"Don't know him."

I drive to the same spot at Fairmont where I was before. I take out my binos, peer through them to look at the corner near 14th. A small group is hanging on the stoop of the apartment on the north side.

I hand the binos to Calvin. "Take a look. Tell me if you know any of those boys."

He takes the binos, looks. "Damn, these small things is strong."

"Anyone familiar?"

"Lot of young 'uns is all. Couple of them be so obvious."

"I don't care about that, whether they're slinging or not."

He turns away from the binos like I said something wrong.

"Shit, man. You still talk like a cop."

"And you talk like a thug. Anyone that looks like Ty or Marlon?"

Puts his eyes to the binos, scans the area.

"Naw."

"We'll sit for a bit, see if any of them show."

He scoots his seat farther back using the power button so his head is at the blind side between the front and rear window. Looks like he's done this sort of thing before. I recline my seat, too.

"Tell me if you see anything."

"A'right. Damn, look at these fools."

Miniature snowmen in the park. Not enough snow to make them bigger. Some of them lined up one beside the other, like pawns. I slide the window down partway, let some of that nice cold air slap my face.

For the first time in a while, I get a real urge. Not like in the bathroom at 7-Eleven when I just thought about it. My body is aching with the need. I breathe in at a four-count, hold, and slowly exhale. I do this a few times before the racy feeling goes away.

Thirty-Six

I drop Calvin off at home in the early evening. Overall, not a pro-
ductive day. For the remainder of the surveillance, we both sat in
silence. I called it when it became too dark to make anything out and
when Calvin got a bit too antsy.

I pull out a wad of money from my pocket. It's my stash
money—money I earned through nefarious means. Hell, I'm not
going to pay him with money that I have to account for.

"Six hours," I tell him while counting tens and twenties. "Buck
fifty."

I hand him the cash. He doesn't count it out, just slips it in his
right front pants pocket.

"I need to find these two guys. Don't want to waste any more
time on it if it's going to prove worthless. I'll pick you up at noon
tomorrow."

"A'right." He opens the door.

"And you never work on your own. I ain't gonna pay you for that.
We only work together."

"Don't have to worry about that." He steps out of the car, shuts
the door.

I pull away. Make my way to Al's.

When I hit his block, I notice an older-model four-door Chevy, like the kind district detectives drive. Shitty and not well maintained. Driver's window is rolled down and the exhaust puffs out the rear of the vehicle, but the lights are off. I drive by it, look in. It's getting dark, but I can make out the driver. Scraggly beard, trying to look like he can blend in. Definitely a cop, probably with that new Crime-Stopping-Something-or-Other unit. When I pass, I notice the front tag through the rearview. DC gov tags.

I park up the block. Looks like Al's living room light is on. I walk to the vehicle. I'm still wearing a suit with my overcoat, and I'm relatively clean-shaven, so I doubt if I'll raise alarm. I stop ahead of their parked car, wave toward their front windshield. They don't get out of the car, so I step to the street, see the driver through the window.

"I'm Frank Marr, retired DC police."

Driver nods, like, *So what?*

"Glad to see you guys here," I tell them. "Thank Sergeant Kendall for me."

The driver nods again, says, "Sure." I know they don't fucking want to be here. Look like a couple of young gung-ho types who'd probably rather be doing jump-outs or some shit like that. Instead, they're stuck watching Al's house for the remainder.

"All right. I just wanted to make myself known," I say, and cross the street toward Al's house.

Leslie answers the door when I knock.

"Frank," she says like a hello.

I enter.

"I left a message with your receptionist," I tell her.

"And I was going to call. I'm in trial through the rest of the week. Sorry."

"No worries."

Al is sitting in his armchair with a drink in his hand. Chinese carryout is spread out on the coffee table. Looks like they've managed to get through most of it. Al still looks better, like he's slowed down a bit. Nothing like when I first saw him. He's strong that way. Won't ever let the shit get the best of him. Unlike me.

"What's up, Al?"

"Feel like a prisoner. House arrest."

Leslie sits on an old wooden chair that looks like it's been brought in from the dining room.

"Couple of news people have been knocking on my door," he says.

"You knew that was going to happen, some fuck leaking your name," I tell him. "You didn't talk to them, right?"

"No."

I sit on the sofa.

"Damn people in front of 300 are like a lynch mob."

"Let them have their time," I say.

"Saw on the news about those officers getting shot near your house. Little close to home for you, Frank."

He doesn't know I was involved?

"Too close to home," is all I say.

Why didn't the detectives talk to him? I told them about the SUV that followed me from here. Maybe they've got other leads to run down first. I want to ask why Leslie didn't call me, knowing that something like that happened so close to my house. But then that'd be like I'm looking for attention.

I'll give Rattan a call tomorrow, ask if they have any leads, see if I can find out why they didn't talk to Al.

"I heard that one of them didn't make it," Al says.

"Yeah, that's what I've heard."

"Where are the protesters for him?" he asks.

Leslie is quiet. I should be, too.

145

"You wanna drink?"

I look toward Leslie, like I need her approval, but then notice she's nursing a bit of whiskey.

"Yeah. Sure."

He gets up, grabs a glass from the dining area.

"Ice?"

"No. Neat is good."

Pours and hands me the glass, sits back down.

"In your investigations, the names Little T or Ty or Marlon ever come up?" I ask Al.

Thinks for a moment. "No. Why?"

"Couple of names that came up associated with Arthur Taylor."

"What are you thinking?" Leslie asks.

"I don't know. Just following through is all."

"Someone had to take the gun from the scene," Al says. "Right?"

"Only explanation, Al," I try to say with confidence. "Probably best that you play hermit for a while. I know it's hard, but you need to stay low."

"And stop watching the news," Leslie advises.

"Hard not to," he says.

"You still have a personal weapon here, right?"

"Of course. Couple of them. Why? I should be more concerned?"

"No. Always prepared. Like they drilled into our heads in the academy."

"Right, Frankie. I noticed an unmarked vehicle parked across the street. Why do I get that treatment?"

"I'll ask when I leave," I say, but I don't mean it, because I already know why.

"They wouldn't be out there unless I'm under surveillance— which they ain't doing a good job of—or there's a known threat. So don't bullshit me, Frank."

"Okay, okay. A sergeant I know did me a courtesy is all. Nothing known, just a precaution. All the protesting and cop hating going on, and you live in the District, after all. If you were in Maryland or Virginia, it'd be different."

"Damn, Frank. I don't want them outside my house, baby-sitting me."

"What's the big deal, Al?" And I want to add, *It's keeping Darling away from your door.*

By the slight smile I shoot him after and the slight turned-up lips he hits me back with, I know he knows what I mean. We've been partners and friends for too many years not to be able to read each other well.

Leslie finishes off her drink. "I'm going to call a cab. I have to be in court first thing in the morning."

"I should go home, too. I'll give you a ride."

"No, thank you. It's out of your way, and I'd rather cab it."

"Let me give you a ride home, Leslie. I just had one drink. I'm fine."

"That's all right."

"Fucking knock it off, you two. Driving me batty. Let him give you a damn ride, Les."

"Couple things we should talk about anyway," I add.

She picks up her satchel bag. "Okay. We should go. I'll call you tomorrow, Al. On my lunch break."

He nods, shakes his head after.

Thirty-Seven

I fill her in on what I'm doing but leave out Calvin. She agrees that it's a good idea to find those two kids and talk to them, at least rule them out if it proves to be nothing.

It's clear to me that Leslie is preparing a defense strategy for Al, nothing more. Everything I'm trying to do is like grasping for something that can't be seen. In Leslie's mind, keeping him from going to jail is about the best thing she can hope for. We drive in silence for the remainder. I put on the radio, her favorite station.

"Would you mind? I'm not in the mood for music right now. Sorry."

"No problem." I turn it off.

The Capitol building is all lit up. It always looks its best during the winter season. The dark-gray, overcast clouds above serve as a backdrop to the lights, makes the dome pop. I turn to Leslie, but only for a split second.

"I was beyond stupid back then," I say. "I'm not like that anymore."

I want to believe that. I hope she does, too.

"The past is the past. Time to move on."

I want to say, *You're not over it, though.*

"I know it'll never be the same with us——"

Time to shut up.

"Frank, leave it alone. Give it time."

It's been almost three years. How much time does she need? I'm not talking getting back together, just friendship, a working relationship. Occasional drink. Something.

"I've got time." I smile so she can see. She smiles back, but it's an ambiguous sort of smile.

I drop her off in front of her Capitol Hill row house, watch her walk up the steps, open the door, and then wave before she shuts it behind her.

I cannot find parking when I get home. I can't see the unmarked vehicle, either, the one that was supposed to be posted on the block. Is that all the time they're going to give me? Kendall probably got shot down by his commander for having a unit at my house. No manpower, something like that. I can take care of myself. No worries there. I park a couple of blocks from my house, walk with caution. No hand-on-the-grip-of-my-gun paranoia, just being aware of my surroundings.

I make it home safely, lock the door. Double-check it and then check the back door, too.

I scrape up some leftover food, what remains of a large plate of spaghetti and meatballs. I want to watch television while eating, but change my mind. It'll only suck me in, and the next thing I know it'll be morning and I'll be staring at the ceiling instead of sleeping. So I eat in silence, have a couple of drinks after, with a Klonopin.

I wake up later than normal. After my morning coffee and the remainder of the leftover spaghetti for breakfast, I put on my favorite suit, the one that makes me look and feel like a detective. I stuff my pack with snacks, a couple of full flasks containing whiskey, and a large bottled water. Flex cuffs, stun gun, and an ASP are also in there, but they are always in there. Haven't had the need to use any of them for a while now. Maybe the stun gun, if Calvin pisses me off again with his thug-life thinking.

When I exit, I'm surprised by a reporter, holding a mic and standing just outside my property. A news van is double-parked on the other side of the street, a cameraman now walking toward me with the camera on his shoulder.

"Mr. Marr," the reporter says.

He looks familiar, but he's not anyone I know. I think about going back inside, but what good would that do? So I lock my door and walk by him.

"Just a minute of your time, Mr. Marr."

"I don't know you," I say while walking.

"Just a couple of questions, please."

I'm curious, so I stop.

"Thank you. Why would Detective Al Luna hire a private investigator?" He jumps right into it.

Fuck. How'd he find out about me?

I give him my best confused look. "I don't know what the hell you're talking about."

"Detective Luna hired you, Mr. Marr. Why would he need a private investigator for a shooting of an unarmed man when the department has already made that determination?"

"Again, I don't know what the hell you're talking about and how my name came up in all this. You should check your source."

"The officer-related shooting that occurred here the other night, what do you know about that? Were you involved?"

I walk away. He keeps up with me. I wanna punch him. He gets ahead of me, gives his cameraman the "cut" signal with his index finger. I notice the cameraman take the camera off his shoulder.

"Off the record, then, Mr. Marr."

"There is no *off the record*. There's never anything off the record."

"We're not the enemy. I know you were here on the night of the shooting. That was a tragedy. With everything that's going on, I can understand why you wouldn't want your face on the news. Talk to me about Detective Luna. Off the record. Is there something more than what the department is saying?"

"I told you I don't know what you're talking about. Your source is confused."

I walk away.

He doesn't seem to be following. I pass my car because I don't want this guy seeing it, but then he probably already knows the car I drive.

Fucking sources. Leaks. When I find out who it is, they'll get a lot more than a piece of my mind.

I walk south on 12th, to U Street.

I have a bit of time before I have to pick up Calvin. The last thing I want or need is for this reporter to find Calvin. He's still a long way off from earning my trust.

Thirty-Eight

Feels good to walk. Sidewalks are salted. What little snow wasn't shoveled away has frozen. Colder today. Patchy clouds. Doesn't look like a possibility of snow, though.

I walk to 14th, take a right and take my time walking up to W, where I go left toward 12th. A nice walk. Not that long, but I hope long enough that the reporter got bored and moved on to something else. When I get to the corner of 12th and W, I peek around. No news van, just a couple of neighborhood people walking a mop dog. Looks clear. I cross the street and walk the couple of blocks to where my car is parked.

Calvin is sitting on the porch when I arrive. Apparently he doesn't want me in the house. I get it. I feel the same way about him being in my house or even knowing where I live. I double-park and wait for him. Looks like he's wearing the same clothes as yesterday. His puffy winter coat is unzipped, revealing a plain black T-shirt, and it's made puffier as he hops down the stairs and it's caught by the breeze. He gets in the passenger seat, but this time he hits his head on his way in.

"Damn, this car short."

"It's not short. The seat's high. Push down the third button on the panel to lower it."

He shuts the door, pushes the button, and the seat drops low. He reclines the back just as low.

"How the fuck can you see anything sitting like that?" I ask.

"What I got to see?"

"Part of your job is having eyes on, being aware."

"You really are having a hard time not being the *police*, aren't you?"

I don't answer that.

I take 14th to Euclid, make the left to University and a right to Fairmont.

Kids playing in the park this morning. Supervising adults/parents sitting around paying more attention to their smartphones. Makes me happy not to have a kid, knowing all that I know.

Bigger kids hanging at the corner of Fairmont and 14th. Damn cold to be out just to lean against cars, sit on cold steps, and shoot the shit. A couple of them on smartphones as well, but also interacting with one another.

"Can I get those binos?" Calvin asks.

I find them in my backpack, hand them over to him. My cell rings. Calvin jumps off his seat a little. I huff.

"Frank Marr," I answer.

"Lustig, Frank. What's up?"

"Hey, Gary. What's up with you?"

"Got some info on one of those boys you were asking about. Little T or Tyrone Biggs."

"That's some kinda contrast."

Takes him a second. Then, "Oh, the name. Yeah. Funny. Here it is, though. He's sixteen years of age, lives at 1401 Fairmont. I don't have his juvie record, but one of the plainclothes guys here that gave me this info locked him up for PWID about two months ago."

"What kind of drugs?"

"Heroin. He was known to hang with Arthur Taylor and the other boy, Marlon Owen, who is known to carry a gun."

"Marlon ever arrested for CPWL?"

"Yes, more than once. Proverbial revolving door, though."

"No shit. Juvenile paradise."

"Oh, they also like to run and will fight the police, even though they're short, wiry little fucks and always lose."

"Appreciate the info, Gary."

"You're not the police anymore, so don't get into any shit."

"Always careful, bro. Thanks again."

"Yeah." Disconnects.

"I know what CPWL and PWID is, you know," Calvin says.

"I'm sure you do."

"Sounds like these young 'uns ain't to be trifled with."

"But I thought you already knew that?"

"Yeah, I did. That why I told you I won't be the one talking to them."

"Ha! I get it."

"Don't know what you expect to find out, either, 'cause they ain't gonna tell you shit."

"Names are Marlon Owen and Tyrone Biggs."

"Biggs? Shit, he's a Biggs? That family is definitely not to be trifled with. Even Cordell Holm stayed clear of those boys. They run everything up here."

"What kind of drugs?"

"What that matter for?"

"Because I like to know as much as I can."

"Mostly hairon, crack, even powder and chronic. That was back when I knew what was going on, but things don't change much here."

"Do they smoke that chronic, too?"

"Wouldn't be surprised. Gives even the little men bigger balls."

"Well, right now all I care about is Little T and Marlon. Don't want to get wrapped up with his family shit."

I grab the binos and hand them to him. He's happy to take them, like some kid playing spy. I give him a second.

"Anyone you know?"

"Naw. Familiar, but don't think they be there."

A car is coming up University. See it in my rearview. I recline.

"Drop down a bit," I tell him. "Let this car pass."

He tucks down. The vehicle passes, an older two-door red Toyota with Maryland dealer tags. Occupied a couple times at least. Young boys. Calvin peeks out the front windshield as the car makes the right turn onto Fairmont almost directly in front of us.

"Shit. Driver looks like Marlon," Calvin says.

"You sure?"

"Pretty sure."

"Those are Maryland dealer tags."

"Man, you can buy those for a couple bills at just about any corner dealership 'round here."

The car pulls to the curb on the north side of the street. Couple of boys from the steps walk to it, lean down to talk to the driver. Calvin raises the binos.

"Looks like they gettin' re-upped or some shit like that," Calvin says. "Rear window too tinted out to see through."

"Engine still running?"

"Think so."

"Well, if they pull out, we'll follow. It'll be your first lesson."

"Huh?" he asks, breaking away from the binos.

"Tailing a vehicle."

Back on the binos. "Look like they just shootin' the shit," he says. "One of the boys is walkin' back to the steps, carrying somethin'."

"You don't have to give me a play-by-play. This ain't a drug bust."

He looks at me, confused, maybe even thinking twice about this.

"Car's pulling away," I say. "Looks like it's gonna head north on 14th." I pull out, make the turn. "Keep down," I tell him. "Until we pass the buildings."

"Man, I feel like a fucking snitch."

"Shut the fuck up."

Thirty-Nine

We follow the car for almost forty-five minutes. It makes a few stops along the way, re-upping some of their other boys. It takes side streets to the 1200 block of Queen Street NE and parks. Four boys hop out of the small Toyota.

"That be Little T," Calvin says.

"The one who got out of the front passenger seat?"

"Yeah."

"You know the other two?"

"Naw."

They walk to an old, beat-down, attached redbrick two-story and enter.

"This is fucking good," I say. I note the address. "Do you know this house?"

"Why'd I know this house? I don't even know these peoples."

"Let's make an agreement here," I say. "I won't ask any more questions if you just tell me when we see a person or a spot that you know. Sound reasonable?"

"Sound good."

"Let's sit on this here for a bit, see how long they stay."

I grab a flask out of my backpack. Enough of this *good example* shit.

I offer it to him.

"What is it?"

"Whiskey to warm the bones."

He accepts with what is probably a smile but looks like a sneer.

Takes a drink. Coughs. Some of the whiskey dribbles out of the corner of his lip. He wipes it away.

"An acquired taste."

"I'll stick to my Rémy. That shit's rough goin' down."

He hands it back. I take a nice swig, return it to my bag.

"That somethin' you do a lot?"

"What?"

"Drinking."

"No, man. I don't drink and drive." I smile.

I sit back. Calvin pulls a smartphone out of his coat pocket, types in a code.

"Can I wear my earbuds?"

"You need to keep alert."

"I got my eyes open."

"As long as I can't hear it. I like silence."

He plugs the earbuds in and sticks them in his ears.

Not even two minutes later he says to himself, "This is some sick shit here," and laughs.

I look over to see what he's watching. He looks up and shows me.

Two large women are fighting on the front lawn of a house wearing tight spandex and torn shirts. They're tumbling around, slapping, scratching, with occasional hard punches to the faces. Fucking disgusting.

"What are you watching that shit for?"

"Huh?" he says, then pulls out the earbuds.

"What the fuck are you watching?"

"Silly shit, man. The fat women fightin'. Funny as shit."

"Sad is what it is."

"Sad? Naw, man, it's silly. Look here."

He taps the screen to show another recording. Two young boys face up to each other. One is tall and lanky, nothing but skin and bone. The other one is a big boy. I can't hear the sound, but they're arguing, and suddenly the lanky kid sucker punches the big one and drops him like nothing. Out for the count.

"This is what you watch for entertainment?"

"Just some silly shit. This one's got, like, more than two hundred thousand views."

"Turn that off and pay attention. Shit."

"You need to get yourself some humor, man."

He unplugs the earbuds, balls them up, and puts the phone and earbuds back in his coat pocket.

Not much conversation after that. I slide down the window, light up a smoke, and am surprised by a man who appears from behind the car and taps on the window. Calvin jerks up, turns to see. Looks like a young crackhead.

"What the fuck you want?" I ask.

He looks over toward Calvin, then back to me.

"You a couple of faggots?" he asks.

I slide my hand to my side, grip my gun, but try not to show what I'm doing.

"What the fuck you think comin' up to my car like that? Move on," I say.

He lifts his jacket to reveal a gun tucked in the pants of his waist area. First thing I notice is where the magazine should drop out at the butt of the grip, there's a release lever for something like a CO_2 cartridge. Fucking pellet gun.

"Oh shit, man," Calvin snaps.

"Yeah, oh shit. Now give me what I needs."

"I don't know. What do you need?" I ask.

He looks stunned, grips the gun, pulls it out and points it at the window toward my head.

Calvin ducks down and says, "Aww fuck."

I roll down the window.

"I don't want you cracking my window with that thing."

"Wha—"

I open the car door hard, knocking him back, but not to the ground. He straightens up, aims the gun at me as I step out.

"You crazy fool. I'm gonna cap your ass."

"Most you're gonna do with that thing is sting my ass."

I draw my gun. He squeaks out a yelp. Comical. I almost laugh.

"Don't shoot me. Don't shoot. This ain't real!" He drops it at his feet.

"I know it ain't real. You think I'd step up to you if it was? Shit."

"C'mon, now," he begs.

"Calvin, step on out here," I say.

"Fuck no," he says.

"Just step out here."

He opens the door, slowly steps around the front of the car, stands there.

"You tell me what we should do here, have him arrested or beat the shit outta him for being simpleminded?"

"And calling us faggots."

"Yeah, that too."

"C'mon…c'mon now…," he whimpers.

"How many views you think this would get on YouTube?" I ask Calvin.

"Y'all got to be kidding me."

"He ain't nothin' but a crackhead," Calvin says.

"You showing pity?"

"Do whatever the fuck you want. He nothin' but a fool. I ain't gonna get none of his blood on me," Calvin says.

"Kick that pellet gun to me," I tell the crackhead.

He does. I bend down and pick it up, holster my weapon.

"You the police?"

"Do we look like the police?"

"Yeah, well, now that I can see you better, you do. I don't know about him there," he says, looking toward Calvin.

"What you sayin'?" Calvin asks, pissed now.

"I ain't mean nothin', man. Really."

"You better watch your mouth, then, fool," Calvin says.

I take the pellet gun in my right hand and shoot the big toe of the crackhead's left foot. He shrieks, bounces on his right foot as he lifts the left to try to hold the tip of his shoe.

"Didn't know it even worked. You could've taken my eye out with this."

"Shit, man. Shit, shit."

"Fucking hobble on out of here. I see you again, you'll get more than a pellet in the big toe."

He limps away at a fast pace, but not quite a run.

"Can I have that pellet pistol?"

"No," I say.

I sit back in the car, stick the pellet gun in my backpack and pull out the flask. Take a nice hard swig and put it back.

Calvin gets in.

"That some crazy shit there. How you know it wasn't a real gun?"

"It's older. Some of the newer ones you can't tell."

"Shoulda caught all that on my phone."

"You want to lose that phone of yours, then try."

"You the one that mentioned YouTube."

"I was being sarcastic."

"Why you didn't call the police on him?"

"We don't have time for that. Besides, that'd make me a fucking complainant on a report and I'd probably have to go to court. I don't need that."

"Yeah, makes sense."

After about two more hours I call it, and we roll out.

"I think that might be a crash place for them. What do you think?" I say.

"Yeah, they probably be bedding down there."

"You hungry?"

"Like McDonald's, somethin' like that?"

"Fuck no. I don't eat at McDonald's."

"I gave my uncle most of that money you paid me."

"It's on me this time. I got this spot."

"In fact, my uncle was wondering why I'm getting paid in cash. He thinks I'm back to dealing or somethin'."

"You want me to talk to him?"

"Hell no!"

"Why you afraid of me talking to him?"

He gives me a look, not hard, just like I should know better. I leave it there.

FORTY

There's a Salvadoran restaurant on 14th I sometimes go to. No frills, just good, authentic food. We sit at a table against a wall and close to the bar. I set the backpack at my feet. Not a lot of folks here, just a few regulars at the bar and at a couple tables in the middle of the room. It's the time of day, I suppose, too late for lunch and too early for dinner.

"I like me some good Mexican food sometimes," Calvin says.

"This is mostly Salvadoran, but they serve Mexican, too."

"A 'migo is a 'migo."

"No talking like that in here, all right?"

"What?"

"You like I should call you a mope?"

Smiles. "I don't give a fuck what you call me, 'cept if it's 'migo."

I don't respond. Just like a few cops I know, even me. I'm no different, so what the hell am I preaching for.

A young, pretty waitress wearing tight jeans approaches.

"*Hola,*" she says.

"*Hola. Cómo estás?*" I say.

"Muy bien, gracias." She smiles.

She hands each of us a menu.

"Would you like drinks?" she asks.

"Two cervezas, *por favor.*"

I notice Calvin looking up at her, smiling. She gives a slight nod and walks toward the bar.

"I know that means beer, right?" he asks me.

"Yeah. You like beer, don't you?"

"Yeah."

"Pretty, isn't she?"

"She be all right."

Yeah right, Playboy.

My cell rings.

"Frank Marr," I answer.

"This is Rattan. You busy?"

"No. Hold on for a second, though." I cup the mouthpiece. "I gotta take this outside," I tell Calvin. "What's up?" I ask Rattan while walking out.

"We pulled some photos from the bodycam of one of the officers," she begins.

I open the glass front door and step out. Walk toward the curb.

"That's good news. Right?"

"Not really the images we hoped for, but I would still like to show them to you, see if you can recognize the subject."

"Of course. When?"

"Now would be great, if you're available."

"Okay, I'm at the Salvadoran spot at Fourteenth near Newton. Just got here. You know where I'm talking about?"

"I can find it. About twenty minutes?"

"We'll be here."

"Thank you." She disconnects.

I realize I just said *We'll* be here.

164

I enter, notice the beers are on the table. He's already halfway through his. I sit.

Calvin doesn't mention anything about the phone conversation. Smart enough to know when something is not his business. I sip the beer.

"You know what you want?" I ask.

"No, man. I don't know what any of this shit is."

"I'm going to have the stuffed pupusas. That's what they're known for here."

"What's a *pupooza*?"

"It's like a closed-up sandwich, stuffed with goodness."

He looks at me, like, *What the fuck...?*

"Beans, cheese, and meat. It's good comfort food. Try it."

The waitress returns, and I order for both of us. I hand her my menu, but she has to pick up Calvin's. He smiles at her, and she returns the smile. *Fucking Romeo.*

"I better not get sick on those pupoozas."

"I haven't yet."

He finishes his beer with an "Ahh..." Sets the glass down. "So, this is what you do every day, huh?"

"Not always."

"That was some shit with that crackhead, huh?"

"Yeah" is all I say, but have to admit, only to myself, that I love when something like that happens. It gives me an adrenaline boost, a bit like coke but without the sudden surge, more like waves, one right after the other. Stays with me for a while after. Little spike of energy. That's why I still like to bust into drug houses. You get that feeling right before you go in because you don't know what to expect. You get it again if you're hit with the unexpected. That's when the training kicks in.

"How you expect to talk to those boys we seen?"

"Haven't worked that one out yet. Maybe you can come up with something. Earn that money."

"I don't know this shit. You gotta teach me, remember?"

"How would Cordell have you handle it?"

Huffs a laugh and says, "He didn't play by the rules."

"And you think I do?"

"That shit slipped my mind," he says, and I know he's referring to the time I got the information out of him and almost killed him after.

"Maybe you two be like the same and I just worked myself from one bad situation into another."

"No, you didn't, 'cause I'll never make you do something you don't want to do."

Except that one time, a few years ago.

"Can I get another one of these *sirvezas* here?"

"Yeah. We're almost done with the day." I look at him. He's got that wandering eye again, trying to catch the backside of the waitress. "How old were you when you first started working for Cordell?"

He looks surprised, I'm sure wondering why I asked that.

"Table conversation," I say. "Nothing more."

"I don't know. Little kid."

"I mean, just like that—from Clifton Terrace to Seventeenth and Euclid?"

"Man, what you diggin' for? Why you wanna know all this?"

"I wanna know better the man I'm working with."

"Shiet."

I don't push it.

"My pops. He the one that introduced me to him," he says after a couple of seconds.

"Your dad knew Cordell?"

"Fuck, how you think Cordell got that name of his, and all the money and shit? He ran with my pops."

"Your dad's responsible for who Cordell is—was?"

Doesn't respond, but I think that crooked smile is an answer.

"He still alive? Your dad."

"I don't know. Man, they got into the shit, though. Serious shit."

"Kill people?"

"My pops had a reputation," he says proudly. "No one fucked with him. The way they rolled, man, that was some old-school shit."

Didn't answer my question. Don't expect him to.

"Drugs?"

"Yeah, but not like you think. Home invasion shit, but they hit the suppliers. The big boys."

"That's some shit," I say, and I'm thinking I'd probably get along with his dad. "So he just, like, disappear on you and your mom?"

"Yeah, 'cause he had to. At least that what I remember. Things got hot after one hit. This rich man's house in Upper Northwest. Nothin' but a dope dealer with a big house and a family to pretend he like something normal."

"They got a good score, then?"

"Hell no. What I heard, it all went bad, but that was mostly 'cause of Cordell, not my pops. He went off, killed the man and his family."

Fuck. I remember hearing about that. I was in plainclothes then. The man was politically connected, but I never heard anything about drugs.

"I think I remember that," I say.

"Fuck, it was all over the news."

"Cordell tell you all this?"

"Hell no. Just heard the stories from everyone else mostly."

"Must be tough, your dad being behind something like that?"

"Naw. Why'd that be tough?" he says bluntly.

"I mean the kids."

"Yeah, I guess. But I know my pops wasn't a part of killing kids. I suppose that's why he had to roll out, though."

"DC police were all over that case," I say.

"Aw fuck. So now you gonna try to bring me in on this 'cause I got stupid with a conversation?"

"Give me a break," I say, but I think how satisfying it'd be to connect Cordell with something like that. Give him life. I mean, damn, after only one beer, the kid's got a seriously loose tongue.

The cute waitress returns with the meals just in time. I order two more beers, wonder how loose he's gonna get after the second one.

"I ain't talkin' about this shit no more," he says, like he knows what I was thinking.

Calvin examines the pupusas on his plate like he expects to find bugs crawling on them. He opens one up to look inside. I take a good bite from one of mine. Hard not to finish with a "Yum." He gives it a try. A small bite at first, and shortly after a large bite.

"Uhm, uhm...," he mumbles.

Waitress returns with the beers. Calvin doesn't look up from his food. Good thing. His dick doesn't control everything.

Forty-One

Rattan rolls in before I'm finished. Calvin came close to polishing his plate. He notices her as she walks toward us, badge hanging around her neck and cradling a case jacket. She's alone.

"That's Detective Rattan with Homicide," I tell him. "She's the one who called me."

He looks nervous.

"Have a seat," I tell her.

She pulls out a chair, gives Calvin the once-over before she sits.

"This is Calvin," I say. "He's an associate in training."

"Okay," she says with some hesitance, offers her hand to shake. "Detective Rattan."

Calvin looks at me like he needs permission, then extends his hand and they shake. It's awkward.

"Just finishing up a late lunch," I say.

She sets the case jacket on her lap, looks at Calvin again and smiles. Reluctant, but he smiles back.

"Might want to have Calvin look at the photos, too."

He straightens in his seat, looks at me again with question. Probably should have told him that Rattan was coming. I'm sure his mind is working nervously, maybe thinking about that day he was the driver when Little Monster took out the dirty-as-shit officer and tried to take me out, too.

"This is about the shooting I was telling you about involving the two officers and me," I tell him.

"Oh yeah. Yeah."

I can tell she's hesitant to pull the photos. Just like thugs can make a cop, cops can make a thug. Unfortunately, Calvin still has a bit of thug left in him—or maybe a lot. Hard to wash away that shit, just like it's hard to wash away the cop left in me.

"You want me to look at those photos now?" I ask.

The waitress interrupts. "Would you like a menu?"

"No, thank you," Rattan says.

"Anything to drink?"

"I'm good, thank you."

The waitress leaves. Rattan pulls the eight-by-ten photographs out of her case jacket.

"Not the greatest, but it's all we have."

I look at the first image. It's definitely the angle, catching the driver in the shadows and only the profile. I look at the second one. The primary officer is closer to the window now, the driver's head turned slightly toward him. Still shadowy and grainy, but better.

"That's the best one," she tells me.

I look through the other photos, which include the one of the driver pointing a gun. Totally blurred out because the officer was running backward. I pick up the second photo again. Suspect looks to be in his twenties, maybe younger. So hard to tell. Gaunt face revealing sharp cheekbones. Shadow falls over the top of his head to his nose and chin. Eyes. Fucking dark, dangerous eyes.

"He doesn't look familiar," I say. "What about the other officer's bodycam?"

"Nothing."

"Can I show this one to Calvin?"

Thinks about it, then says, "Yes."

I hand it over the table to Calvin. He holds it but doesn't look at it right away. I know he's thinking *snitch* again. After a moment, he looks. His eyebrows rise for a split second.

Did Rattan notice?

It's like he recognizes him, but I can't be sure.

"Naw. No. I don't know this guy. He the one that shot the police-man?"

"He's one of them," Rattan says.

"Can I have that one?" I ask, pointing to the second photo. "There's a couple of people I might be able to show it to."

"It's going to be released to the media, so why not."

Calvin returns the photo to me. I carefully slip it into my back-pack so it doesn't bend.

"Anything new you can share concerning Luna?" I ask.

"No. It is where it is."

"Meaning?"

"With IA. Most of us have been pulled to work this and the other homicide."

"Officer Wiebe?" I ask. "You think all this is related?"

"We're looking into it" is all she says.

"I appreciate the photo. I'll keep you informed."

"All right, then," she says while slipping the other photos back in the case jacket and then standing.

She shoots Calvin a smile and turns to exit.

When she's out the door Calvin asks, "Why you didn't bring up about those boys Ty and Marlon?"

"You heard her. They're swamped with working these officers

that got shot. Besides, even if she did follow through and try to interview those boys, all they'll do is shut down."

"True that."

"You sure you didn't recognize that dude in the photo? Sort of looked like you did."

"No. I don't know him."

FORTY-TWO

I can feel the drunkenness. It's not like it used to be, when one
substance balanced out the other. Now I feel like an ordinary
drunk. I never liked that feeling, but hell, I need something. I've said
it before: I prefer the ups over the downs. I miss the ups. So, here's
to the chemically induced ups, nothing but a distant memory.

I dropped Calvin off after the late lunch, drove back to sit on the
house on Queen Street. Lights were on, but no action. It doesn't
appear to be a drug house. More than likely, as we already guessed,
a place to bed down, a stash house, or both.

Damn press has been lurking around my neighborhood, fishing.
Curtains are drawn, and the only light on is dim, emitted by the
small end-table lamp beside my sofa.

Before bed I check in with Al.

"Hey, Frank," he answers.

"I located those two friends of the kid. Looks like they're a couple of drug boys."

"Yeah?"

"Just need to figure out how to play it."

"To what purpose?"

What do I say? 'Cause all I'm doing is fishing.

"A hunch."

Hunch?

"Because you've got a hunch?"

"Yeah, because I've got a hunch. You talk to Leslie?"

"Yes, briefly. She's in trial."

"Anything other than that going on?" I ask, meaning pending grand jury or some shit like that.

"That I should be prepared for administrative leave without pay."

"Yeah, you knew that was coming. US attorney's office moves slow, so of course that's the department's next step. You tell your union rep?"

"I'll call her tomorrow."

"All right, brother. Keep the faith."

He cackles something like a laugh.

"Talk later."

"Yeah." And then he hangs up.

Keep the faith.

FORTY-THREE

P repare for record-breaking cold weather to hit the DC Metro area today," the weatherman advises on the morning news. Unfortunately, no snow. I do prefer the winter's ear-nipping cold over the summer's sticky humidity, though.

I fill a couple of flasks with Jameson, grab a bottled water out of the fridge, put everything in the backpack, and exit through the rear kitchen door to avoid any reporters, or someone worse, who might be lurking around.

I find my car, let it warm up, and then drive around the block to check out if any suspicious vehicles might be parked in the area. When I feel comfortable, I drive to Calvin's.

He's not sitting on the patio chair when I get there. I double-park and wait. After a few minutes, I call him on his cell, but it goes to an automated voice mail.

Where are you, Calvin?

I wait a couple more minutes, then find a parking spot, grab my backpack, and walk to his house. I give the door a couple of hard raps. A few seconds after, I hear scuffling inside, then close to the door, probably someone looking through the peephole.

"Who is it?" a man who is not Calvin says.

"Frank Marr. I'm here for Calvin."

"Are you the police? He in trouble again?"

"No, sir. He works for me. Part-time. I've been picking him up here."

"He works for you?" he asks through the door, like it's hard to believe.

I pull out my wallet, put the badge up toward the peephole. Don't bother to hide the "Retired" that is etched at the bottom.

"I'm a retired police detective. A private investigator now. I hired Calvin because I need the help."

He unlocks the door and opens it. He's wearing a bathrobe with polka-dot-patterned pajama bottoms and leather slippers.

"Sorry. It's my day off."

"I didn't mean to bother you."

"No bother. Private investigations, huh?"

"Yes, sir. It's good work."

"I apologize. Come in." He opens the door for me. I stomp my feet on the outdoor rug and step in.

"Thanks. It's a bit cold out."

"Record breaking, they say."

He closes the door.

The house is well kept. Older furniture that carries that musty, old-house smell, but not intolerable.

"So, you the one who been paying the boy cash?"

"Yes, for now. Is that a problem?"

"No, not with that, now that I know it's good work. It is legitimate work, right?"

My best smile. "Of course it is."

"Well, he was gone when I got home from work yesterday. Left two hundred dollars cash on the dining room table with a note that said, 'For rent.' I don't know where he is now."

"Does he have a room here?"

"Yes. Of course. He's been living here for close to three years now."

"Have you checked his room to see if his belongings are still there?"

"No. I don't make it my business to go through his room. I just figured he was up to his old ways. I don't mean he's—"

"Don't worry, Mr...."

"Tolson. Mackolson." He extends his hand to shake.

I take it.

"Mr. Tolson, I didn't mean to interrupt, but I know about Calvin's old ways, so no worries. Maybe we should check his room, though, just to see if his belongings are still there."

"He doesn't have much in the way of belongings. Few clothes items, couple pairs of shoes. We can look in there. It's down the hall."

I follow him to a door at the end of the hallway. He opens it, moves aside so I can look in.

Bed is actually made.

"He make the bed?"

"Of course."

For some reason, that surprises me.

It looks sterile, like a simple guest room that no one has been staying in. I walk in, open the closet.

Fucking empty.

"His closet is empty," I tell Mr. Tolson. "Did he have a suitcase or anything like that?"

"Just a backpack. I don't see it, though. Damn. This is all my fault."

"Why?"

"Would you like some coffee?"

Shake my head.

He steps out of the room. I follow. He shuts the door.

"I was really on him about the cash he was bringing in. Thought it was drug money, so I would have nothing to do with it. Didn't take it when he offered it to me. We fought about it. Do you want to sit down?"

"I'm fine. Does he have any other family he would stay with?"

"No. I'm it."

"Good friends maybe?"

"He never talked about having any friends. Most of them got locked up a few years ago."

That would be by or because of me.

"Can you try to call him on his cell?"

"Yes, I can do that."

He walks into the living room, picks up a landline phone, dials. After a minute, he hangs up.

"Went to his voice mail."

"Well, he's not the type to sleep on the streets or in some abandoned building, so he has to be somewhere near," I say.

"I should have believed him."

"Don't blame yourself. Has he ever left over an argument before?"

"No. Never."

"Well, I'll find him. More than likely, though, he'll find his way back here. It's damn cold out."

"Too damn cold. He may freeze himself to death."

I pull out one of my legitimate business cards with my regular cell number on it, hand it to him.

"If he shows up, call me or just have him call."

Takes the card. "I will."

He looks torn up. I feel bad for him.

Forty-Four

I don't think that's why Calvin left, over some little argument with his uncle. Well, not so little, but still, Calvin wasn't kicked out. My opinion, he left because of something else. He's been there for three years or so and has probably had similar arguments. He left his job at the deli because of me, and I'm sure he left his uncle's house because of something having to do with me. I don't know where to begin to look for him, or if I even should. I think I have fucked his life up more than enough.

There was a time I allowed myself to get close to another guy. Unlike Calvin, Biddy was addicted to crack. Not a good substance to be addicted to. He was sent to jail, and once inside, he wasn't using. He committed suicide. Wrote a note to me, saying he didn't like himself sober and not only that, but life was too hard to handle without the self-medication. I feel responsible for what happened to him. Calvin is different because he doesn't have an addiction (that I know of), but not so different because there's a part of him, like Biddy, that's like me. So maybe I should leave it alone. But then I remember that look he had when he saw the bodycam photo. *Is that the something else?* Is that alone worth my time trying to look for him?

Shit. I don't even know what my next move is for Luna, and here I am posing all these fucking questions.

For some reason it's hard to move on.

I sit in the car, parked on Hobart. The house Calvin stayed in is in view. I'm halfway through one of my flasks, now lighting another cigarette. The car is turned off and my window is partway down so it won't get fogged up inside. I'm dressed appropriately. The cold nipping at the tip of my nose is all.

Phone rings.

Leslie.

"Hello, Leslie."

"Can you get to Luna's house? There's been an incident, and I'm stuck in trial."

"Incident? Al okay?"

"Yes. He's okay. Some rounds were fired through his window. I don't know if he was the target or if they were stray bullets from a nearby shooting."

"Shit. I'm on my way."

"Call me when you get the info from the police. I need to know. Leave a message if I don't answer."

"Okay."

"Thank you, Frank."

She disconnects before I can say anything.

I start the car and head to Al's as fast as I can.

When I get there, I park behind a Crime Scene Search van that's double-parked in front of the house. A marked cruiser and two un-marked units are also double-parked near the front of Al's house.

As I'm walking, I notice the front window to the left of the door is broken out. Sharp, jagged pieces of all sizes still line the frame. I hustle up there, but I'm stopped at the door by a uniform.

"I'm sorry, sir. Can I ask who you are?"

"Frank Marr, a friend of Al Luna."

"Let him in," a familiar voice from inside says.

The officer moves aside.

I walk in, notice the familiar voice as Freudiger's, and wonder what the hell he's doing here. Al is sitting in his armchair, wearing a winter coat and being interviewed by a district detective. He acknowledges me with a tilt of his head. I notice a shattered bottle of scotch on the end table, a pool of scotch still on the surface. His personal weapon, a Glock 23, is on the sofa, unsecured. He's still a detective on administrative leave, so they aren't worried.

Another uniform officer is taking notes. Two Crime Scene techs are in the living room area, one taking photos and the other on a ladder cutting into the ceiling, where I notice several bullet holes. Freudiger walks toward me, extends his hand to shake. I take it.

"What are you doing here, Johnny?"

"Believe it or not, I was only a few blocks away when this happened. Afraid I was on my way here to serve Al a subpoena."

Subpoena. Has to be for information regarding Al's source, Tamie. I don't respond to that.

"You see anything?" I ask.

"No. By the time I got here, it was over. I was the first here."

"It looks like it was a drive-by, intentionally targeting Al's house?"

"Yes. That's what it appears to be."

"He looks okay. Damn. You think it's related to the shooting? Retaliation?"

"I don't know about retaliation or anything like that. It could just be the result of all the protesting and his name and address getting leaked somehow. District detectives are going to look into everything."

"I need to talk to him."

"That's up to him."

I don't know the young detective interviewing him. I notice he has an investigator badge hanging on his neck, so he hasn't made detective yet.

"Don't want to interrupt," I say. "You okay, Al?"

"Lost a damn good bottle of scotch."

The uniform officer chuckles. Al shoots him a hard glare.

"Leslie called me. I came over right away. I'll let the detective here finish up, and then we'll talk, okay?"

"Yeah. You mind pouring me some Jameson on ice? It's in the kitchen. You know where the glasses are."

"Of course. But I should call Leslie first. She's worried about you."

"All right."

I walk to the kitchen, pull out my phone and tap to call Leslie. It rings and goes to voice mail.

"I'm here. Window is shot out, but he's okay, just a little rattled. Johnny Freudiger is here. He has a subpoena. I assume it's for information revealing the source who was with him prior to the shooting. Call me. Bye."

I find the half-empty bottle of Jameson on the counter near the sink, grab two glasses from a cabinet and ice out of the freezer for Al's glass. I give him a good pour and myself a three-finger shot, which I down right away. I think about my breath. Forgot my mints in the car, but who gives a shit.

I bring the drink to Al. He takes a nice sip right away.

"Calm my nerves."

I'm obviously here toward the end of the interview.

"Anything else you would like to add?" the investigator asks.

"You got everything," says Al.

The investigator hands Al his business card.

"My personal cell is on there. Call me if you remember anything else."

"Yeah," he says, taking the card and then setting it on the end table in the pool of scotch.

The investigator grins, turns and walks to the officer taking notes.

"Can you guys stick around until Crime Scene is done here?"

"No problem," the uniform says.

"Talk later." He nods toward Freudiger and exits.

The uniform officer who was taking notes is an older 5D guy, an MPO patch sewn onto the left shoulder of his shirt. He has a scruffy beard, like he hasn't been home for a while.

"I thought you guys had a unit sitting outside?" I ask him.

"No, man. Sarge pulled that last night. All these robberies and shootings going on, you know. Low manpower and shit."

"Well, what about now? You gonna see about getting a unit to sit on the block now?"

"I'll talk to my sarge," he says. "If he won't, we won't clear the scene and we'll stay out there through the end of my tour." He looks at Freudiger, worried because he heard him say that.

Freudiger smiles. He doesn't give a shit about something petty like that. At least the Freudiger I remember doesn't.

I look back at Al. He's sitting there sipping his scotch. Looks like a fucking lost puppy.

FORTY-FIVE

Crime Scene finishes up and leaves the mess for Al to take care of. "We'll be in the car out front, working on the report," the MPO tells Al.

"Appreciate you sticking around out there."

"No problem."

They exit. The only one left is Freudiger, and we know why he's here.

"Like I said, Detective Luna, I was already on my way here when all this broke out. Wish I was on the block when it did."

Al looks up to him from his chair, weary smile on his face.

"I have to serve you with this subpoena for you to provide us with the information that can identify the confidential informant you said you were with prior to the shooting. We need to interview the person. You know that."

"I know, but I also have to protect it. You know that."

"We will not release any information that can identify your CI."

"Right, just like my name and address were not supposed to be released. You can see what came of that."

"Our office had nothing to do with that leak. The information will stay with my office, and I'll be the only one to interview the person. It goes without saying, but you do know the consequences of not responding to this subpoena."

"I know the consequences." He downs what is left of the Jameson.

"Leave the subpoena," I say. "He'll get with his lawyer and we'll figure this out."

"Figure what out, Frank?" Al snaps.

"Give us time, Johnny."

"End of the week." He turns to exit, looks at Al again. "I'm sorry this happened, Al."

"What? The window or the subpoena?"

"Everything."

"Never say you're sorry," Al says.

Al's looking at his empty glass of Jameson with only one melting cube of ice in it.

I walk Johnny to the door.

"I'm going to stick around here until we get the window fixed," I tell him. "And if Al says the CI doesn't know anything, then the CI doesn't know anything."

"We'll talk soon." He walks out the door, closing it behind him.

Al turns to me. "It's freezing in here."

"I can make a run to Home Depot, get what you need to board it up until you can get a new window."

"No, no. I got a guy who'll come right out and do that."

"I don't mind."

"No, Frank. I'll take care of it. I'll give him a call now."

"All right, then. You want a refill?"

"Why not."

I grab his glass and go to the kitchen. I can hear him talking on his cell.

When I return with his drink, and a bit for me, he's off the phone. I hand him his glass and sit on the sofa. I look at the broken bottle of scotch on the end table.

"Don't worry about that, either. I like the smell."

"Shit. I'll clean up the glass at least," I say while standing.

"Sit down, Frank. You're driving me nuts with your need to help. It's not like you, and it's freaking me out."

I sit, sip the whiskey.

"You can be a real hardhead, you know."

"Yeah."

"Your guy coming now for the window?"

"Be here in about an hour."

"I don't want to *freak* you out any more, but you should come stay with me."

He snorts a short laugh. "You're a good friend, bro. Don't want you to think otherwise, but I'm staying here."

"Stay away from the windows, then."

My phone rings. I pull it out. It's Leslie.

"Yeah," I answer.

"Judge called a brief recess. Was Al the target?"

"Seriously doubt it was random."

"He still with the police?"

"They're all gone. You want to talk to him?"

"Yes."

I hand the cell over to Al.

"It's Leslie. I'm going to step out onto the porch to have a smoke."

He nods, takes the phone.

"Hello."

I exit, tap out a cigarette from the pack and light it. The MPO and his partner are in the marked cruiser double-parked in front of the house. The nonemergency lights are on. He sees me when I step out, gives a half salute instead of a wave.

I sit on an old wooden chair. I can hear Al through the broken window as he talks to Leslie. I notice three bullet holes in the siding near the window, all the holes made larger after Crime Scene dug out the spent rounds. More repairs he'll need to do.

My butt's getting cold.

When I finish the smoke, I flick it to the sidewalk beyond the front yard, watch it roll to the gutter, and then walk back in the house.

Al's off the phone. The phone is on the coffee table. I snatch it up before I sit and slip it back into my coat pocket.

"Getting cold as shit," I say, and then pick up my glass and take a drink. "That makes it better, though."

"Sure does."

"By the way, have any of your investigations ever led to a house on Queen Street?"

He thinks for a moment. "No. Why?"

"Those two mopes I was telling you about, Ty and Marlon. Looks like they have something going there."

He rests his head back on the armchair, staring at the ceiling.

"Like what?"

"No foot traffic, so I'm thinking a safe house."

"Sorry I brought you into this, Frank."

"Now you're being a dope."

"Really, I am sorry. I figured if anyone could get to the bottom of this, it's you. Honestly, though, I don't know how the hell you can." He looks at me direct. "I am telling you the truth, Frankie. The kid had a gun." Rests his head back on the armchair, not expecting me to reply. I don't.

I finish off the glass and wait for the guy who'll board up the frame where the window once was.

Al is sitting on the chair, head slumped back, hand on the glass that's sitting on the end table, snoring.

When the repairman shows and Al looks like he's fully awake, I leave.

"Call you later," I say.

"Thanks, Frank."

Before I get in the car, I walk to the MPO's cruiser. He rolls down the driver's window.

"I appreciate you boys sticking around."

"No worries. Talked to my sarge at 5D. He said he'd post a unit on the block for the next shift."

"Thank him for me."

"Will do."

"You guys stay safe and warm, all right?"

"A good officer always does."

I extend my hand to shake. He accepts.

I get in the car and drive.

The dark drops hard in winter. I decide to take advantage of that and drive around, maybe hit the 17th and Euclid area. This cold will keep most people inside. I'm not looking for *most* people, just certain knuckleheads, the ones who are up to no good, braving the freezing weather to make a few more dollars.

A couple of guys are standing on the corner, huddled together in their overly large bloated black jackets, looking like a couple of bear cubs left out of the den.

I'm parked on Euclid, half a block away, and look through my binos. They don't look familiar. I decide to hang out for a bit.

About an hour passes, when I notice a newer-model Explorer pull to the curb at the corner. The two guys walk over to it as the rear door behind the passenger seat opens. Someone steps onto the sidewalk, wearing a puffy white winter coat. Can't make the person out until she turns and reveals her profile. *Fucking Darling.* What the hell? I thought she was sober. Is she trying to score something from them? But then the Explorer pulls away. She stays there talking to the boys for a bit and walks up the stairs to the row house on 17th, the one that was—maybe still is—a brothel, and where I discovered the other runaway a few years back. Tamie opens the door and steps in.

Holy fuck.

More than two hours later the Explorer returns, double-parks in front of the house and waits. A couple of minutes after that Tamie exits, says something to the two boys on the corner. They nod, keep a respectful distance, like she's their queen. After a minute she steps back into the car and it drives north on 17th.

I follow.

I'm fucking ready to jump outta my skin now, especially when I follow the car to Queen Street and it parks near the house we followed Ty and Marlon to.

The driver and another guy step out of the front as Tamie steps out of the rear.

Peering through the binos, I can't make the boys out. The street is not well lit. They enter the house.

It's late. Al's probably sleeping. I know Leslie is. I'll keep this to myself for now. I have to take it all in first.

I hang out there for more than an hour, then head home. I have Darling's contact information and the Explorer's tag number. I'll give Lustig a call tomorrow, see if he'll run it for me. I pull out the Polaroid of Tamie that's in my backpack. Damn, she's rough-looking. *You fucking played me well.*

Forty-Six

I drive around my neighborhood for a few minutes, like I did before. Looks clear, so I park down the street from my house and walk home.

I'm hungry, but too tired to fix anything. Too late to order anything, so the best option is sleep.

My good friend Klonopin helps.

I immediately fade into a dream.

Phone rings. Wakes me up.

Was I dreaming?

It rings again.

I roll over, look at it on the nightstand. I don't recognize the number. Still a little groggy.

I answer with a scratchy "Hello."

"Frank Marr?" a somewhat familiar voice asks.

"Yeah.. Who's this?"

"Sounds like I woke you. Sorry. This is Officer Russ Smith, 4D."

"Russ, what time is it?"

I sit on the edge of the bed, turn the light on. I notice the time on my cell. Oh-three-thirty.

"Oh-three-thirty."

"Damn. Haven't talked to you in ages, man. Is something wrong?"

"I don't know. Need you to tell me that."

"Okay."

What the fuck's this about?

"I have this young man here, stopped him when he was wandering the outer perimeter of the zoo's fenced area at Adams Mill and Clydesdale. Says his name is Calvin Tolson and he works for you."

Takes me a second.

"Calvin? Is he under arrest?"

"Stopped him for suspicious behavior. Had a large baggie of weed, more than personal use, but no, didn't arrest him."

"Yeah, he works for me. Did he say what he was doing up there?"

"Said he got locked out of his uncle's home on Hobart. Didn't want to wake him, so he was just finding a spot to rest. Has a backpack with personal items and clothing, so I thought that was odd."

"We were doing a two-day surveillance gig on a cheating husband. That's why he's packed," I make up on the spot.

"Well, I ran him and he's clear. No record."

"Yeah, I know he is. Sorry about this shit, Russ. He probably was too worried to call me. He always forgets his keys. Can you hold him there and I'll come pick him up?"

"No problem."

"Can I talk to him?"

"Here he is."

"Yeah," Calvin says.

"That's all you got for me is a *yeah*?"

"Only thing I could think of."

"You the only one that can hear me?"

"Yeah."

"I told Officer Smith you had a backpack of clothes because we were working a two-day surveillance case and that you forgot your keys. Got it?"

"Yeah."

"And do you know what would have happened if you got yourself locked up?"

"For what?"

"Weed is legal in the city, but not if you have more than a certain amount. You know that."

"I know. I get locked up, then I'd have an adult record."

"Fuck that. They would've run your prints, and it would've come back to a hit on the nickname Playboy. The fucking drive-by. You understand now?"

A bit of an exaggeration. I'm only trying to scare him. Like I said, I'd have to identify Calvin as the driver, too. That is, unless his prints are also on the shooter's weapon. That'd fuck him.

"Fuck."

"You're lucky the officer knows me. I'll be there in a few. You treat Officer Smith with respect for the courtesy he's shown you."

"Yeah."

"Let me talk to him."

"What's up, Marr?"

"I'll be there in about twenty. I appreciate what you did, man. I owe you. Calvin's a good kid."

"Drinks on you at Rebellion next time I see you."

"Hell yeah."

I disconnect, step out of bed, and shake off the sleep.

I don't even have time to make coffee. It'll have to be by willpower alone.

When I get there, Calvin is sitting on the curb in front of the patrol car. The headlights are off, but the parking lights are on. Smith and his partner are in the car. It's a no-parking area, so there are no other cars around. I can pull ahead of Calvin and park along the curb. When I step out, Smith is already out. His partner, a young woman, probably still in training, also steps out. Calvin stands up and shoulders his backpack.

I shake my head at Calvin, like I've had to pick him up before.

"Good to see ya, Smith."

We shake hands.

I turn to his partner and introduce myself. "Hi. Frank Marr."

"Officer King," she says.

"Calvin, I'll say it again. You can't keep forgetting your keys, man."

"I know."

"Thanks for not locking his ass up for the weed, Russ."

"Looked more than for personal use, but hell, I don't have a scale. Do you, Officer King?"

"No."

"'Sides, Mr. Tolson seems like a good young man who knows in the future to carry only a couple of joints, right?"

"Yes, sir."

"Well, we'll get out of your hair, man. Be safe."

"You too, Marr. See you around."

They both step into the cruiser in sync.

"It's freezing out here," I say, and walk to the car.

Calvin follows.

FORTY-SEVEN

S till don't trust him enough to take him to my house, so we head
to an all-night food joint in Georgetown. I am curious why he
chose to call me.

I never asked how old he is, but I figure no older than his
midtwenties. Hard to tell, though. He could be younger. I don't
want to say I feel like a dad right now even though I'm old enough
to have a son his age. Let's just say I feel like a big brother, and we'll
leave it there.

"Why'd you disappear?"

"I don't know." He shrugs, but I know he does know.

"Why'd you think to call me?"

"Couldn't call my uncle. I guess I was afraid they might have paper on me, so figured you being an ex-cop might help. At least I was
bankin' on you helpin'."

"If there was paper on you, the officer would have locked you
up after he ran your name. It would've been under your nickname,
Playboy, with your description, but more than likely, what we call
an unnumbered warrant, so the only way they would've found out

194

is if you got locked up and your prints were run. Then the detective who got the warrant on you would be notified."

"Unnumbered?"

"Not in the system, but still a warrant for your arrest. You're lucky that officer knows me. Most cops won't waste their time processing an arrest for weed anymore. It'll just be a no-paper, but some of the young ones like the overtime money that comes with going to court at the end of their shift even if the case is going to get thrown out."

"Weed's legal."

"Technically."

"Appreciate what you did." He says it sincerely. Sounds like a different person saying it, a little uncomfortable.

"You get back with your uncle, tell him you met a girl, some shit like that. Tell him you'll call next time instead of disappearing like that, or I'll turn you in to the detective myself. You're an adult. You make your own decisions, but your uncle's not like a roommate. You can't just run off, not tell him. He's gonna worry, 'cause he's family."

"Yeah."

The city is different around this time. Quiet, and there's a certain light glow in the night sky as it begins its turn to day. There was a time I pulled a lot of all-nighters, but it's harder to stay awake these days. I am up now and may as well stay up, as hard as that might be.

When we get to the diner, we grab a couple of stools at the counter. Not a busy night, just a few tables taken up by college-type kids still trying to sober up.

First thing I do is order coffee, Calvin just water. I'm not hungry. It's too early. My body has its set routine. I don't like to disrupt it or it'll fuck up my system.

Calvin orders the steak and eggs with toast.

"Where did you think you were going to go after you left your uncle's?"

"I don't know." Sips water. "Thought about goin' to the house where I bought weed, but didn't take long to change my mind 'bout that. Knew I'd be walking into trouble if I did. Fall back into that old shit. Don't know, really, what I was thinking. Where I'd go."

"So, you got this job back if you want it. No strings."

Seems bothered.

"What's the problem here, Calvin?"

"I can't say."

"Can't say 'cause you don't know or you won't say? Something happen I should know about? Someone step to you?"

"Naw. Nothin' like that." He turns to me, makes good eye contact. "No strings attached?"

"No, but it is a job and you work for me. You want to quit, you tell me. Give me notice. Don't just up and disappear."

"Those are strings."

"No they aren't." I smile. "That's called being an adult."

Something I know little about, but I'm learning.

"Being a man comes with strings," he tells me.

"Yeah, and just so you know, I did meet with your uncle the morning I came to pick you up. Knocked on the door, thinking you overslept, and he answered."

He doesn't say anything. Looks down.

"You were right. He's a good man."

"I know."

A couple of minutes later the counter man sets Calvin's plate in front of him.

He digs in right away. I finish my coffee, signal for a refill. It's like drinking the coffee I used to have at the branch, tastes like it's been sitting from the night before.

I think about Darling and what's going on there. Still hard for me to take in. I reach down to my backpack on the floor at my feet, dig through it and find the Polaroid. I pull it out, look at it, but only a second. The image is tough to look at, and I've seen almost everything.

"I have a photo I want you to look at and tell me if you know her."

Calvin looks up from his food, his face almost buried in the plate.

"A'right."

I hand it to him.

He nearly jumps out of his seat.

"Aww…fuck. Damn. Disgusting crackhead pussy. Shit. Right when I'm enjoying my food."

I notice a couple of the guys at a table to the side of us look up from their drunken slumber.

"What the fuck you wanna go and show me this for?"

I take the photo, cover the lower extremities.

"Look at the face. You know her?"

"This an old picture?"

"Yes."

"Looks like some crackhead whore is all. I seen hundreds of them, just not their pussies. Aww…"

"Think of her a little older, cleaned up."

Studies it.

"Naw. I don't know her. But like I said, I been out of this shit for a bit now."

"All right." I return it to the backpack.

"Why she important?"

"I don't know yet."

He looks down at his plate.

"Damn, man, I done lost my appetite."

FORTY-EIGHT

I pull the car up near the front of his uncle's house. It's almost 7:00 a.m.

"I'll wait here to make sure you get in."

"He'll be up by now."

"Let me know if you need me to talk to him."

"Won't have to. I'll tell him I got temporarily confused."

I almost chuckle after he says that. I don't know if it's a dry humor or he's serious.

"You're not confused now?"

"Not as much."

"All right, dude. Stay home and get some rest. I'll be by tomorrow morning to pick you up."

He grabs his backpack and steps out, looks back at me briefly. Can't read him. Maybe 'cause I said *dude*. He closes the door and walks up the stairs, has to pull his pants up after a few steps.

I wait while he knocks on the door. His uncle answers. I give a couple of taps on my horn so the uncle can see me. He waves.

I drive home, make myself some more coffee when I get there, check the time. Lustig should be in the detectives' office for day-work by now. I want to see if he'll run the Explorer's tag.

"Hey, Gary. This is Frank Marr."

"What's up, Frankie?"

"This a bad time?"

"It's always a bad time when I'm working."

"I can imagine. Listen, I'm working Luna's shooting and have a tag to run, if that's cool."

"Yeah, I don't give a shit. Stand by. Let me log on."

"Thanks."

"Okay, go."

I give him the tag. I hear his fingers hitting a keyboard. I have my notepad and pen at the ready.

"Ready to copy?"

"Yeah."

"Comes back to a Patricia Holm, with a DOB of 02/01/1939."

Patricia Holm?

He gives me her address. It's on the 1600 block of Euclid Street.

"Everything looks up to date. Anything else?"

"No. That's good. Thanks."

"No problem, bud. Hope it helps, and keep me informed with Luna's situation."

"Will do."

I power on my laptop. Open LexisNexis and run Patricia Holm with her DOB. I can run basic background checks through this ser-vice—nothing like what I could work when I was a cop, though. I check prior addresses, and it appears as though she has always had the same address. She's also had only one job: file clerk at Superior Court. Been retired for several years now. Associates are just about everyone in the Holm family, most prominent, her son, Cordell Holm. I laugh to myself. Sort of a nervous laugh, 'cause I don't know what the fuck's going on.

Does she know these boys are using her car?

My experience tells me she does, but hell, it's family, and what a connection that family must have had when she used to work for Superior Court.

So how do I play this? I go back with Tamie Darling, like Al does. Well, not exactly like Al does. Mine was a working relationship, far from that shit he was into with her. I hope it doesn't go further than that. I consider him a best friend, but shit, you never know someone as well as you think you do. Look at me.

My next call is Leslie, but again, straight to voice mail. I leave a message for her to call me back when she gets a chance.

I also don't have a clue as to how all this is going to play into the shooting, if at all, but I have to work it through.

I call Al, tell him I'll be out and about and ask if he wants me to bring him lunch.

"I have leftover takeout from last night, but thanks."

"Man, you can't survive on that shit. It's gonna rip a hole in your stomach."

"I have an iron stomach."

"You get the window in yet?"

"Still boarded up. The window is a special order, so it's going to take a few days before I can get it put in. He used three-quarter-inch board, though."

"Yeah, I remember. Stronger than the window, then."

"And more private. Maybe I'll keep it."

"I meant to ask you something before." *Not true, of course.* "I was recently thinking about the Cordell Holm case—"

"What the hell you thinking about that piece of shit for?"

"'Cause no one ever told me where he got sent after sentencing."

"Some federal prison up in New Jersey. Why?"

"Was driving by 17th and Euclid the other day and thought about it is all."

"Yeah, okay."

"Maybe I'll stop by later this evening and we can have a drink."

"Yeah, sure."

"Later."

Damn, and I thought I was paranoid when I was putting that shit up my nose. Not a good feeling now, especially when you have to keep things from your good friend.

FORTY-NINE

I wake up later than normal. Had one too many with Al and Leslie last night. I didn't have a chance to get with Leslie privately, fill her in on what I know. She does need to know. After all, it could come back to bite Al, especially now, with the connection between Darling and members of Cordell's crew. I don't have long until Freudiger forces Al's hand with the subpoena, so I need to get to the bottom of this, which means Tamie Darling.

Before I leave, I open my stash wall and count out Calvin's pay for the day. I also count out another two grand.

Calvin is already on the sidewalk by the time I roll up to the front of his uncle's house. He lets the backpack slide off his shoulder and carries it to the front-passenger door, sets the backpack at his feet when he sits.

"What's the plan here today?" he says with a quiet tone, as if embarrassed.

"There are a couple of things we need to work."

Him taking off the way he did is one of the things. I reach into my backpack, which is sitting on the floor in back, find the folder that contains the photo Rattan gave me, the one Calvin had appeared to have a reaction to.

I drop it on his lap.

"Who is this?" I ask.

He doesn't pick it up, just eyeballs it and looks out the front windshield, then back to me, and says, "I told you, I don't know."

"Bullshit. I think seeing this before is the reason you took off. Who is it?"

"Man, you startin' to sound a lot like my uncle."

"Right now I'm your boss, and I expect answers."

I give him time but don't take my eyes off him.

He picks up the photo, looks like he's studying it.

Shakes his head.

"Can't say for sure, 'cause the quality ain't that good, but he looks a lot like a dude I know as Rule."

"Why'd you keep this from me?"

"Why you think? First off, I ain't hundred percent on it, and second, you show me it in front of that detective woman. I knew she'd ask too many questions just like I know you about to. Difference is, she don't know my background like you do."

He sets the photo on the center console. I take it and slip it back into the folder in my backpack.

"Where does he stay?"

"Back when I knew him, he stayed at one of those buildings on Fairmont."

"Fourteen hundred block?"

"Yeah."

"So he knows those boys we followed to the house on Queen?"

"I used to see him with Ty, but that was a few years back."

"He connected to Cordell in any way?"

He hesitates, but says, "Cordell was his supplier. I don't know about now, especially since Cordell got sent up."

"Crack, heroin?"

"Mostly crack."

"Listen up. We work together, which means you never hold things back from me. You want to learn this business, then there has to be trust, and some rules, like any other job."

He looks at me like *trust* and *rules* are words that are difficult to comprehend.

"I can understand you not wanting to say anything in front of Detective Rattan. Hell, I've kept things from the police until they need to know. Sometimes even keep things from them I don't want them to know. But you should've come to me after, not fucking take off like you did because you didn't know how to handle it. I can keep you out of this one here. No worries."

He nods.

"You never went back to the neighborhood, then?"

"Naw."

"Really?"

"For real, man. How many times I got to tell you? Shiet, I took that advice you gave me when you decided not to kill me and I didn't go back. Between you and thinkin' the cops knew I was the driver for that police killing, I stayed away. I don't want to go to fucking jail."

"Yeah, you stayed away, like three blocks away. I mean, the day I followed you to your uncle's, you passed Seventeenth, which is about two blocks north of Euclid. You're telling me you never ran into any of the old crew on Columbia?"

"No, man. I be like a ghost when I walk."

"Shit. Ghost. If I can see ghosts, so can they. What I'm starting to think is Cordell put a hit out on me after he got sentenced, which wasn't that long ago. Maybe even Luna, too, 'cause he was one of the lead detectives."

"How you fucking think that?"

"'Cause this boy here killed a cop, wounded another one, and almost got me. And it all happened too close to my home. Not to mention his connection to Cordell."

"He like Little Monster. He a crazy fool, and that right there ain't a good combination. If it is something like that, he be acting on his own. Cordell ain't stupid like that. I never known him to order a hit on a cop, even an ex-cop like you. Shiet."

"He was stupid enough to allow you and Little Monster to do the drive-by that killed Officer Tommy, and again, almost me."

"That was all Monster. He acted fast 'cause you were taking that girl, Cordell's property. He didn't think. He just act."

"Property?"

"Fuck yeah, man. Property. She knew it, too. You talk this trust shit, then trust me that I ain't part of that no more. I got some PTSD over all this shit here."

PTSD? That wouldn't surprise me. Almost makes me laugh.

"Do you know who is running things for Cordell now?"

"Fuck no, and please don't say you want me to try to find out."

"I wouldn't put you in that kind of situation."

Intentionally, anyway.

"We can't keep this info about Rule from the police. It could endanger lives. I have to give it to Detective Rattan."

"How you gonna say you got his name?"

"I'll keep you out of it. We'll tell her it came from a source. They won't care as long as they have a name or a nickname to work. I have to make a quick stop first."

FIFTY

I drive to Riggs, to a house I hit a while back. A bedridden old lady lived there—or rather, was kept prisoner by her two drug-dealing grandkids. Needless to say, those youngsters are doing good time now and the old lady's been freed of their shit.

Depending on what the outcome of a stash house hit is, I try to help her out financially at least once a month. She doesn't know the money is dirty. At least I hope she doesn't. She's not stupid, though. I told her when I first gave her a bag of money that it was from neighborhood donations. Now my story has changed, and I collect donations from different philanthropic sources, all cash, of course, because they want to remain anonymous. She still calls me the tax man. I forget why. But I advised her she doesn't have to claim this income on her taxes.

Calvin wants to wait in the car, but I make him go with me.

"What's this about?" he asks.

"An elderly woman who needs help on occasion, that's all."

"What kind of help?"

"All kinds of help. Don't worry about it. Just go with my story."

"Story?"

"Yes, story, and if you talk, watch your mouth. In fact, maybe don't talk."

"Shiet."

I knock on the front door. A couple of minutes later, I hear someone moving around on the inside, near the door.

"It's Frank," I call through the door.

"Frank?" she says softly, like she doesn't know.

"The tax man," I say, and roll my eyes at Calvin.

"Oh, for—" I hear her begin, and the dead bolts unlock and the door opens.

First thing she does is give Calvin a hard look. He takes a sliding half step back on the porch.

"How are you, sweetie?" she says to me, and bends her frail self over to give me a hug. "Come in, now."

She steps away from the door, and I walk in. Calvin stays where he is.

"This is Calvin. He's one of our volunteers."

"Oh, you come in, too, then, young man."

His eyebrows furrow, but he obeys.

I sit on the sofa, set my backpack at my feet.

"You sit, too," she tells Calvin.

He looks at the armchair covered with protective plastic. The only place to sit.

"You go and sit there," she tells him.

He does. It squeaks and crinkles when he sits and even more when he adjusts himself. He gives me a hard look.

It's a new chair. Didn't see it last time I was here. Looks like she's putting some of the money to good use.

"I like the new armchair," I say.

"That was delivered last week. Good for watching that big television."

The large flat-screen is sitting on a console against a wall on the other side of the living room. It is too big for the room, but I bought it anyway. Like having her own little theater.

"I can make tea," she offers.

"No, thank you. We can't stay long. Today's a busy day for us."

"Must be. All the good you do, and now you have this young volunteer to help."

"Yes, I'm thankful for that." I smile.

Calvin sits very still, staring straight ahead, clearly not in his element.

The old lady moves slowly, sits on the sofa beside me. I grab a brown paper sandwich bag out of my pack. It's folded over to not reveal what's inside. I hand it to her.

"God bless you, son," she says.

"We're happy to do it."

"You sure you boys don't want some tea? I can make coffee, too, if you prefer."

"No. We really have to be going. Shouldn't have even sat down. Now it'll be hard to get up. It is a comfortable sofa."

I remember the old one, coated with crusty vomit and soaked with blood. Not mine, but the two thug grandkids who took over her house. I almost killed those bastards.

"Those boys haven't tried to contact you from prison, have they?"

"No. Thank the Lord."

"You tell me if they do."

"I surely will."

"You need anything done around here before we go?"

"No, thank you, sweetie. I have a wonderful lady that comes in now three times a week to help around here and go to the grocery store for me. You two go on about your business. You stay longer next time."

"I will."

I lean over and give her a hug, grab my pack, and stand. Hugging her is like hugging a cricket. Calvin does the same.

She starts to pull herself up from the sofa. Her arms look double-jointed, as if they'll snap in two.

"Don't get up. We'll let ourselves out."

"Okay, now," she says.

"G'day, ma'am," Calvin says uncomfortably.

I have a key, so I lock the door when we exit.

Walking back to the car, Calvin says, "I'm afraid to know what was in the bag you gave her."

"Does look suspicious, huh?" I leave it at that.

FIFTY-ONE

I called Rattan. She agreed to meet me in front of 300, police headquarters, because she has court and can't break away.

It'll take too long to find parking, so I don't bother. I pull the car to the curb in front of 300.

"Man, this place make me naus…nausea…makes me wanna puke."

"Yeah, makes me nauseous, too," I say. He gives me an odd look.

Rattan is on the steps, talking to a uniform cop. She's wearing black tight-fit suit pants and a teal in color overcoat. The beanie cap is what gets me. Makes her look cuter. I shake away the thought and tap the horn a couple of times to get her attention. She takes notice, slaps the uniform on the back, and walks over to my side of the car.

"Parking's a bitch," I say.

"Tell me about it."

"Like I said when I called, we might have some good information on the shooter in that photo."

I hand her the bodycam photo.

"A source said it's pretty confident that this is a guy known as Rule."

"Rule?"

I spell the name for her. She notebooks it.

"He's known to hang at the fourteen hundred block of Fairmont

NW, and lives in one of the buildings located at the north and south corners of Fairmont and Fourteenth. Not sure which one. Also known to deal drugs."

"Not a real common nickname or name, so I'll get with 3D and Narcotics Branch, see if they know of him. This is good. Thanks."

"Anytime. And can you let me know if you get him and it turns out to be good information? I had to pay the source."

"Yes. If it is, I'll personally reimburse you."

"You can buy me a couple of drinks."

"Deal."

She hands me back the photo. "Hold on to this."

"All right, then. Stay safe."

"Thanks again, Marr."

She offers her hand, and we shake. Soft, cold hands.

When she steps onto the sidewalk, I pull out.

"Why you didn't give up Ty and Marlon, that they might be runnin' together?"

"Remember when I said some things we keep to ourselves?"

"Oh. Yeah. Why them?"

"Because we want to get to those mopes first."

"Mopes." He chuckles. "That what you all called me?"

"Fuck yes. You were the worst kind of mope."

"Fuck you."

"What, you can't take someone bustin' your balls?"

"Yeah, with the best of them."

That's good.

"You also lied to the detective woman—"

"Rattan. Her name is Rattan."

"Rattan. You lied to her about payin' a snitch."

"No I didn't. I got to pay you, don't I?"

"You playin' that shit again?"

"No. You're saying it. And we call them a source of information."

He rolls down the window and spits, rolls it up again and says, "Just call them what they are."

"Listen, you did good, possibly identifying the shooter. And you're not a source of information. You're a coworker. If they get him, then we're owed a favor down the road. And trust me when I say in this business we need all the favors we can get."

"Makes sense. And you hot on that Detective Rattan, ain't ya? That the kind of favor you talkin' about down the road?"

"She's cute, but business first."

"Yeah, I learned that, too, when I worked for Cordell."

"No comparison."

"Haven't known you long enough to know if that's true," he says.

I drive to the Salvadoran restaurant we went to before and find parking.

"Early for lunch, ain't it?"

"This is work."

I roll down the window and light up a smoke. Calvin pulls out a pack of Swisher Sweets Tip Cigarillos.

"Mind if I light one of these up?"

"No. Unless you got something more than tobacco in there."

Huffs a laugh. "Naw."

He takes one out of the pack, unwraps it from the plastic. I hand him my lighter. Funny, Luna used to smoke those before he was spoiled with good cigars. Bought them at 7-Eleven. Must've had a death wish, 'cause he inhaled.

They have a sweet smell. Sort of upsets my stomach.

"Roll your window down a bit," I tell him.

He does, then hands back my lighter. Inhales.

"So, here's what I got. You know what an okeydoke is?"

"Yeah, some sort of con."

"Yes, except the kind I'm talking about is legal. Well, sometimes legal. Depends on if it's something that's going to go to court or not."

"We talkin' something that's goin' to court here?"

"No."

I grab a burner phone out of a side pocket of my backpack, hand it to him. It's an old-style flip phone. He looks at it as if it's some sort of oddity.

I want to be careful how I handle this with Calvin, because I don't want to give up Tamie Darling as someone who was/is a CI for me but who is now playing for the other side.

"I have a contact number for this girl who might be working with Ty and Marlon. I want to try to set it up so I can get to her. So I have this idea."

"How you get the number?"

"One step at a time, rookie. Some things you're not ready to learn." *Or, rather, there are some things I don't want to tell you.*

I grab a roll of money out of my pants pocket, peel off two twenties, and hand them to Calvin.

"This is your expense money."

"Meaning it don't come off my pay?"

"Yeah, meaning that. What I want you to do is take the burner and go into the restaurant, sit at a table, order food if you want or just coffee or beer."

"Don't like coffee and it's a bit early for beer. Just make me tired. Maybe a screwdriver, something like that?"

"Yeah, whatever. Just sit in there and wait for me, and with any luck I'll have additional info when I come in. Got it?"

"A'right."

He opens the door, but before he steps out, I say, "Don't go flirting with that waitress. Her brothers might not like that. Get your ass kicked."

"Yeah, right." And he exits, shutting the door behind him.

I wait for a couple of minutes after he enters, to make sure he doesn't step back out. Then I grab my phone and call Darling.

Fifty-Two

I walk into the restaurant, see Calvin sitting at a small table, drinking what looks like a screwdriver and eating chips with salsa. It's before the lunch rush, so there's hardly anyone here. I sit across from him.

"That didn't take long," he tells me.

The waitress approaches, offers a menu.

"You order something?" I ask Calvin.

"Yeah, one of them pupusas."

"I'll have what he's having, and a Baileys and coffee. Thanks."

She smiles and takes the menu back.

"Gracias," she says.

I notice Calvin watching her as she walks away.

"Careful there, hombre."

"Wouldn't be normal if I didn't take notice."

"Is your uncle at work today?"

"Yeah. Why?"

"I set something up and will be meeting a source—"

"Snitch," he says, then sips his drink from the little red straw.

"With a source. I'll drop you off at home, but you'll still be on the clock. If it works out through this source, you'll be getting a call on that burner."

"Why I can't go with you?"

"Source will only meet with me."

I have to lead Calvin to believe that the source I'm meeting, Tamie Darling, and the person who will be calling him on the burner, also Darling, are two different people. I don't fully trust Calvin yet. If it doesn't pan out, I don't want to burn Tamie.

I am playing them both, but Darling's the target. If she takes the bait, then Calvin will know they are the same person and it won't matter. With any luck, Calvin won't recognize her voice from about three years ago, when I had her play him. Shit, I'm pushing the line. This is a fishing expedition, and I'm testing the waters of Darling, who may have been playing me and Al for a long time.

"Here's how you have to play it. I want this person who might be calling you to believe you're a big player, slinging ounces of crack."

"What? No the fuck way. You tryin' to get me jammed up?"

"I do this kinda stuff all the time. The person who will be calling you won't know who the hell you are. Like I said, it's an okeydoke and you're one of the players in the con. But it's also a part of the investigation, so it's important to stay the part."

"Sound like I'm just gonna get caught up in something that might get me arrested."

"Calvin, for shit's sake, an okeydoke can't get you arrested, unless you're really going to be dealing an ounce of crack. And you're not."

"Hell no."

"This kind of thing is going to be a regular part of what we do."

Takes him a moment to think about it. "So what I got to do, then?"

"I'm hoping it'll be a girl that will call you," I say, knowing it will

215

be. "When she does, don't play into it right away. Ask how she got the number. To play the part well, you need to be suspicious of her. I'll feed the source a code word that she'll give you, that only you and your other fake buyers know for the product you sell."

"Yeah, we used to do that shit. Like 'jellybeans.'"

Fuck, that was the code word Darling used on Calvin back then. I almost want to laugh.

"Yeah, that's good, but let's think of something a little more common, like 'blizzard,' or something like that."

"Blizzard?"

"Heavy snow."

"Ain't that a bit obvious?"

"'Rock' would be a bit obvious. This is simple shit here. We're going with 'blizzard.' Once the caller tells you she got your number from Arthur—"

"The kid who got shot?"

"Yeah, that's a part of the okeydoke. So she gives you that name and calls it 'blizzard,' which is what you call the product you sell. You will call the meeting spot. Make it the little circle park at Sixteenth and Columbia, the one you hit before Mount Pleasant."

"A'right."

"Of course, you won't show, but both of us will be there to see if she shows."

"So then you'll know who it is?"

"Yeah, I hope."

She won't show, though, because Tamie will think I'll be there on surveillance. It's what happens after that I'm looking for.

"But then what?"

"We let her walk with the idea that she'll call you again."

The call after is what I want. Something she does on her own. That'll be what gives her up. If that happens, who the fuck knows what I'm gonna do.

"She ain't gonna have my real name?"

"No. Make one up. Who you want to be?"

He thinks hard, does everything but rub his chin with two fingers.

"Idris," he says.

"Idris? What kind of name is that?"

"He an actor I like. Tough as shit."

"Idris, then."

We eat our brunch, have another drink, and I take Calvin home.

On the way, I feed him questions, some of which I'll feed Darling to ask him, until I feel comfortable he's playing the part well.

I pull up in front of his house.

"Don't go using that burner for your own calls."

"C'mon, now."

"Keep it on you at all times and just play the part."

"I can play the part. Don't worry 'bout that."

"I should be back within a couple hours."

He grabs his pack and exits. Hops up the stairs to the front door. I don't have to meet her for about an hour, so I go home to have a couple of drinks and fill my flask.

FIFTY-THREE

S ame spot as the last meet. Eleven hundred block of Kenyon, by the mural. And there she is, wearing tight jeans and her puffy white coat. I scan the area a few times and then roll up. She hops in the back seat.

"Two times in the same week. I feel special," she says.

"Lot going on, and who else am I gonna call?"

I feel uncomfortable with her in the back seat now. Not like before, when I didn't doubt her. Like having an unaccompanied prisoner in the back for a drive-around. Doesn't matter if they're in shackles. It's just not something you do. Tamie's not a prisoner, but it sure feels the same.

"How'd you get here?" I say.

"Same as last time. I walked. I like walking the city."

I pull the car out. "Let's go around the corner where we were last time, try to find parking."

She cracks the window open, lights up a smoke.

I find a place to park on the school side, closer to 11th.

I look at her through the rearview as she flicks the cigarette out the window and pushes the button to slide it up. She dabs the right side of her upper lip with her middle finger, tightening the skin where there's a little wrinkle smile.

"Here's the deal. You know I'm working the shooting that Al was involved in?"

"Yes."

"Well, I started by looking into the background of the kid he shot, and it's not a good background."

I keep my eyes on her through the rearview. I know she knows I'm looking, but I still want to see if I get a reaction out of her.

"What's the kid's name again?"

Again? I don't recall ever giving her the kid's name.

I play stupid and say, "Arthur," because it doesn't matter if she knows. It's been on the news.

"I was able to get the name of a drug-dealing associate of his. This guy who goes by the name Idris."

Again. Nothing.

"Like that handsome actor?"

"Actor?"

"Ain't nothin'. Just playing."

"Idris is all I have on him."

"Why he so important in all this?"

"I need to find as much dirt on this kid, Arthur, as I can. I'm hoping, in some way, it'll help Al out, maybe even lead to something that can clear him."

"I see."

"The information I got is Idris is dealing large amounts of crack. He was getting supplied by Arthur. I'm talking ounces."

Still no reaction. Stone-cold. She does reach into her purse and take another cigarette. Lights it but doesn't roll the window down.

"Window," I remind her.

She does.

"Like I said, Arthur was supplying him ounces at a time, at least once a week."

"How you get this information?"

"What does that fucking matter, Darling?"

"Thought maybe it can help me when I talk to him."

"It won't. I don't even know what area he's working, but I'm thinking the fourteen hundred block of Fairmont, because that's where Arthur was known to hang. I do have a cell for Idris, and I want you to give him a call, say you got his number from a friend of Arthur's 'cause Arthur used to be your supplier, but now he's dead so you got nowhere else to go. Got that so far?"

"Easy."

"The word from my source is the shit he sells is called blizzard."

"Like the Dairy Queen drink?"

"I don't fucking know. Just blizzard. Just play him like you always do, and see if he'll sell you a quarter of an ounce or something. Nothing big, but you're a regular buyer. I want to get a meeting spot, where I'll be set up, and get him snatched up."

"By the police?"

"By me, baby."

I give her one of my burner phones.

"So, what's his name?" I ask, testing her.

"Idris, and don't bother asking the other shit. It's called blizzard, and you want me to get a quarter ounce of crack."

"That's what I love about working with you, Darling. You got a sharp memory. Also, make up your description and an outfit you'll be wearing so that he'll recognize you. And get one from him, too."

I gotta play the story as much as I can. Has to feel real.

"Okay."

"Here's the number."

FIFTY-FOUR

S ounded like Calvin played it well. Maybe got a little hard at first, but that's expected with drug boys getting cold calls. According to Darling, he agreed to meet her tomorrow at noon at the circle park area near 16th and Columbia. Again, I know she won't show because she thinks I'll be there, which I will, because I have to play Calvin, too. I'm hoping that sharp memory of hers memorized his cell.

It's a good sign when Darling looks at the cell screen briefly before handing it back to me.

I don't want to keep her, fill her head with anything else, so I say, "Might need to get with you later."

"Anytime, baby."

I hand her forty bucks. She folds it up, drops it in her purse, and steps out of the car, walks away. I swear she's working on that walking sway. Hate to admit it, but that ass ain't looking bad. I shake the thought away, like something perverted that managed to creep in.

Now it's Calvin's turn. I call him to let him know I'm on my way.

When I make the right to go south on 11th, I notice what looks like a black Explorer driving north. The tint is heavy, but what else is new. There are lots of Explorers in DC with heavy tint. But I can't help thinking about the one I saw drop Tamie Darling off at 17th and Euclid.

I get to Calvin's and stay double-parked with him in the car.

"You got my cell?"

"Yeah."

He pulls it out of his pack and hands it to me.

"My source said he got your number to the girl, and she called you," I say.

"Yeah. She called."

"So break it down for me."

Playing both sides can get frustrating and even confusing. You have to have a script in your head, be quick with a comeback just in case. Even when I was a cop and Luna was my partner, I played him, hid the fact that I was using blow. Had to lie to him on more than one occasion. I was pretty good at it. Now that I think about it, I'm sure he did the same, but his passion was sex.

"Your snitch works fast, 'cause she call quick."

"My *source* is one of the best. I swear you use the word 'snitch' one more time, unless we're really talking about a snitch, I'm gonna kick your ass from this car."

"I got ya."

"So tell me how the conversation went."

"She sound cute, but I played hard with her for a little bit, acted like, 'Who the fuck are you to call me?' Some shit like that. We settle on a quarter and a meet tomorrow at noon at the circle park."

"How you gonna recognize her?"

"She say she gonna be carrying a pink purse and wearing a white puffer coat. I made up something about myself, too."

I notebook everything he says like it's for real.

"Okay. Calling it a day. A short workday 'cause we got what we need. I'll pick you up at around ten thirty tomorrow morning. We'll set up somewhere near the meet spot, see if she shows. What are your plans today?"

"I don't know. Play some games on the box. You know. What-ever."

"Keep your cell near just in case something comes up, all right?"

"A'right."

I pay him for the day and give him a little extra because I had to lie.

FIFTY-FIVE

F atigue. Something to get used to. Again.

The alarm surprises me. I tap it off and sit up. Still tired. Good sipping rum will help that. All the sugars. I need all the help I can get. I'm meeting Leslie at Rebellion for drinks, maybe something to eat.

After I shower, I slip into my jeans and my favorite designer black V-neck. Trying to impress, I guess. What can I lose? She's already lost.

I walk to Rebellion. It's on 18th Street, near S, and a nice walk for a cold evening. Not so far that it'll be unbearable, but far enough to get the blood flowing, so that rum will warm up the body after.

I smile before I walk up the stairs to enter. There's no reason to smile, but I heard somewhere that smiling, even a fake smile, can shoot some mild adrenaline to the brain and, if you do it enough times, even reboot it. I know she's not there yet because she's always late, but I have to give it a try. And yeah, I sorta feel something. So I smile again.

Lucky for me, I spot a couple of stools at the end of the bar. It's only five thirty, and people are beginning to fill the room.

I take off my coat, put it over the end stool, and sit. I pull the other stool close to me so I can save it for Leslie. I get my boy's attention behind the bar. He finishes serving another customer and walks over.

We knock knuckles and he says, "Seeing more of you these days, Frank."

"Yeah, you're too close to my home, and that's dangerous."

Chuckles and says, "Bourbon or Zacapa?" 'Cause he knows me well. That's dangerous, too.

"Double Zacapa. One cube."

"Comin' up."

A young, college-aged girl walks up. She smiles. "This seat taken?"

"Yes. Sorry. She's on her way."

Slight smile this time, and she turns and walks to the other side of the bar. The person on the other side of the stool I'm saving is also a young college-type girl, but with another equally young man. If Leslie weren't about to show, that stool would be more than available, maybe this older guy in his midforties, too.

The bartender sets my drink down. "Anything to eat with that?"

"Maybe when Leslie gets here."

"Haven't seen her for a while. That's nice."

"Yeah." And I shoot him a fake smile, but don't feel anything.

Leslie shows up at about 6:40, which is early for her. I'm impressed. Also impressed with the outfit I see she's wearing after she takes off her overcoat—tight-fitting maroon corduroy pants and an unbuttoned, fleece-lined plaid flannel shirt over a white T-shirt.

Damn.

I pull out the stool for her.

"You look nice," I say.

A soft smile is the answer I get.

She sets her purse between the stools, at her feet, carefully folds the overcoat and places it on top of the purse.

I'm almost finished with my drink, so I signal my guy behind the bar. It takes him a few seconds, but he walks up.

"Hey there, Les," he says, and stretches his tattoo-ridden arm across the bar counter to offer his hand.

They shake.

"How're you doing? It has been a while," she says.

"Everything's good. As you can see, things are busy here."

"Happy to see that."

"What'll you have?"

"Moscow Mule."

"You guys want a menu?"

"I'm good for now," she says, and looks at me.

"I'm good, too. I'll have another one of these, though."

Leslie sets her cell phone on the counter.

"How's the trial going?"

"I convinced my client to take a plea."

"That's good, I guess."

"Never good when you waste the court's time with a trial you know you can't win."

"Sorry."

"No reason to be sorry. I've been there before."

Bartender returns with our drinks, serves hers in a copper cup, the way it should be served.

"Thanks," she says.

He taps the counter with his knuckles and goes to the next customer.

I finish what remains of my first Zacapa, slide it over.

"I'm afraid to ask what news it is you have," she says.

"I'm going to be honest. It's not good."

She sips her drink, looks up after like she doesn't want to hear it.

"Al's been having a sexual relationship with his CI," I say.

"Oh shit."

I notice the young woman sitting next to Leslie turn toward me.

"That's why he doesn't want IA to get to her," I say a bit more discreetly.

"What the hell was he thinking?"

"He wasn't."

"Have you met with her?"

"Yes." I sip some more.

"And?"

"And she confirmed they're having a thing, but said it was her who initiated it, not him. Not that that matters."

"It doesn't."

"If it means anything, she's not going to tell Johnny at IA, if they get to her. She doesn't want to jeopardize the extra income. Ching, ching, baby."

"How noble of her. Does Al know you know?"

"Of course he does. It's up to you whether you want to tell him you know."

"If it gets out, I'll deal with it. That's enough to get him fired or, at the least, kicked out of NSID to work behind the counter at Court Liaison for the rest of his career. And that's hoping he gets through the shooting."

"Well, the good news is I can't see how it has anything to do with the shooting. The CI said she only heard the shots, but by that time she was a couple of blocks away and didn't know where they came from."

"Dammit, Al."

"Yeah."

"Anything else you want to tell me?" Like she senses there's more because she can still read me well.

"No."

I don't want to go there until I know more.

"I'm just following through with the decedent's associates. Couple of thugs. It's like I'm trying to reach for nothing, but I still gotta try."

"I understand."

I know what I want to reach for now, but I trash the thought.

FIFTY-SIX

S econd drink in for Les. Fourth for me. Candied bacon on the side. One tasty-looking piece left.

"It's yours if you want it," I say.

"And I do."

She picks it up between two fingers, nibbles it at the edge, then takes a nice bite. Her eyes roll up, savoring it. Something she does with food. Don't think she realizes it. I can tell she's more than buzzed. Never could hold her liquor, more of a wine person. I'm also feeling a bit more than buzzed. They pour well for me here.

Two businessmen have now taken the place of the young couple that were sitting beside Leslie. They're nursing fine single malts and deep into some political conversation. The guy on the other side of the one sitting next to Leslie will occasionally peer over, looking at her, like he's trying to catch her eye, but only gets mine. I think the last glare scared him off, but we'll see. What makes him think I'm not with her? She might be my wife, for all he knows. Rude fucking bastard.

"Want to order something else to eat?" I say.

"No. The two orders of candied bacon did me in. Go ahead if you want to."

"Naw. I'm good."

This feels strained, not like it used to be with us, where we enjoyed each other's company. I feel like she's here only because she has to be, nothing having to do with me.

"I'm sorry about everything." I don't want to say it, but it comes out anyway.

She turns to me. "I'm sorry, too."

Didn't expect that.

"You didn't do anything."

"I know I didn't, but I can still feel sorry for all that has happened."

Damn, I want to hold her, smell her hair again. Perish the thought. I'll only embarrass myself. Again.

She finishes her drink.

"Want another?"

"No. I should be going."

"You sure?" Like I'm begging.

"I'm sure."

She reaches for her coat and her purse underneath. Takes out her wallet.

"I got this," I say.

"Okay. Thanks," I'm surprised to hear her say.

"I'll walk you to your car."

"I Ubered it."

She looks at her cell, taps the Uber icon.

"In fact, there's one two minutes away."

"All right, then."

She stands, puts on her coat. The rude bastard watches while she does.

"Keep me in the loop, Frankie."

Frankie?

"I will."

I stand, step to her and give her an awkward hug and a quick kiss on the cheek. She shoots me an uncomfortable smile, turns and walks out the door. I should walk her out, but she'd probably kick me back, so I return to my drink.

FIFTY-SEVEN

I'm about the only one left in here. Even the suits are gone. I think I've had one too many. I know I've had one too many. I don't want to be the last one out, so I pay my tab and leave.

Temperature has dropped a few more degrees. I put on my leather gloves and stagger toward home.

From 18th, I cut up Florida Ave. The Third District is on V, the next block down. By the time I cross 16th to W, I feel like I'm on autopilot. I walk on the Meridian Hill Park side. This cold air needs to do its job and start sobering me up, but not so much that I won't be able to sleep when I get home. Should've cabbed it. Fingertips are starting to tingle. These gloves aren't lined. More like driving gloves.

When I get close to the end of the park at 15th Street, I notice a couple of younger-looking kids taking the steps out of the park onto the corner. Looks like they're about to cross to the other side, possibly make their way south on 15th, but then they see me.

I get close enough so that I can make out their faces. Couple of fucking juvies. And they're not waiting at the corner for a cab or because traffic is so heavy they can't cross. I know the fucking look. I could cross the street, but that would only postpone the inevitable. They'd follow. I decide to stand my ground like I learned when I was a rookie cop, even as a kid growing up in DC. You don't give up your ground. I feel for my weapon's grip. It's secured in an in-the-pants holster and placed near where my wallet would be. I'll keep my hand there until I'm sure they don't have a gun or any other kind of weapon. They might just try to strongarm me, which I'm pretty sure would be a mistake on their part.

They break apart, like they're going to let me cross between them. I take my hand off the grip of my gun in case there's going to be a fight. Last thing I want is the gun falling out of the holster. It has a retention grip, so it's better that my hand is not gripping it unless I'm fighting for my life. I move to walk along the curb, but they move in the same direction. They're not crackheads. Look like a couple of corner mopes who want to make some extra cash for a new pair of shoes or some shit like that.

They don't have to ask. I know what time it is. I keep an eye on their hands as I try to pass between them.

The fatter of the two blocks my path, while the thinner moves behind me. I feel something sharp poke my left side, but I think/ hope it didn't penetrate my skin. I'm so drunk I might be impervious to pain and not realize.

"You know what this here is, right?" Railboy asks.

Damn, he can't be more than fifteen years old.

I'm worried he might try to search for my wallet himself, feel my gun instead, so I turn so my left side is toward him. Bigboy moves to my front. He looks a few years older. I see the knife Railboy is holding with his right hand. It looks like an old-style switchblade. It'd cause some damage.

"I can see now what it is," I say, but try not to sound too calm.

Bigboy moves to my right side, grabs my arm to escort me. I don't fight him off because the knife is too close to my rib area.

"Let me give you my wallet. No need for all this."

"Shut the fuck up," Railboy says.

We begin to walk up the short flight of stone steps at the edge of the park where the shrubs make better concealment. This ain't good, but again, the knife is too close for me to try to break away. One quick thrust and that could be it. Stupid position I got myself into.

"Okay, now, I have a wallet with some cash and credit cards."

"Get up them stairs," Bigboy orders.

At this point, that's probably the best thing I can do, get up there and get a bit of distance between us. Not ideal, but even a foot or so away from me is better than this. Fucking gotta be kidding me, letting myself get caught up in this.

They lead me up the steps and then toward the bushes.

I turn so Railboy's knife is at my stomach now, and Bigboy is to my left. I step back. Railboy thrusts the knife toward me, but not in an attempt to stab, just scare. I stop.

"Don't be a fool, big man. Jus' give us what you got, and it better be fucking good," Railboy says.

"No problem. I'll even give you the PIN numbers for the cards I have. Just don't hurt me."

"C'mon, now," Bigboy says. "Give it up."

I can still get stabbed at this distance if he gets an eyeball on my gun, unless he freezes for a second. That's not a chance I wanna take. I pull out my wallet and hold it up so they can see. Bigboy stretches his hand out to take it from me, but I throw it at Railboy's feet and at the same time back up a couple more steps and draw my gun. It takes them by surprise, Bigboy looking at the wallet on the ground and Railboy at the Glock pointed at his head. I'm about two feet from both of them, so I keep it at a tuck position so they won't try to slap it out of my hand.

"You know what this here is, right?" I say.

Bigboy finally realizes. He steps back.

"Make one fucking move and that'll be the end of both of you. Tryin' to run will just get you shot. Drop the fucking knife at your feet."

Railboy hesitates. I put my finger on the trigger so he can see.

"They say you can get me at nineteen feet, but that's if my weapon is holstered. I'll drop your ass before the first step, and then I'm gonna shoot Bigboy's kneecaps out. Drop the knife. Now."

He drops it, almost like it's involuntary.

I was right. It's an old switchblade, black handle, shiny long blade. The tip of the knife hits the stone walkway, next to his toe, takes a little bounce and falls to its side.

"Slowly kick the knife toward me."

"What you gonna do?"

"Cap your ass unless you do what I say. Gently kick it over."

He does. The knife stops just to the side of my right foot.

"Get on your knees," I demand.

"C'mon, now," Bigboy says.

"You keep saying that," I say while taking a couple more steps back.

I grip my gun with both hands now, more directly at Railboy's head.

"Do it."

They are reluctant, but they obey.

I notice my wallet on the ground between the two of them. It opened, but not so my badge can be seen, just the credit cards.

"Hands on your heads and clasp your fingers."

"You a cop, ain't ya?" Railboy says.

I don't answer.

I kneel, pick up the knife with my left hand, and walk around Railboy, to his right, so I don't go between them.

"What ya gonna do, sir?" Railboy says.

"Sir?"

"Yes, sir. We weren't gonna use that knife. Just scare you is all," Railboy says.

"Well, you managed to scare me, but just a bit."

I get behind Bigboy, still holding the knife in my left hand. I put the gun to his head, pat him down and search his pockets, find a baggie of weed and drop it on the ground to my side.

"C'mo—" He stops himself.

"Just let us go. You ain't gonna see us around here again," Railboy says with a quiver in his voice.

"Make a move and your boy here gets most of his head blown. Brains look like little marbles on the ground when that happens."

I stand and grab Railboy by the fingers of his clasped hands and squeeze hard.

"Ahh—" he belts.

I make him scoot closer to Bigboy, where I pat him down and search his pockets, too. Another baggie of weed and then a zip.

I pull it out. Looks like about a gram of powder.

"What the fuck you two doing with blow? Lacing this shit with your weed?"

They don't answer.

"Where'd you get this shit?"

Still no answer.

"Fucking not playing."

"Adams Morgan," Bigboy says.

"Shut up, fool."

"No, don't be a fool. Go on," I tell him.

"Off some dude with his girl at one of them clubs."

"I'm assuming he didn't sell it to you."

I don't expect them to answer. I know they robbed him. I put it in my pocket and then think to myself, *Why the fuck I do that?*

I stand up, looking down at them.

236

Fourteen hundred block of Fairmont is just a few blocks from here, Clifton closer.

I scan the area. It's like a ghost town it's so fucking late.

"I'm thinking as long as I got myself a captive audience, I'm gonna ask you a couple of questions. I'm not going to ask your fat friend here 'cause I think all he knows what to say is *c'mon now.*"

"You a cop, then? Just arrest us. You can ask us then," Railboy says.

Been through the system a few times.

"How old are you? Fifteen?"

"Sixteen."

"No, I'm not going to arrest you. You're going to answer a couple of questions, though, and if you answer them right, I'm gonna let you two walk right outta here."

They both look at each other.

"Think hard. Here's the first question."

FIFTY-EIGHT

I would have been justified in shooting Railboy because he was close enough with the knife to be a threat. Only seconds, and everything your mind processes is massive. First thing that came up for me is, *Fuck no, not another shooting.* Like someone outside of me telling me. All the attention it would bring, shooting a sixteen-year-old kid, justified or not, is not something I need—not something this city needs right now. That little pack of protesters in front of 300 will grow into a much larger pack. Some will even be bused in—black bloc and fucking Antifa-ucks, 'cause most of them are paid to cause trouble. They wouldn't give a shit about some kid losing his life. Fuck no. They want to destroy property and fight the police. They get trained for that shit.

"I swear, we ain't hear nothin' about no cops getting shot."

No, I did the right thing, or more accurately, they did the right thing by obeying my commands. Could have gone bad otherwise.

"You speaking for your friend here, too?" I say.

"Naw. He can speak for himself."

"So, then *you* tell me. You know anything about those two cops that got shot on Twelfth?"

"No. I ain't hear nothin'," Bigboy says quietly.

"Hear nothin', say nothin', huh?"

They don't know how to answer that.

"I'm not going to ask again," I say.

And how do they respond to that?

They don't.

"I'm waiting."

They look at each other. Railboy looks antsy, like he might take his chances and run. I've seen the look enough times, and the way the feet start to move apart, toes to the ground. I'm close enough to stop him, but then chance having Bigboy try to take off, too. So what do I do?

I poke Bigboy with the knife in the upper-right thigh, hard enough that it cuts through his jeans and penetrates the layers of skin to the fatty tissue.

He yelps, a little too loud.

I pull the knife out fast.

"Shut the fuck up, you big baby. Won't even need stitches. The next one will cut to the bone. So answer me."

Bigboy turns to his running buddy, looking for some help, like he's too stupid to know himself. Tears breaking through. I sort of feel bad 'cause maybe he's slow in the head.

"Okay," I say like a warning.

"Wait! Wait!" Bigboy says.

"We ain't a part of nothin' like that," Railboy says. "All we heard is it's some boys from fourteen hundred."

"Fourteen hundred what?" As if I don't already know.

"Fairmont, man. Fairmont." Bigboy whimpers.

I wipe the blood off the tip of the knife onto Bigboy's jeans. He jumps a little, thinking he's getting stabbed again.

"You got names?"

"No. I swear. We don't know who. We ain't a part of them up there."

"How did you hear about them being involved?" I say.

"Just on the street, man. That's all. Just talk."

"What area you boys from?"

"Garfield," Railboy says.

They're my neighbors. Better not run into these two again. Probably won't remember my face anyway. Too scared.

Switchblades like this are hard to find, so I fold it up and stand, then slip it in my front pants pocket.

I'm not going to push this any further. Even at this hour it'll attract attention, if it hasn't already. I take out my phone, move to the front of Bigboy and snap a couple photos of him. He shakes off the flash. I do the same with Railboy.

"What you gonna do?" Railboy says.

"I'm gonna go home."

I pocket the cell but keep the gun on them.

"Now, you two mopes, get up, hit Fifteenth Street, and walk south until I can't see you anymore."

Before Railboy gets up, he asks, "Which way is south?"

I point toward the direction they should go and move back to give them room.

They get up, Bigboy having a harder time, but he manages anyway. He limps behind Railboy, down the steps, to 15th. They cross the street, look back toward me.

"Go on, now," I say.

They head south.

I stay there until I can't see them. Then I go to the corner and look down 15th. I see them nearing U Street. That's good enough for me. I notice Bigboy turn to look back. I know he can see me, so I wave.

Damn kid lifts his hand up to his chest like he's going to wave back but changes his mind and drops it to his side. They walk left on U, out of sight.

FIFTY-NINE

W hen I get to my stoop, I pull the zip of powder outta my pocket.

Fuck.

I sit on the top step, my back to the front door.

Recreational purposes?

I could do the whole thing with two easy snorts. That'd be that. Easy peasy. Or just go inside, make it last for as long as I can, like when I first started. That was years ago, when I could make a half gram last me most of the night.

Shit. This is too easy. I want it bad, now more than ever.

I quickly stand, walk to the sidewalk, and step onto the street.

I drop the zip at my feet and, without hesitation, scrunch it into the pavement, breaking open the zip, letting that fine powdery white substance turn to nothing but dirt.

I go into the house.

I slip out of my clothes, keeping my boxer briefs and undershirt on—and socks. I toss my clothes in the washer and open my stash wall, place the switchblade on a shelf under the money, where I used to keep a nice collection of confiscated—or rather, stolen—

weapons. I like this switchblade. It'll be safe here. I go into the kitchen to wash my hands.

I wash them twice.

I'm too wired for sleep. With all that happened, the adrenaline is staying with me. I pour myself a nice glass of Jameson and sit on the sofa to see if any cable news is on. It's too early. Most of what's on is paid programming. I turn it off, take a Klonopin and down it with a bit of whiskey.

I wake up in a sitting position. Drool is on the sofa cushion where my head was resting and on the left side of my face. I wipe it away with the back of my hand.

"Fuck me," I mumble.

It's almost 7:00 a.m. Too damn early. Don't even waste the time for coffee. It'll be of little use. I grab the remote, power on the TV to watch Fox 5 News and recline on the sofa, resting my head on a small square pillow.

Possibility of snow, a light coating.

Top of the hour, the news begins again. Top local stories are the growing number of protesters in front of 300, demanding justice for the "child-killing cop"; the city's out-of-control crime rate, specifically homicides and robberies; and the funeral arrangements for the officer who was killed on my block. They cut that in with Officer Wiebe's funeral procession, blocks of cop cars crossing 14th Street Bridge, every jurisdiction from New York to Virginia. That always gets me, sometimes even a tear.

I hope the robbery stats will drop slightly in my neighborhood because of last night's encounter, but I doubt it. I don't think it's possible to scare any of these young thugs straight. They'll just be more careful who they target next time.

I turn the television off. Like I've said, it's nothing but an anxiety channel. Gonna have to be careful what I fill my brain with.

So smile.

After a couple hours of doing nothing but lying on my back, I call Detective Rattan.

"Rattan," a groggy voice answers.

"Sorry. Did I wake you?"

"It's okay. Have to get up anyway."

"You working midnights?"

"Evenings, but caught a double and worked it through the night."

"I can call you later."

"No. No. What's up?"

"I met with another source of information last night, not connected with the one who looked at the photos. The source confirmed what the first one said, that a crew from the fourteen hundred block of Fairmont is responsible for the shooting on my block."

"Did the source give names?"

"No, but like the first one said, Rule is known to hang at 1400 Fairmont."

"That's good. Thanks. It's looking good on our end, too."

"You got Rule and his crew identified?"

"Just him. And that is his real last name. He's a piece of work."

"You have enough for an arrest?"

"I've been working on it, and I think so. It'd be great if I could talk to your sources."

"One is a possible. The other one, doubtful."

"Try for me."

"I will." Obviously won't. "How's the other officer?"

"Stable condition."

"Good. I'll let you go. Get some rest."

"Yeah, right. Thanks again."

"Anytime."

I know I'll start getting pressured to reveal my sources. I wasn't totally lying. Calvin might come through, but he still needs time, especially with that whole snitch mentality instead of a reasonably good work ethic.

One of my three burner cells is ringing in the backpack. I unzip the pocket where I keep them and pick up the one that's ringing. It's the cell I let Calvin use to call Tamie. I don't answer, but look at the screen.

"Yeah," I say to myself. "Fucking Tamie Darling."

I let it go to voice mail, but she doesn't leave a message.

SIXTY

C alvin is reclining in the front seat and we're heading to the circle park at 16th. I still have to play Calvin on this one, but it
won't matter soon, because it looks like Tamie is playing both sides.
Why else would she call who she thought was Idris, someone she believes I'm working?

"Almost forgot," I say.

I pull to the curb before crossing 13th, put the car in park, and
reach into my pack for the burner Calvin used. I hand it to him.

"Pocket this just in case she calls back or something."

"Why she gonna do that if we're already set up to meet?"

"One thing you'll learn is it doesn't always go as planned."

"Oh, I learned that already. I learned that a long time ago."

I look at him, think about asking why. But we're on a mission. I
pull the car out and drive on.

Not even two blocks out and his burner rings.

"Hold on," I say.

By the time it's on the third ring, I'm parked along a curb again,
but illegally this time.

"Let me see the number."

He does, and it's her.

"Put it on speaker and answer."

"You sure? People know when it's on speaker. Most in this business don't like that shit."

"Put it on speaker, and if she asks, tell her you're driving and it's on Bluetooth. Answer."

He taps the screen for speaker. "Yeah," he says.

"Hey, Idris. You supposed to be meeting me today for a blizzard," she says.

"Yeah, but that ain't till later. What you callin' now for?"

Damn, he's a natural.

"Are you on speaker?"

He looks at me like, *I told you.*

"Yeah, baby. Bluetooth. I'm drivin'."

"You alone?"

"Yeah. What the hell goin' on here? You callin' me like this?"

"We need to change the meet location."

"The fuck for? I called the spot."

"Yeah, baby, and I have information it got burned."

"Burned? You playin' me?"

"No, no. I got ways of knowing things."

I write in my notebook what I want him to say and show it to him.

"How do I know you ain't the police or a snitch?"

"We meet and you'll know."

I write in the notebook for him to play along and then give her a new spot, public—parking lot of McDonald's at 7th, by Howard.

"How I know that?"

"All kinds of ways, baby. You can call the spot, but not at the circle."

"All kinds of ways?"

He looks at me, smiles, and raises his eyebrows 'cause he knows what that means. Shit. Fucking Darling.

"Okay, in an hour. Meet me at the McDonald's parking lot on 7th, the one at Howard U. What you gonna be wearin', again?"

"White parka and tight black jeans. I'll be carrying a pink purse."

"Tight jeans, huh? All right, then."

"See you there, baby."

He disconnects.

"Damn, she got a sexy voice."

Fucking black widow spider is what she is.

"Damn good job, Calvin. You're a natural."

"You burned, man. You know that, right? She smart."

"No, not burned. I didn't really want it to get played this way, but I had my suspicions."

"How you mean?"

"She's playing both sides, and now we gotta learn the extent of the damage she's caused."

"I don't understand."

"You will, rookie."

"Shiet."

The question is, do I take Calvin with me when I snatch up Darling?

"I'm going to have to go do this one on my own," I tell him.

"You not taking me?"

"It's too risky, and I don't know if it's a setup for a robbery, thinking you have all that crack," I lie.

"Fuck that shit, man. I know how to handle myself."

"It's best I keep you out of this one, Calvin."

"What be my purpose here, then? I ain't learnin' shit, except what I already know. Seems like you just using me like you would one them *sources* you say you work with."

"It's not like that. I don't want to put you in a position where the cops might get involved. I still don't know if they have a warrant on you for that shit at Euclid."

"You said they'd have to get my prints to put me with a warrant, if there is one."

"Yeah, unless one of your old running mates worked out a plea deal and gave everyone up."

"You never mentioned anything like that. You sayin' the police might have my real name associated with that shooting?"

"I thought we talked about all this."

"No. You didn't share all that."

"Listen, I'm going to do this one on my own. You sit tight at home, still on the clock, and when I'm done, I'll make a couple of calls and see what the police have on your old Playboy days. All right?"

"Seems to me you shoulda already done that. I been runnin' with you all this time, gettin' with that female detective and shit, and they might know me by name? I been takin' some big chances here."

"I don't think they do know you by name. Shouldn't have even said anything. I'll make that call and let you know. I'm confident they just got you by nickname and physical description."

"And you'll put it on speakerphone so I can hear?"

"I said I'll make the call later. No worries."

"Right. No worries. And I gotta trust you with that?"

"Yeah, you do."

Sixty-One

I messed up with Calvin. Didn't mean to go there. I want to keep him away from Darling, though. For now. I'm getting closer to trusting him, but only with certain things.

I get to the parking lot at McDonald's half an hour early and set up at a spot where I can see the side and the rear area. It's busy, mostly college students.

I notice a black SUV pull in from Georgia Avenue and park on the side facing Barry Place. I'm backed into a space about five cars west of them, so I can't make out the occupants. I will notice if anyone steps out, and yes, I'm skeptical of most dark-colored SUVs now, because of what happened. I notice thick smoke wafting up and taken by the slight breeze toward me. Too thick to be a cigarette, and I doubt it's a cigar.

I roll down the window and light up a smoke. Supposed to get flurries today, but the clouds overhead don't look like they're holding snow. Darker clouds east of here. The slight breeze blowing west might bring some my way.

Thirty-five minutes and a couple cigarettes later, I notice Darling step out from the passenger side of the black SUV. *There you go.* I'm not being paranoid, after all. Like she told Calvin, she's wearing the white puffy jacket/parka and tight, nicely fitting jeans, and she's carrying a pink purse you could see from a mile away. This is not the Darling I once knew. I wonder who might be at the driver's side of that vehicle. Is she planning to rob Idris, and her muscle is waiting in the car?

She walks to the side entrance area of McDonald's, turns to scan the parking lot. I tuck down. She pulls a pack of smokes out of her jacket pocket, taps one out and lights it with a pink Bic lighter. She smiles at a couple of knuckleheads wearing lowrider jeans and nothing but T-shirts as they walk in the side entrance to McDonald's. They both tip their heads toward her and smile back, look at her backside through the window once they're inside.

Now I know. But I still don't know enough. Like who the fuck is waiting in the car while she's standing there waiting for the fictional Idris?

It doesn't take me long to figure out what needs to be done. Now might be my only chance. I roll up the window, turn off the car, and cautiously step out, walk to the sidewalk on the Barry side, toward Georgia. I keep my body low, my head turned away from her view, which isn't that close, but still she could recognize me. I hold my overcoat at the collar with my right hand, clutching it closed, like I'm cold and that's why I'm tucking my head down.

I pass the SUV, hesitate to peer in because they might know me. I quickly walk by, turn right on Georgia, and then go to the front entrance of the McDonald's.

I look out the side window. Darling is still standing there, patiently waiting. Fucking dirty snake. Never thought about smacking a girl—well, maybe once—but now I want to for sure. There's a small line at the order counter. I stand behind a cute college girl shouldering a book bag. I keep my eye on Darling, and when my turn comes around, I order a coffee.

"Anything else with that?"

"Just coffee, thanks."

I exit using the side door. When I step out, Tamie turns to me. I try to look as surprised as she does.

"Tamie?"

"Frankie."

"What are you doing standing out here in the cold?"

Doesn't even take her a second. "Waiting on a blind date, sweetie."

"A blind date at McDonald's? You can do better than that."

"C'mon, now, Frankie. It's just a meeting place."

"Blind date? It ain't Luna, right?" I play her.

"You know better than to ask that."

"I must say, Tamie, you really got yourself together. Real good."

"Why, thank you, sweetie."

"So, I'm spoiling your action by standing here talking to you?" I say, and have a sip of coffee.

"Yeah, I'd say you are."

"Sorry. Wouldn't want to do that, but I'm afraid I'll have to."

Looks at me, tilting her head sideways.

"Idris is gonna be a no-show, *sweetheart*."

She steps back, looks toward the SUV.

"You fucking asshole," she says, not sounding so sweet anymore.

A big guy steps out of the driver's seat. He looks to be about my age. He shuts the door behind him and looks our way, like he's waiting for orders.

"*That* your blind date?"

"What did you do, Frankie?"

"I did my job, Darling. What the fuck did you do?"

The big man starts walking toward us. Tamie stretches her arm out, hand open in a stopping motion.

He obeys, stops in the middle of the parking lot.

251

"You and I need to take a drive, Darling."

"I don't think I can do that today, Frankie."

"Don't let this go sideways, Tamie. It's only gonna be you that'll suffer."

"It ain't what you think."

She playing me for a fool?

All I can do is smile.

"We're going to take a walk to my car, have a talk. Tell your boy to stand down and have some more of whatever it is he's been smoking, but back in the car he came out of."

"I can't do that, Frankie."

She walks away from me, toward her body man.

I follow closely behind, stop her by the arms when she's a couple feet away from him. He steps up to me. Without hesitation, I sidekick him hard on the right knee. When he buckles, I hit him with the side of my right hand on his jaw near his ear. He falls hard.

"What the fuck did you do, Frankie?"

"Let's go."

"You okay there, sweet pea?" one of the knuckleheads with lowriding jeans says. He's holding a milkshake with a straw. Knucklehead two is by his side.

Sweet pea?

"Ain't nothin' but a lover's spat, doll. Thank you."

I keep my eyes on them. They look at me hard but continue on their way.

"I can't just leave him there," she says.

He moves, trying to roll to his back. Moans.

"Cops are gonna be here any second. They'll take care of him."

"He has a gun. Don't let him go to jail."

I lean down again, grab the Sig Sauer he has wedged in the front area of his pants. I look around. There's a few onlookers, so I try to be discreet. Fucking surveillance cameras, too. My car is far enough away that, with any luck, all they'll get is a description and not the tag.

She notices what I'm looking at and says, "He ain't going to make a police report about this, so you don't have to worry yourself."

"Let's go," I tell her.

She struggles, but only a little. She thinks she knows me well enough that I won't hurt her. I don't know, though.

I open the front passenger door for her.

"Hold on," I tell her before she gets in the car.

I squeeze the pocket areas of her parka and around her waist.

"I ain't stupid, Frankie. You never had to check me like that before."

"It ain't the same as before. Get in."

She steps in with some attitude. I close the door for her.

I walk to the driver's side. People are gathered in the lot, looking at me like I'm her pimp or some shit. I start the car, drop the gun inside the backpack behind my seat. When I pull the car out, I notice the muscle trying to push himself up from the cold pavement.

Sixty-Two

P ut your seat belt on," I say.
   She does.

I take a quick left on the narrow road, more like an alley, behind McDonald's. It stretches from Barry Place to V Street, where the 9:30 Club is. I hear a siren close by as I near V. I make another quick right and then a left, heading back toward Barry, the way we came, and barely make the green light to pass Barry.

"Where are we going?" she asks.

"What used to be our favorite spot."

"Why'd you have to hit him like that?"

"He stepped up to me."

"He wouldn't of done anything unless I told him to."

"I wasn't about to take that chance. You're not the same person I once knew."

"And that's a bad thing?"

"You know what I mean."

I turn into the construction lot where Al shot Arthur Taylor, park between the two detached semitrailers. I keep the engine running, roll down my window and light a smoke.

254

"Why are you bringing me here?"

"Isn't this where it all began?" I look at her, throw her a slight, knowing smile. "What the hell did you do, Tamie?" But before she can answer—"Why did you set Al up?"

"I didn't. Why would I mess up a good thing?"

"You mean a good source of information?"

She doesn't answer.

"You been playing both sides. For how long?"

She taps a cigarette out of her pack, lights it.

"Window," I say.

She rolls it down halfway.

"All this time I believed you got yourself healthy because you got smart."

"I did. I got smart."

"Yeah, you were smart, playing us. Using the information we gave you as a trusted CI for your own personal gain."

"That ain't true."

"Then how the fuck did you get a number for Idris unless you memorized it? What, you were going to rob him of his stash? You got your own drug-dealing network now?"

She doesn't answer.

"How many other targets of mine did you get to? How does it even work? You get that piece of muscle and a few other crew boys and start taking over shit based on the information you get from us? Damn, you think you're Elektra or something?"

I keep Ty and Marlon to myself for now. Don't want to give up everything I know. Then she really won't have anything to talk about.

"You know if Idris was real, what kind of danger you could have put me in?"

"I never would have let that happen."

"Oh, you have that kind of power now? Fucking tell me something, Tamie."

She looks at me. I've known her for a lot of years. Granted, we used the hell out of her, didn't give a shit that she was smoking up all that crack because it was good motivation for her. But still…

"I got a bigger taste for money than crack. Sure as hell wasn't making enough working for you all. In fact, you and Al are mostly responsible for making me who I am today. In fact, I should be grateful."

"Don't pull that shit on me. You cleaned up nice. You could have got yourself a real job."

"What? Retail? McDonald's? Make myself less than minimum wage? Fuck you, Frankie Marr."

"You broke the cardinal rule as a paid CI. In fact, you could find yourself in jail, not for what you did to me as a PI, but what you did to Al, 'cause he's law enforcement. You remember what you signed?"

"I never did anything that could come back to Al, or even you. You know if Idris was real, he'd know nothin' about you until you made yourself known."

"But you don't know that I didn't make myself known. That'd make me a possible target."

"I knew. It was all in the way you presented it to me when you wanted me to call your snitch boyfriend."

I almost slap her. She flinches. I back off, close my eyes for a second. I don't do that kinda shit.

"You want to beat me down, Frankie? You think I'm your property?"

"No, I…don't fucking turn this shit around. You know, it doesn't matter, Tamie. You fucked up bad. And don't try to lie your way out of this one. I know you know Arthur Taylor. Why you think I'd waste my time trying to set you up if I didn't already know that? I just wouldn't work with you again. But this is Al we're talking about. Why would Arthur Taylor be at this lot at the same time as you and Al were meeting if you had nothing to do with it?"

"You ain't going to believe me if I tell you."

"Tell me."

"I didn't know. That's the truth. But I sure been trying to find out, 'cause it makes no sense."

"And I'm supposed to believe you?"

"Yeah."

I know she knows Ty and Marlon, and now Arthur. First spotted her at the old brothel at 17th and Euclid, so I know she also somehow worked her way in with Cordell's crew. Can't even guess how the fuck she accomplished that. Unless Cordell is a part of it. I realize now it was a good idea I didn't let Calvin come with me.

She flicks her smoke out the window. That's when I notice it's starting to snow. A light flurry.

She rolls the window up.

"You honestly gonna tell me you didn't know one of your boys was there?"

"That's exactly what I'm telling you. And he wasn't *one of my boys.* He wanted to be, though."

"But he hung out with your boys."

"That he did."

"How do I know you weren't setting Al up to get killed and when it went wrong you were already there, hiding behind one of these construction trucks? Maybe it was you who took the gun from the scene."

"No!"

That was anger.

"Al used me and I used him. Fair trade, far as I'm concerned. Besides, I like him. He's funny. And like I said, I was careful not to use any kinda information I got that would get back to him or maybe get him hurt. Same with you."

She's full of shit.

"How can we fix this, Frankie?"

"I don't have to fix anything."

"You want some of what Al's getting? Maybe more?"

"Fuck you."

She's too tough to be offended.

"Al's got a subpoena to give up your information so that an Internal Affairs detective can interview you."

"Hell no."

"Yeah, that's exactly what Al said. Protecting your ass. But he doesn't know what I know now. And he won't, and IA won't either, if you do what I say."

"Tell me, then."

"Simple—you let the detective interview you about why you and Al were here, because he was talking to you about a crack house he wanted to work you in. Nothing about your sexual exploits with him. I hear you mention that, game over for you, not only with the police, but with your little crew. You just tell the detective what you told me when we first talked, that after you left and were a few blocks away, you heard the gunshots. That's all you gotta do. For Al, anyway. Me, that's gonna be a different matter."

"Oh, I got to work this shit off with you now?"

"Darling, do I have to say it again—how bad you fucked up?"

"You just said it again."

"You don't mention anything about knowing Arthur Taylor to the police. That'll get both you and Al fucked. You are going to find out why he was here, though, and who was here with him, 'cause I believe my friend. I believe the kid had a gun; otherwise he'd be alive right now. Someone in your crew knows. You do that for me and we're clear. But it can't be some made-up shit. I'll know if it is."

"I still say it'd be more fun if we work it out the other way."

"You need to take this seriously, Tamie. We've known each other for a long time, so I'm sure you know how bad I can fuck up your life."

"Yes, I know, Frankie."

"And as far as the boys you work with now, you can't trust any of them."

"I can trust the man you beat down."

"You can't trust anyone, and I didn't beat him down, 'cause he'd never get up if I did."

"Can I get his gun back?"

I reach behind my seat, grab the pellet pistol I got off the crack-head who tried to rob me and Calvin. Don't think she'll know the difference.

I hand it over to her. She takes it and slips it in a nylon pocket of her jacket.

She hasn't learned anything.

SIXTY-THREE

More than flurries coming down now. Far from a snowstorm, but it should leave an inch or two if the ground's cold enough.

Tamie is sitting comfortably in the front passenger seat, just like we're getting ready to do an okeydoke. No sign of worry at all. Is she that good?

"So, tell me, how did you work your way in? Was it through Cordell, while he was still in prison, or one of his lieutenants who took over?"

"Cordell?" she asks, trying to look convincing and like she doesn't know who I'm talking about.

"Cordell Holm. You remember him, right? When I was looking for that missing teenage girl?"

"Oh, yes. But what makes you think I'm doing something with him?"

"I know about you at the house on Seventeenth and Euclid. Tamie, no more shit. I know more than you think, so be careful, now."

I won't give up Queen Street. For all I know, that's her new house. A safe house or a stash house. I want her to feel comfortable with still going there.

"How long you known Cordell?"

"A little over two years," she says too easily.

"You got to him through me, then?"

Taps out another cigarette, rolls down the window, then lights it up.

"You know that whole thing became Al's case after me, right?" I say.

"Cordell was already charged and in jail, just waiting to be sentenced. I'd be visiting Al at his house and listen to him talking on the phone about the case. A prosecutor, I think."

"All the players, locations, shit like that?"

"Yes. Then it was just a matter of working myself in, getting an introduction."

"And how did you manage that?"

"Frankie, this is not me being your *special employee* no more. So what you need to know all this other shit for? You ain't been the police for a long time."

"Because you owe me the information. Simple as that. I could give a shit that you're some sort of queen bee running things out there. Keep doing what you do. I don't care. I need to know how fucked this is and how to fix it if I have to." Her lips tighten. She's frustrated now. "Was it that dude I had you call—what's his name? Playboy? Remember him?"

"Yes, I remember him, and no, never even met him after. Never tried to call him, either."

"Like you did Idris?"

"Right."

"Then you got to Cordell before he got sent into the federal system? When he was still in DC jail?"

"That man you knocked down. He was running some shit for Cordell. Trying to, at least. Big heart, big man, but...not sharp, you know? I got to know him. He helped me clean up. In fact, you should let me call him so he doesn't put out a search party."

"You can call in a bit. It's good to let a man worry. Go on with the story."

"Just because the police raided the house on University Place and locked up Cordell and a lot of his crew doesn't mean business stopped. It just quieted down for a while. Cordell needed a new face to get dope inside so he could make a bit of money until things on the outside started rolling again. When I cleaned myself up, my man introduced me to Cordell. It all began there."

"And now you're being trusted with more, huh?"

"Damn you, Frankie. We shouldn't be here like this."

"Yeah, and that kid shouldn't have gotten killed and you shouldn't have tried to play both sides, either."

"Your Idris boy mentioned Tay—"

"Taylor?"

"Yes. You also played me well, 'cause he made it sound like a couple of the boys were running their own thing, outside of me and Cordell. I had to find out."

"You and Cordell. Shiet."

"I found something I'm real good at, Frankie, other than smokin' up my life and getting paid nothin' so that you and the police got everything and all I got was enough money to buy a day's worth of rock."

I don't respond to that. Instead I ask, "Was there anyone else before Cordell that you got to through working with me or Al, or both of us when I was on the job partnered with Al?"

"No. Only Cordell."

"Don't forget Idris."

"You set me up for that."

"Does that matter? Shit, Darling."

"You need to let me go or make a call, 'cause shit's gonna start rollin' the wrong way."

"One more question. You know anything about the police that got shot on Twelfth or any other officer that got killed?"

"Of course not. You know I wouldn't be a part of something like that. I only know what I get on the news."

Should I mention Rule? Show her the photo?

"I don't know what you're capable of anymore," I say. "And you know, Al got his window blown out in a drive-by."

"Damn. He okay? You don't think that has anything to do with me?"

"I hope not. And yeah, he's okay. You don't call him, though, and if he tries to call you, don't pick up. I mean that. Also, I saw what looked like the SUV you're driving parked on Al's block. Before the shooting. It followed me when I left. Saw someone who looked a lot like you in front." That part's not true.

"That's bullshit."

"No, it's not."

"Well, you didn't see me. It wasn't my car. Might want to talk to your police buddies. I don't have the only black SUV in this city."

"Just go," I say. "Call your man while walkin'."

She opens the door, turns to me before getting out. "I'd never hurt Al, and—as much as I hate you right now—you, either."

"I call. You answer," I tell her.

"Like always, sweetie."

"When the time comes, I'll personally take you to meet with the detective from Internal Affairs. You play the CI bit, and it'll all be good."

She steps out.

"And you fucking be sure to find out why Tay was here that day," I add.

She smiles at me, flicks her cigarette like spit to the ground, and walks away.

SIXTY-FOUR

I don't trust her and certainly don't believe her. And damn, I hate being played. Played is a kind word for what she did. You can never trust a CI. I rarely have, but Tamie did win me over, and now that trust has been violated. Depending on how far she went with Al, or me when I was on the job, maybe it was even something criminal.

Before leaving to pick up Calvin, I call Millhoff on my cell, like I told Calvin I would.

"What's up, Frankie?" he answers.

"Not a whole lot." *Shiet, right.* "Quick question if you have a minute."

"Go on."

"About the Cordell Holm case."

"Yeah."

"Remember that dude, Playboy, I told you about?"

"Yeah, the guy you said was the driver."

"You ever get him?"

"No. Why are you asking after all this time?"

"Because I saw someone who looks a little like him earlier and was wondering if you got him or identified him for a warrant yet."

"Where'd you see him?"

"Don't know for sure if it was him, but it was in PG County, walking out of the Burger King on Bladensburg and Fortieth."

"Why didn't you call?"

"Like I said, I wasn't sure, and by the time I turned my car around so I could get a closer look, he was gone. Must have rolled out in a car. Didn't see it."

"Well, we don't have anything on him. Just what you gave us, and the nickname. Prints were negative. Give me a description."

"Wearing a Ravens jacket and black jeans. Really hasn't changed much."

"All right. You see him in your travels again, give a call. Nothing else, just call. How's it going with Luna?"

"He's a mess. Stands by his story, and I believe him."

"In our prayers, man. Don't want to see him go down like that. Be an awful shame."

"It would be, brother. Everything good with you?"

"Same ol', same ol'."

"Appreciate you filling me in. You stay safe."

That was a good story I came up with. I don't believe Playboy has anything to worry about.

I call Calvin to let him know I'll be there in about an hour. He doesn't sound enthusiastic, but he never does so I don't take it personally. I need to get with Luna first, tell him not to fight with Freudiger about meeting Darling. I know he'll fight me, too. The fear of their relationship being revealed, on top of everything else, is more than enough motivation to fight it.

When I get to his house, I see the window is boarded up and the siding around the boarded-up window has been replaced. No more holes that I can see.

I knock on the door, smile to myself, but don't feel anything this time. I'll keep trying. It takes Al a couple minutes to get to the door. He's wearing his old gray MPDC sweatpants and a faded blue T-shirt. Still clean-shaven. That's promising. I smile again. Damn. This positive brain-feed crap doesn't work for shit.

"Hey, Frankie."

"Al. I met with Tamie again and thought it best to talk in person."

"Oh yeah?" he says with reservation.

"No worries. You gonna let me in?"

"Sorry."

He steps aside to allow me in, closes the door after I enter, and locks the doorknob and the dead bolt, checks it after.

I walk into the living room. Wall and ceiling areas where rounds were removed by Crime Scene are patched but not painted. The curtain is closed, hiding the boarded-up window.

"When's the window coming in?"

"I hope in a couple days. It's gonna be a nice window. Want a drink?"

"Good stuff?"

"Laphroaig 18."

"Dude, you should take it easy on the expensive shit. Remember, you're on leave without pay."

"I broke into my scotch reserve."

"I'll just have some Jameson."

"Fuck you," he says, and grabs a clean glass that happened to be on the coffee table, like it was waiting for me, or someone else. He pours a nice double, hands it to me.

I take it and sit in the armchair. He sits on the sofa, picks up his glass and sips.

"What do you have, then?"

I'm not going to give it to him like that. I don't think he can take it. For all I know, he's suicidal right now, and what I learned about Tamie might throw him over the edge.

"First off, you have to stay away from her. I don't give a shit how real you think the relationship might be."

"Another fuck you."

"I'm not kidding, Al. Let's get you through all this crap first. Get your life back, and then you can make all the stupid relationship decisions you want. For now please listen to me and stay away, not even a phone call. I told her the same thing, and she won't accept your calls."

He takes a deep breath, long exhale, as if to calm himself. Takes another sip but says nothing.

"And I want you to know in advance that I'm going to take her to see Freudiger."

"What? No, you're not."

"Al, you get served that subpoena and don't comply, you're fucked. Hear me?" I don't let him respond. "She knows how to play the part, the special employee, confidential informant, and all that shit. She knows what will happen to her—and you—if she gives up anything else. I don't know why, but I believe she does like you."

"Well, here's to that." He lifts his glass, finishes what's left in one gulp, and then an "Ahh..."

I take my glass and do the same, but only because I need another drink.

"You with me on this, bro?"

"I'm with ya."

"Okay. Just a quick visit because I gotta go," I say while standing. "You need me to get you anything?"

"No, thanks."

"You'll get through this. Don't let the department beat you down, 'cause that's what they're going to do and they're not going to ease up."

"I know that."

"Lock up behind me."

I open the door, but before I can leave, he says, "I do sincerely appreciate everything, Frank."

I smile. Tingles in my brain. All righty, then.

SIXTY-FIVE

Y eah. A little over an inch on the ground. People driving like it's twelve inches. I grew up in this city, been through all the major blizzards, couple of the worst when I was on the department and a state of emergency was declared. We'd roll around answering dispatched calls in Humvees driven by DC National Guard, living on MREs. I miss those times, as stupid crazy as they were. But an inch on the ground, and the city goes crazy.

I don't have Freudiger saved as a contact, so I can't use Bluetooth to call him. I find an open space and park.

"This is Freudiger," he answers.

"Frank Marr here, Johnny."

"What can I do for you, Marr?"

"More like what I can do for you. I spoke with Luna's SE, and she can meet with you this week. I'll have to pick her up, though."

"That's great. I'm jammed this week. Can you bring her to the office Monday morning, say around eleven hundred?"

"I'm sure that'll work for her. If you don't hear back from me then it's good."

"All right. Appreciate the call."

"Talk later."

It was a priority, but now it's like he wants to drag it out, wear Luna down in the process.

Tamie is my next call. Surprisingly, she answers right away.

"Give me a second," she says. "I'll be right back, babe. I gotta take this call," she says to someone else, and sounds like she's walking. "Okay, I can talk now."

"I need to pick you up at ten thirty Monday morning to go meet with the detective I told you about."

"I don't know, Frank. I don't know if that works for me right now. You almost broke my man's jaw. You're lucky he got himself up and left before the police came."

"Well, I'm sure you gave him a good story."

"Yes, I did."

I don't ask because I don't want to know. Might make me mad.

"You have to meet with the detective on Monday at eleven a.m."

"Maybe later. I don't know if Monday works."

"Make it work. We need to get this out of the way so it doesn't look like Al's hiding something."

She laughs a short laugh and says, "Hiding somethin'?"

"You know what I mean."

"Yes, babe, I know. By the way, you also put me in some shit giving me that pellet pistol instead of his real gun."

"Oh, my bad."

"No, seriously, Frank. I need his gun back. It makes me look bad here."

"I'll give it to you after you meet with the detective on Monday."

"You swear to me now."

"I'm not going to swear to shit. You're in no position to make any demands, Darling."

"Please bring it. You can pick me up at the same place on Kenyon."

"Ten thirty in the a.m., Monday. I'll see you then."

"I'll be there. And bring that—"

I disconnect.

Calvin is on the sidewalk waiting for me when I pull up. What little bit of snow has fallen has been shoveled off the stairs to his house and the stretch of sidewalk in front. He's wearing a gray hoodie under his jacket and shouldering his backpack. Like a kid waiting for a school bus, but he's in his twenties.

When he gets in the car and shuts the door, I say, "Sorry about being a bit late. Some last-minute shit happened."

"Like you said, I'm on the clock, so waitin' is easy money. Am I gonna learn somethin' today?"

"Yeah, actually, go sit in the back. We're going to set up on that house on Queen, conduct a little surveillance."

His brows rise. I think he likes that idea.

He opens the door.

"You have something to drink, eat, and piss in?"

"Piss in?"

"You think we can break away from surveilling so you can go piss?"

"Never thought about that."

"You just learned something new, then. You got a jar with a lid, or something like a Gatorade bottle in the house?"

"You serious, right?"

"Yes, I'm not playing you. Go get something."

"A'right."

He takes his backpack and walks up the stairs.

A couple minutes later he returns with a large glass orange juice bottle, shows it to me through the side window like he's proud of it. He gets in the back, sitting behind the front passenger seat.

"Damn, that's a big bottle. You piss that much?"

"All I could find on short notice."

"Set it on your side of the floor, not my seat."

"It's clean."

"I know, but put it on the floor anyway."

I remember the gun in my backpack. I grab the backpack from the floor behind my seat and set it on the front passenger seat. I unzip an outside compartment and pull out the binos, hand them to Calvin.

"There you go. You'll be the eyes."

I pull out, notice him in the rearview mirror, looking through the front window with the binos.

"Put your seat belt on."

"Who gonna know?"

"Me," I tell him.

"It's restricting, man."

"Better that than being thrown into me or out the front windshield if I get in an accident."

"Shiet, that ain't likely."

"I know. I have good driving skills, but all the same."

"I meant me being thrown into you or out the window."

"Just put your fucking seat belt on. My car, my rules."

"Damn, you sounding like my uncle."

"I'll take that as a compliment."

Sixty-Six

B ack to flurries, but melting when they hit the front windshield, which is good because I can't turn the wipers on while on sur-veillance. We've been set up for more than an hour, and all is quiet. We can't see anything inside the house. The shades are pulled down. Doesn't look like anyone is home, or maybe they had a late night and are sleeping.

I do love the surveillance part of this job, despite these dull mo-ments. I loved it even more when I was a cop, though. It's like I had more control, leverage. It's different not being sworn, having lost an impenetrable oath.

"Why you wear that suit? You don't work in no office," Calvin says from the back seat.

He catches me by surprise, and I say, "My suit?"

"Yeah. Seems like it'd be uncomfortable, restricting, even."

"Like the seat belt, right?"

"Yeah."

"Not if you're wearing a nice suit."

"But it seems that most of the work you do is in this car. I can understand if you at an office and behind some desk meeting with people."

"This car is my office, and I do dress down on occasion. It's just a matter of looking professional."

Truth is, it's more than that. Something like magical thinking. I sometimes feel vulnerable without it, like I used to feel when I first hit the street as an officer and had to wear that heavy Kevlar vest. I won't tell him that shit, though.

My cell vibrates.

"Frank Marr," I answer.

"Hello, Marr. This is Rattan."

"How are you doing, Detective?"

"Always working. We identified the guy your source says is Rule."

"Yeah, you mentioned that before. What's his full name?"

"Jonas Rule. He has a substantial record, so I obtained a current Live Scan photo of him. It looks a lot like the guy in the bodycam photo, but I'd like to get your source to look at the photo I have and confirm that it's the same guy your source knows as Rule."

I turn to Calvin. He's peering through the binos.

"I can arrange that," I say.

"And I can be there with you?"

"Yes. Where are you now?"

"At the office, but I can meet you."

"How about the construction lot off Sherman?"

"Where the kid got shot?"

"It's not a crime scene anymore, right?"

"It's not."

"I can be there in about an hour."

"Okay, I'll see you there."

"All right."

I disconnect and slip the cell back in my inner coat pocket, turn to Calvin, who is looking at me.

"What that about?" he asks.

"Detective Rattan. She identified a possible suspect based on who you said the guy in the bodycam photo was and needs you to look at an arrest photo of him to confirm."

"They arrested Rule?"

"No. It's an older arrest photo, but this is how the police work. It's a part of the process."

"So she gonna know I'm the guy who said it looked like Rule?"

"Yep."

"I don't want to get jammed up with that, possibly have to go to court or something."

"I'll keep you out of court." *Somehow.* "You work with me now. And remember when I said it's good to do certain things for the police?"

"Yeah, favors and shit like that."

"Right."

"When she asks how you know him——"

"I said I don't know him," he snaps back.

"I know, but she'll probably ask, so tell her simply, you grew up in the Clifton area and know a lot of the boys that hang or live around there, but you don't know Rule personally, just seen him around. Nothing more."

"She give you his real name?"

"I'll let her tell you that."

"You people act like you've got all these rules."

"What do you mean, 'you people'?"

"Investigators, police—people like that."

"Then what the hell do you mean by 'act'?"

He doesn't answer.

"Listen, Calvin, without it, you might screw up what you're working on," I tell him.

"I guess."

He goes back to the binos, scanning the block like he's about to catch something good.

We give it another forty-five minutes here and then make our way to the lot. I'm going to have to work this out, how to handle Ty and Marlon. One of them has to get snatched up so we can have a chat.

Sixty-Seven

R attan is parked in the middle of the lot, the front of her car
facing the entrance that we drive through. Calvin is sitting in
the front seat now. She's seen him before, when I told her he works
with me, so I'll have to explain why I didn't identify him then as the
source of information. I park with my window beside hers, with the
back of my car facing the entrance.

We roll down our windows in sync. She notices Calvin, scans the
rear seats of my car.

"You remember Calvin," I say.

"Yes. You said he works with you. He your source?"

"I ain't—"

"He's not my source," I cut Calvin off. "He does work with me
part-time, learning the PI biz."

"So what's the big deal not revealing him?"

"No big deal. Just wanted to keep him out of the possibility of all
that court shit. Still learning, you know."

"All right, then," she says with a hint of skepticism. "How are you
doing, Calvin?"

"Doing fine."

"I want to show you a photo, but first I want to ask a couple of questions."

Calvin looks at me.

"You don't need my permission," I tell him. "Answer her questions."

"This is just common procedure, Calvin. I have to ask these questions whenever I show one photo for a confirmation."

"Okay."

"The person you identified in the bodycam photo as Rule, do you know his full name?"

"No. Just Rule. Don't even know if that's his real name."

"Is he a friend?"

"Hell no. I only know him from seeing him around the neighborhood. I grew up around Clifton."

"When was the last time you saw him?"

"Had to be more than three years. Before working with Investigator Marr, I was working at a deli and living with my uncle, so I'm not around that area no more."

"Okay. How many times have you seen him when you were in that area?"

"I couldn't say for sure."

"More than ten times?"

"Oh, hell—I mean yes."

"Okay. I want to show you this photo. Tell me if you know him." She hands the photo to me, and I hand it to Calvin.

He looks at it and says right away, "That's Rule, all right."

"Okay. Thanks, Calvin."

I take the photo from him, look at it for a second, and hand it back to her.

"I'll give you a copy of the BOLO in case you see him in your travels. Keep it to yourself, though. It's not public yet. I know I don't have to tell you this, but if you do see him, please don't try to stop him yourselves. Call nine one one and then call me."

"That mean you have enough for a warrant?"

"The bodycam photo is just barely identifiable, but with any luck it's enough to get it by a judge."

"I hope you will."

"Thanks again, Calvin. Oh, I'll need your full name, but don't worry, it won't be on the affidavit."

"Affydavid?" Calvin says.

"Affidavit. It's what the police write up to get a warrant signed," I say.

I can tell he's scared. I hope Rattan can't read him like I can.

"Tolson," he says.

"Good, and I'll just get in touch with him through you, Marr. That is, if I even have to."

"No problem," I say.

"I have to roll."

"Stay safe."

She raises her window, drives out, and when traffic is clear she makes a right turn. I keep the window down and light up a cigarette.

"Now the police got my full name."

"Will you stop it with that shit already?" I say.

I drive to make our way back to Queen Street.

Sixty-Eight

I find a good parking space on the same block as the house, about half a block down. Calvin's in the back seat again, working the binos. There's nothing to see, though. Maybe he likes birds.

I notice through the rearview mirror a black, older-model SUV coming up. I recline back.

"Stay still," I tell Calvin.

It drives past us. Heavy tint, of course, so I can't make out anyone inside.

"Can you see anyone inside?" I say.

"Naw. Tint too heavy."

The car stops at the end of the block and takes a right.

Calvin repositions himself in the seat so he can get a better view through the front windshield.

"Don't bounce around back there," I say.

"I ain't bouncin'."

"You know what I mean. People can notice movement when you do that."

"I'll be smooth about it next time."

I sneak back up in my seat. The SUV is gone.

"We need something to break here."

"What you mean?"

"I want to snatch up Ty or Marlon. I have questions."

"How you plan on doin' that? Can't just go and snatch someone up like that."

How do I answer this?

"There are ways."

"What ways?"

"Ways that are usually a spur-of-the-moment kinda thing."

He huffs a laugh and says, "You do that kinda shit when you were the police?"

"Hell no," I lie.

"Yeah, right."

I don't respond. Guess he can see right through me, too.

"If you want my opinion, it should be Marlon you snatch up."

"Why do you think that?"

"'Cause he weak."

"He might have some fight in him."

"Without a doubt, man, but I'm talkin' 'bout his mind is weak. He'll be quicker to talk."

"That's a good observation. I hope we'll get there, 'cause I don't know if we're wasting our time on this shit or not. Might be chasing the wind here."

"I like that—*chasing the wind.*"

I shoot him a hard look.

"What?"

I turn back to the house.

"If anyone's gonna have answers about Taylor, it'll be one of his boys. I don't believe it's a waste of time," he says.

"Hope you're right."

The front door to the house opens. It's Ty, and he's alone. He closes the door behind him. Damn, is this karma or what.

"There's Ty," I say.

"Yeah, that him."

He's standing on the porch, tapping something on his iPhone.

"Keep a close eye on him."

"I got it."

After a few minutes of standing there looking at the screen of his phone, he steps off the porch and walks across the street to our side. We're a few cars down. He's standing on the street close to another car, facing our direction.

"Take cover behind the passenger seat. Slowly."

I recline back as far as I can, but without losing sight of him.

"What the fuck is he doing?" I say.

"Looks like he be texting from what I can see. These binos are the fucking shit."

"Maybe waiting for somebody."

"Look like it."

Ty finishes whatever he's doing on the phone, looks in our direction, like he's staring right at us. He begins to walk toward my car. He stops near the front of the vehicle parked ahead of us. He's still standing in the road.

He points the iPhone straight at my car, keeps it there. Taking pictures?

"Fucking shit."

"Yeah, looks like we been made, man."

"You gotta be kidding me. They had to have a lookout somewhere. Fucking stupid."

"He just standing there, pointing the cell at your car. What are we supposed to do?"

"Now's as good a time as any, I suppose."

"Ty's a fool standing there like that."

"Fuck it," I say. "You stay down, watch my back."

"Naw, this ain't good. Let's roll."

"Stay down."

I check the small of my back, tug at the handcuffs secured over my belt, open the door and step out.

He's still standing there, pointing the phone at me. Recording me?

"Don't go fucking running on me," I tell him.

"I ain't got no reason to run," he says calmly.

I stay behind the front door for cover, then decide to close it so I don't burn Calvin, who is hunkered down in the back. I grip my weapon and take a couple of steps forward.

"I'm an investigator looking into the death of your friend Arthur Taylor."

He doesn't say anything. I step closer, hand still gripping my weapon. The kid won't budge. He has an odd, freaky smile. Makes me uncomfortable, especially since it's coming from such a little kid.

This is a fucking setup.

Before I can pull my weapon out, I feel something like cold steel pressed against the back of my head. I don't have to guess what it is.

"We all know who you are," an unfamiliar voice behind me says.

"Then you know I'm not the police, and I'm trying to find out why Arthur got shot."

"You still the police," the unfamiliar voice says. "You always the police, and you helping out that shit 'migo detective friend of yours."

"I just want to talk, and then I'll be on my way. No need to have that gun at my head."

"Fuck you, bitch. Take your hand off your piece or I blow the brains outta your skull."

I take my hand off the grip, put them in front of me so he can see.

"How about letting me turn so we can talk face-to-face?"

I feel the gun move away from my head, and I start to slowly turn, but a sudden blow crashes into the back of my head, near my right ear, not a fist. It throws me forward and to the ground. I fight not to go out.

I don't draw my gun. I roll to a sitting position, now see the man who was behind me, standing over me and pointing the gun at my chest.

Jonas fucking Rule.

Sixty-Nine

Head is throbbing. I can feel the blood down the back of my neck and dripping down my right ear. I put my left hand on the back of my head.

"That fucking necessary?" I ask.

Look at my hand after, smeared with blood.

I'm going to die here, kissing this cold fucking filthy ground.

"We need to roll out, Rule."

"Shut the fuck up, fool. Fucking calling me out like that."

It's done. I'm gonna get shot at close range. *Dammit, Calvin. Did you call 911?* Not that it'll matter.

He steadies his gun, finger on the trigger. No fear in his eyes.

"You don't have to do this. I'm not out to fuck with your business."

"Naw, but we out to fuck with yours."

I'm dizzy. Feel like throwing up. I reposition myself awkwardly, my hands now on the freezing pavement to hold myself up, keep from going out. It's going to be the last thing I see.

"Rule!" I hear Ty yell.

"Drop the fucking gun or I blow *your* brains outta your skull," I hear a beautifully familiar voice say.

I look up.

Calvin is behind Rule, pointing a gun at his head. It's the gun I took off Tamie's man. He must've gone into my backpack and gotten it.

I struggle to stand. Waver a bit, but I manage to find my balance. When I turn toward Ty, he pivots and bolts. Running so fast he hits the corner and runs north, then out of sight.

Rule still has his gun on me.

"Drop that piece, Rule," Calvin orders.

I choose not to draw my gun 'cause he's only a couple feet in front of me with the gun pointed right at me.

He lowers it to his side. That gives me the chance to pull my weapon and aim.

"Drop the gun, Rule!" I command.

He turns to me, gun still at his side. I can tell he's thinking hard.

"Drop it now," I order again.

He does. It lands at his feet.

"Kick it my way," I order him.

He hesitates but kicks it halfway and steps forward to turn his head and look at who is behind him.

He is surprised, almost smiles.

"Playboy? You a fucking snitch for the feds, just like Tamie D, but you a snitch with a gun, boy."

"I ain't no snitch."

Rule doesn't seem to be afraid. He's either a fool or a maniac. I hope not both.

"Get on your knees, Rule," I say.

"Fuck you and your bitch snitch."

He's both.

"I said I ain't no snitch. This a job."

Calvin steps back, aims the gun at Rule's left foot.

"Oh fuck," I mumble.

He fires, blows the tip of Rule's designer high-top sneaker off, along with what appears to be his big toe. Calvin didn't expect that. The recoil was too much, and the gun falls from his hand close to the front tire of my car, near Rule's gun.

"Fuck," Calvin says.

"My toes! My fucking toes! You fucking shot off my toes!"

Rule's frantic, a crazy kinda rage, and doesn't seem to care that I'm standing there with a gun aimed at him.

"I'm gonna fucking kill you!" Rule says, and makes a dive for one of the fallen guns, gets his hand on the grip of the one Calvin was holding.

Calvin jumps back, at least a couple of feet.

"Stop, Rule, or I'll shoot you!" I yell.

He doesn't hear me or chooses not to.

I fire two times, hitting him in the stomach, maybe the right shoulder. His hand is gripping the gun. He turns to me.

"And fuck you," he says to me, trying to sit up with the gun still in his hand.

Like he doesn't even know he's been shot.

I double tap him in the chest. The impact rolls him to his back. His head falls to the pavement, and the gun falls from his hand.

"Shit. Fuck. We have to get outta here," Calvin says.

"We don't run, Calvin."

I put my gun in a tuck position, still aimed at Rule, and with my right foot I slide the Sig Sauer to me, and then the 9mm Taurus that Rule had. I scan the area, notice a couple of neighbors a few houses back peering out their windows, but no one outside or anywhere else I can see. Possible witnesses, but they're not close.

I holster my weapon, pull my handcuffs out and cuff Rule's hands behind his back. I can hear his labored breathing.

"Fuck, he's gotta be on PCP or some shit like that," I say.

"This crazy. This some crazy shit."

I leave both guns where they are.

"What we gonna do now?"

"Call nine one one and wait for the police," I answer. "I'm justified."

"But I ain't. I got the gun from your pack. I thought it was the pellet gun. I wouldn't have shot his foot otherwise. I ain't got no license. I shot him in the foot after he dropped the gun."

"Oh, and then there's that."

I look around again and then bend down, act like I'm looking under my car, but pick up Rule's gun, keeping it close to my side so it's not easily seen.

"What are you doing?"

I stand up, walk around to the passenger side of my car, open the door, and place the gun at the bottom of my backpack, under a bottle of Jameson, my stun gun, and a few other essential items. I close the door and lock it with the key fob.

"What the fuck you doin'? You gotta talk to me."

"When the police get here they're probably going to interview us separately, so we gotta get the story right. Understand?"

"Fuck me."

"We don't have much time. I have to call nine one one."

"I'm gonna get arrested."

"Shut the fuck up," I say while tapping in the number.

When the dispatcher answers, I identify myself and say, "There's been a shooting. We need the police and an ambulance for one male, suffering from multiple gunshot wounds to the back and chest area. I think he's still conscious."

I quickly give the address and disconnect. Not even ten seconds later, my cell rings. I recognize the number from my police days. It's the dispatcher calling back because I hung up. I don't answer.

Sirens already in the distance. Now I need a good story.

"This is our story," I tell him.

SEVENTY

T his is one of those trigger moments, when I feel the need, that burning desire to snort up a beautiful pile of blow.

Millhoff, Rattan, and Shawn Caine, a detective who worked the officer shooting Calvin was involved in, are here, along with the rest of the homicide squad, including the lieutenant and sergeant. Even though Rule is still alive, they have to show, both because of the severity of his injuries and because he's a suspect in the shooting of the two officers. A couple of district detectives are also on the scene, helping the homicide detectives conduct a door-to-door for possible witnesses. The house Ty was in is secured by uniform officers, pending a search warrant. Of course, the big guns are on the way. The district commander is leaning against his marked unit, waiting for their arrival. Caine is interviewing Calvin, and Rattan and Millhoff are with me. The back of my head has been cleansed and bandaged up. I refused going to the hospital. It's just a gash.

"I'll say it again. I had no idea that Rule was at this location. I got information about this house as a possible safe house where Ty and

Marlon stay. All I wanted to do was interview one of them about their friend Arthur Taylor."

"What do you think they're going to know?" Millhoff asks.

"I don't know until I question them. That's the point. Rule things out. No pun intended."

Rattan smiles. That's a first.

"EMTs advise if they think he's going to make it?"

"No, but he's going to MedStar, so at least he has a chance," Millhoff says. "Afraid we're going to have to take your guns again. We'll get your statements at the office."

"He's gotta be on PCP. He was out of his mind."

Lights and sirens catch me off guard. I flinch.

"You okay?" Rattan says.

"Yeah."

The ambulance rolls out.

"When can I get my nineteen back from the shooting on Twelfth?"

"I'll get that taken care of," Millhoff says. "One gun at a time." He smiles.

I have a new .38 at home. Worst case is I'll have to buy another Glock, but I'm sure I'll get my weapons back. The shootings were justified.

"I'm not going to leave my car here. I'll drive Calvin to Homicide Branch."

"You should come with us," Millhoff says.

"You suggesting I need a lawyer?"

"You're the only one who can decide that."

"I don't."

"We have to keep you two separated—you know that."

"I know. I know that. I'm just forgetting is all."

"You've been retired for a bit," Millhoff says. "I can get a detective to drive your car to our parking lot."

"Appreciate it. I need to sit down now."

"You sure you don't want to go to the hospital?"

"I'm sure. I need to get my backpack out of the car first. I think Calvin has to get his, too."

"No problem."

I walk across the street. Rattan follows me. If I were a suspect I'd be in cuffs, so I'm not that worried.

I walk to the passenger side. Rattan stops at the front of my vehicle. I unlock the door, lift my pack, notice the curb gutter near the back tire. This place is crawling with police. I turn and sit on the edge of the seat with my feet on the curb.

"You okay, Marr?" Rattan says.

"Give me a second. I don't want to have to puke."

"Do it if you have to."

"Just give me a second, please."

"Everything good over there?" I hear Millhoff ask from across the street.

"I think he's going to puke," Rattan says.

"As long as it's not in my car," he says.

I place the backpack on the floor under my dash, lean my head between my knees, look both ways. It's clear. I search for the Taurus with one hand, stick my finger down my throat with my other. Couple of heaves. I feel the grip of the gun and quickly pull it out. Stick my finger down my throat again. Big heave with some vomit, and then I can't stop. I slip the gun under my legs and grab it with my right hand while vomiting, and then slide it like a hockey puck into the gutter. It makes a slight *thud* as it hits the bottom. I cough hard a couple more times and spit.

"You good now?" Rattan asks.

"Yeah, much better."

I stand up, making sure to step over the vomit, shut the door, but don't lock it just in case Calvin wants to get his pack. I walk to the front of my car, set the pack on the hood.

"Need some water," I say.

"You got some?"

"Yeah, side of my pack."

I take out the bottled water, but I really want whiskey. I swish the water in my mouth and spit, then drink some.

"Much better," I say. "Let me advise Calvin what's going on before we leave. He's pretty shaken up about all this."

"I'll go with you."

"Okay. I want to get out of here before the chiefs arrive."

"Me too," she says.

SEVENTY-ONE

DC Homicide. Last time I was here it still smelled like fresh
paint and new carpeting. Not so fresh anymore. They have me
in one of the interview rooms and Calvin in another. This isn't an interview that can take place at a desk, because it has to be recorded.
A camera is positioned at a corner wall to the right of the door.

I refused to sit in the chair they've had suspects sit in. Filthy mon-
sters. I don't even want to rest my arms on the table. Who knows
what's been wiped off that?

Rattan brings in a spare chair from the office.

"Thanks," I say.

She leaves the door open and sits on a chair next to Millhoff,
across from me. Their notebooks are open and pens at the ready.

"We've already made the introductions for the sake of the camera
there," Millhoff says. "And you've waived your rights and agreed to
speak with us, and like I said before, you are not under arrest at this
time."

Get in all the necessary shit, Millhoff.

"Would you start from the beginning, Frank? What brought you to the twelve hundred block of Queen Street NE?"

"Like I told the both of you on the scene, I had information that two subjects I know only as Ty and Marlon were staying at a house on the twelve hundred block of Queen Street NE. They were known associates of Arthur Taylor."

"Do you know the address?" Millhoff asks.

"I was only given a description of the house, wasn't sure which one," I reply, because I don't want to provide them with too much information.

"How did you get this information about Ty and Marlon?" Millhoff asks.

"Interviews on the street. A little money here and there."

"Any names of the subjects you interviewed?"

"I'm not a cop anymore, Tim. I don't have to note anything or get names, unless it can directly help my client."

"Your client being Al Luna?"

"Normally, I would say that's privileged information, but you both have known for some time that I'm helping him out."

"Go on," Millhoff says.

"So my part-time assistant, Calvin, and I go to sit on Queen Street, see if there are any young kids who fit Ty's and Marlon's descriptions so we can try to talk to them about Arthur Taylor, see if they know why he was at that lot where Detective Luna shot him. I've stated to both of you before that I believe Taylor was not there by himself."

"A gut feeling?" Rattan asks.

"You all get those occasionally, don't you?"

They don't answer.

Damn, I fucking need a drink.

"Also, Calvin was pretty sure he might know what Ty and Marlon look like because Calvin grew up in that area, and no, he didn't hang with any of those subjects. I can't remember what time we got there, or even how long we were there. I'm thinking it wasn't that long. I spot this kid who fits the description of Ty. Calvin is in the back of my vehicle with binoculars. The rear windows have good tint, so it's easy for him to conceal himself back there. Calvin tells me he believes that is Ty. We watch him as he stands on the porch of the house, looking like he's texting someone."

"You weren't parked that close, though," Rattan says.

"The binoculars are good, and Calvin thought it looked like he was texting, but I suppose he also could have been playing a game. Doesn't really matter. So, a couple minutes later he steps off the porch, walks across the street, just a few cars ahead of where we were parked. He's standing on the street, still staring at the screen of his phone. He looks up, right in our direction, like he knew we—or rather, I—was there, because I don't think he realized Calvin was in the back."

"What made you think that?" Millhoff says.

"I'm pretty certain if Rule knew Calvin was in the car, he would have had him step out after he put me down, but I'm jumping ahead here. The kid we think is Ty starts walking down the street straight to us, but he stops about a car length ahead of my car. He points the phone at my car, like he's taking pictures or recording. It is weird and a bit unnerving. He had this quirky little smile on his face. Calvin said something like 'He made us.' Even though I was reclined down as far as I could get, I was sure Calvin was right. That's when I decided I would exit and try to talk to him. I advised Calvin to stay in the car and keep low but watch my back. I stepped out of the car. It didn't feel right. And yes, another gut feeling," I say, directing that to Millhoff. "I called the kid by name, 'Ty,' and said something like I'm a private investigator, and I'm looking into the shooting of his friend Arthur Taylor. Again, I'm sort of losing the time frame, but it couldn't have been more than a couple of minutes when I felt what I knew was the barrel of a gun pressed to the back of my head. Sorry, but I can't remember what I said, if I even did say anything. Next thing I know, the gun pulls away, and I'm hit hard on the back of my head. So hard, I'm thrown to the ground, on my knees, I think, using my hands to steady myself, trying not to go out. Can I get some water?"

"I'll get it," Rattan says.

"You can continue," Millhoff says.

"I'll wait for your partner," I say.

She returns with bottled water. I twist the cap open and drink. Fucking like I have cottonmouth.

"Thanks, Rattan. Where was I?"

"On your knees," Millhoff says.

"Yeah, felt like I was going to pass out. I look up, immediately recognize the man standing a couple feet away from me, aiming the gun at my head, as Jonas Rule. Rattan showed a BOLO picture of him to me and Calvin, to confirm whether Calvin knew him as Rule. Calvin was the one who thought the bodycam photo looked like Rule. He confirmed to Rattan that it was. There he is—"

Not doing this pause for effect. It's like my mind goes blank for a second.

"You all right, Frank?" Millhoff asks.

I sip more water. "Yeah. That was weird."

"You need us to take you to the hospital?" Rattan asks again.

"No. I'm fine."

"You sure you can continue?" Millhoff says.

I know all they're doing is trying to cover their asses just in case I drop dead right now.

"I'm sure. It's like I knew I was dead, that he was going to shoot me. I do remember Ty calling something out, not sure what, but he used Rule's name, and that pissed Rule off. I'm looking down at the ground, thinking, *I fucking hope Calvin called nine one one,* and I'm praying to hear the sirens.

"Next thing I know, Calvin is fighting Rule for the gun. I don't know how much time had passed. The gun goes off, though, and I saw it fall to the ground beside the tire of my car. I turned to make sure Ty's not coming up on me. He's not. I draw my weapon. I think I stand up. Yeah, I stand up, position myself so I can see Ty and Rule. Calvin was head-to-head with Rule. I ordered him to get on the ground. I notice a lot of blood on the pavement, and Rule's foot. Calvin later told me that when they were fighting for the gun, it went off and blew a couple of Rule's toes off.

"Rule saw that I had a gun pointed at him, but it's like that didn't mean anything. He was out of his mind. It was crazy, because I ordered him to the ground several times, and he still tried to make a dive for the gun. He landed on his side toward me. I could see that he managed to grab the grip of the gun with his right hand. I fired. I think two times, hitting him in the chest. He yells something, tries to regain himself, raises the gun toward me. I fire again, hitting him in the chest area again. He drops. Gun falls out of his hand. I tuck my gun, keeping it pointed at him, and I walk over, slide his gun in my direction with my foot. Calvin's freaking out at this point, scared. I cuff Rule, then try to calm Calvin down. Don't know how long after, but I call nine one one."

"Damn, Frank," Millhoff says.

"Why did you hang up on nine one one?" Rattan asks.

"Because I remembered Ty. He was gone. For all I knew, he was going to get help, more guns. I needed my hands free."

"We found a witness," Millhoff begins, "said they believed Calvin had a gun in his hand, pointed at Rule."

"I don't know. Maybe he managed to wrestle the gun away from Rule. But from what I saw, which was about two feet away, they both were fighting for the gun and then Rule got shot in his foot."

"The witness was pretty sure Calvin and Rule both had guns."

"Witness is wrong. I had my gun. Calvin doesn't have a gun."

"How do you know?" Rattan says.

"How do I know? Because when I hired him, I made sure. Last thing I want is a young kid working for me, carrying an unregistered concealed weapon. He's a good kid. Smart as fuck. That's why I hired him. Your witness is mistaken. The way I tell it, you would think it took place over several minutes. It was only seconds. He probably had his hands on Rule's gun for a bit, but he definitely didn't have a gun pointed at Rule."

"Everything you said adds up, but we'll reinterview the witness," Millhoff says.

"You do that. I was right there. Your witness was probably halfway down the block, looking out a window."

They don't respond because they know I'm right.

I look directly at Rattan and Millhoff, like they're one person.

"I know Ty was recording all of this, or at least some of it. It was a planned execution."

"Why would you think that?"

"I remember now—something Rule blurted out, that he knew all about Detective Luna. He called him a '*migo* detective."

"When did he say that?"

"When he had the gun on me."

"Why would he mention Luna to you?"

"I told you, I advised Ty that I was looking into the shooting of his friend Arthur Taylor. Maybe Rule heard that. He's probably the one who shot out Luna's window, and was more than likely on Twelfth Street, sitting on my house to kill me then. Maybe because of all the questions I was asking on the street, trying to find out about Taylor. Maybe they didn't want me to find anything out. Or maybe it's just because they found out somehow that I was working to clear Luna. Who knows. Hope the son of a bitch survives so you can find out."

"We haven't been notified yet, so that's good news."

"Yeah, wouldn't that be something."

"What?" Millhoff says.

"That he lives."

"Don't understand," Millhoff says.

"A cop takes one bullet and dies. Rule takes several and will probably live a full, healthy life."

"Funny how that works. Then that full life is spent behind bars," Millhoff says.

Seventy-Two

I t's late afternoon by the time we get out, well past lunchtime, but I'm not hungry. Calvin says he isn't either. My car is parked in the lot, between a marked unit and a detective's cruiser. We hop in. I keep my pack on my lap and start the car.

"Get some heat on in here," Calvin says.

"It'll kick in when it warms up."

I grab a Ruby Red grapefruit out of my pack.

"In the meantime, this should help."

I use my knife and quarter it.

I hand two slices to him.

"How will an orange help with the heat?"

"It's a grapefruit. Ruby Red grapefruit, and it's good for your immune system. It'll keep you healthy."

"Naw, man. I'm good."

"Just take a bite. Suck the juice in."

He tightens his lips. A fucking childlike grimace you give when you don't want to take your medicine. He bites into it, though. Eyes widen a bit after.

"Good, isn't it?"

"Yeah, refreshing-like."

He devours both of them, rolls down the window and tosses the slices out. I finish my half and do the same.

"Shit's gotta bite to it, though."

"A healthy bite."

I zip my pack back up.

"You still have that gun in there?"

"What gun?" I say.

He knows better than to answer back.

"It's about time you meet our client, my best friend and brother," I say.

"Been a long day."

"It's gonna get a bit longer."

I drive out of the lot.

"What did you say when Detective Caine brought up a witness?"

"Like you told me in case there was a witness, that I had control of Rule's gun for a bit, but he got it back and that's when he shot himself in the foot. So, where's it go from here? I mean, they let us walk out."

"Found out just before they finished up with us that Rule is in critical condition and unresponsive. Doesn't look like he's gonna make it. I'll still get in touch with Leslie Costello, a lawyer I know. We got nothing to worry about, though. I'm sure of that."

"Then why the hell we need to lawyer up?"

"We're not lawyering up. I want to run our story by her is all. Keep her in the loop. So keep it all together in your head."

"Yeah, but what if they find Ty, and the phone he was using to record that shit?"

"I guess we have to find him first. Stop fucking worrying."

"You good at that, huh? Finding people."

"Yeah."

I know he's nervous. I'd worry about him if he wasn't.

"You saved my life back there, Calvin. That was some stealthy shit you pulled off."

"You give me a raise, then?"

"Save me twice, and you'll get a raise."

"Fuck, you a hard man, Marr."

"Not hard enough. My head's throbbing like a hammer keeps hitting it."

That reminds me. I think I have some Oxys left from a hit I did a few months ago, but they're at home. I'll suffer through.

We get to Al's house. Calvin notices the boarded-up window.

"Shot out," I tell him. "Probably Rule."

"Shiet."

I knock on the door. Al's looking the same. Beat down. He shoots Calvin an unsure look when he opens the door, looks at me after and says, "What the fuck happened to you?"

SEVENTY-THREE

Calvin is sitting on the sofa closest to the boarded-up window. I'm at the other end, beside the armchair Al is sitting in. We're drinking the good shit. Calvin has his glass filled with ice.

"You're ruining that good scotch with all that ice," Al tells him.

"He'll come around eventually," I say.

"Naw. It's better like this."

I pull out the BOLO of Rule and hand it over to Al. "You know this guy?"

"No."

"He goes back to Cordell Holm. You sure?"

"Yes, I'm sure. Never seen him before. And I don't know how he would know anything about me and my CI. It doesn't make sense."

"Tamie D your CI?" Calvin asks, surprised.

"How the fuck he come up with that?" Al says to me.

"Because I was coming up to Rule when he said it," Calvin begins. "Your name, too. Called you the 'migo detective. Your CI's burned, man. So are you."

Al is visibly angry.

Calvin's stepping up. Al looks at him hard, turns to me, and raises his hand, like, *Who the fuck this kid think he is?*

"If he didn't say it, I would have," I say, defending Calvin. "These mopes aren't fucking around, Al. This goes back. Has something to do with Cordell, with you, and maybe me. Or maybe because I'm just helping you. I don't know anything at this point. Might only have to do with the shooting you got into. He was one of their boys."

"Shit, I don't know. But I never used her to work Cordell. That I do know," Al says.

This is where I've got to be careful, because I did use her, and Tamie played the both of us to get to Cordell. I can't let him know that. I don't know what he might do, and he's got to get through this shooting investigation, not get himself jammed up with her again.

I need to call her.

"Gotta hit the head," I say.

"You know where it is."

"Take it easy on my rookie there. Okay, Al?"

"As long as he doesn't keep killing my fine scotch with all that ice."

I hear Calvin spit out a huff.

I turn the fart fan on when I get in the bathroom. It's older so it makes some noise. I use my burner phone to call Tamie. It rings several times and goes to an automated voice recording. I don't leave a message. I call again. No answer.

I fucking told her to pick up when I call.

Damn, though, I hope she's okay.

I flush the toilet and return to the living room.

I sit on the sofa.

"So, your associate here was just telling me how you two met."

What the...?

Calvin must see the concerned look I have.

"Yeah, turkey on wheat," Calvin says.

"That's right. Kid makes a killer sandwich. Listen, we're going to have to roll," I say suddenly. "You need to sit tight, keep that .38 of yours close."

"Don't worry about me, my friend. I been through the shit before."

"I'll talk to you tomorrow," I say, and then stand. I finish the scotch left in my glass. I notice Calvin doing the same, but with some trouble. He does, though, walks over to Al with the glass.

"You want me to go rinse this in your sink?"

"No, but thanks for asking. Just set it on the coffee table. I'll take care of it."

He does.

"And thanks for saving my boy's life. I owe you one."

"A'right."

"Walk us to the door so you can lock it up," I say.

"Yeah, yeah."

We get in the car, and after I start it up, Calvin turns to me.

"That cop friend of yours ain't so bad."

"He's good people."

"Don't know how you all can stand the scotch. Smells like it been mixed with ash from an old fireplace. Tastes like it, too."

"Hey, you have a good palate."

"Huh?"

I drive around the block to check for any suspicious cars.

"Why you drive around the block?"

"Being safe is all. You ready for the long haul, or you want me to take you home?"

"I'm ready for whatever it takes."

"You should call your uncle, then, let him know you're safe."

"You keep forgetting I'm an adult here. You keep treatin' me like a fucking kid."

"Just do it."

Seventy-Four

T hings change when you save someone's life. It doesn't matter if you're a thug, civilian, military, or a cop. It's like an accelerated bond between the two. Nothing you go on about, like civilians might do, getting all mushy and shit. It's just there. Different. A new level of trust. In my case, a trust that was never there until now.

Evening is settling in. It'll be dark soon, harder to find someone. I drive north on 14th toward Fairmont. I try calling Tamie again, but with negative results.

"That Tamie D you tryin' to call?"

"Yeah."

"She the crack whore from the photo you showed me?"

"Yes, but that was an old photo. She looks nothing like that anymore. In fact, I gotta be honest with you. It looks like she worked her way into Cordell's crew somehow, or some faction of Cordell's crew."

"You mean like some of Cordell's boys broke off to go on their own?"

"Yeah, but I don't know for sure."

"Why you didn't tell me this before?"

"I wasn't ready to tell you before."

"What you mean to say is you didn't trust me."

"Yeah, that too."

"And she the one that called me on the burner?"

"Yes."

I don't tell him how Tamie learned of Cordell because I'm sure it was through me, when I had Tamie set up Calvin for a meet. That's how I originally found Calvin, but he was only known as Playboy back then. He's got my trust now, but certain things I have to keep from him or that will all be taken away.

"So how you think she did all that?"

"Get with Cordell's boys?"

"Yeah."

"I don't have a clue," I say. "Possibly back when she was using crack."

"I don't remember her, though."

"Were you out slinging crack on the corner back then?"

"Naw. I had other business to run."

"Okay, then."

Other business that almost made me kill him, but I won't bring that up again. Ancient history.

I'm certain Queen Street is still locked down. Detectives probably in the house by now with a search warrant. That might be why Tamie hasn't returned my call, because she was in there and is being detained. The only one I know for sure wasn't in there is Ty.

"You gonna have a problem hitting these spots with me?" I say.

"At this point it don't matter, does it?"

"No, it doesn't. Does Ty or any of those boys on Fairmont or Euclid know where your uncle lives?"

"Naw. That I know for sure."

"That's good. It appears they fucking know where I live, though, and Al."

"So you asking to stay at my uncle's?"

"No. I've been through this before. No worries."

"By the way, what happened to the other gun?"

"I'm not going to keep repeating myself here. I don't know what the fuck you're talking about."

"Just one thing, and that's the end of it, 'cause it just came to me."

"All right."

"The gun that the police got was the gun I got out of the pack, right?"

"Yeah."

"But what about the gun Rule had?"

"Got rid of it. Listen, I know what you're thinking. You know about ballistics?"

"Yeah, bullets."

"Little more than that. The bullet that took off Rule's toes has to match the bore of the weapon, the inside of the barrel. The bore is like a fingerprint. That is, unless the bullet mushroomed out, hitting the pavement. Even then there's ways. So that gun had to go with Rule."

"And the other gun?"

"There is no other gun. End of story."

I make the left on Euclid and a right on University Place to Fairmont. We stop at the corner. Calvin uses the binos. I can tell from here that it doesn't look like any real players are out. Makes me wonder if that has anything to do with what happened on Queen Street.

"Anywhere else you can think of that Ty—Little T—might be hanging?"

"Probably nowhere on the outside after what happened."

"Assuming he's a part of whoever Tamie is with, and a possible connection to Cordell's boys, you know of any other safe houses?"

"If they be with Cordell, then he's still in control, working it from the inside, and he has himself a couple places. But if they be working on their own, broke off from him, then I don't fucking know."

"Here's another lesson. It's called ruling things out. So let's check those other safe houses out, assuming they still might be with him."

"A'right. Head to Seventeenth and Euclid, but keep on Seventeenth toward Kalorama."

I roll west on Euclid from Sixteenth. Calvin's in the back seat now. When we get to Euclid, we see that it's also clear. Word travels, unless it's too cold for them, which is something I doubt.

"You forget this is one-way south of Euclid?" I say.

"Man, I don't pay attention to that shit."

I go to Ontario and make the left to go around the block.

We hit 17th, and Calvin says, "Keep up past the cut and slow down."

Calvin is leaning his head between the two front seats and then points over the front passenger seat so I can see. It's a row house on the left.

"That one there. It be a cousin or some shit, but I don't know for sure. But it's a clean house. Never been hit."

I keep driving, make my way around the block again, come back up 17th and park at the corner.

"Remember, this car be burned."

"I know, but it's getting dark."

"How you thinkin' of playin' this shit?"

"I don't have a clue. Lights are on in the house, though."

Calvin looks with the binos. "Can't see shit from here."

I roll down my window a couple inches and turn the car off.

I pick up the cell to call Tamie again.

"What the fuck you do?" she answers, having recognized my number.

SEVENTY-FIVE

After I tell her she's burned and in danger, she says, "I already know that," and agrees to meet, but only if she brings the big man with her.

"As long as he doesn't hold a grudge," I say.

"And you bring his gun with you."

"Damn, Tamie, you've really changed. I remember when you used to call me hon and I called you sweetie."

"You don't know the half of it. But you can still call me sweetie, hon."

She picks the spot. Coincidentally, the same location where those two knuckleheads tried to rob me.

"Why don't we compromise and say the west side at the corner of Sixteenth," I say. "More traffic, less that can happen."

"Ain't nothin' gonna happen, Frankie, unless it's you that make it happen, but all right. Give me an hour."

"See you there, Darling."

I disconnect.

"So?" Calvin says.

"An hour, but we're going to find a spot to set up now."

It's only a couple of blocks from here, which makes me wonder if we should stay where we are, that she might come out of that house. I decide to roll.

I park on W Street, with the rear of the car at 16th and the corner we're meeting at across the street from us. Like the side I was robbed at, there's a small courtyard off the sidewalk with steps that lead into the park. Darling knows my car, so if her man is smart, they'll drive the block and I'll get made. I'm not worried about that.

Calvin is still in the rear of the car.

"This is where you have to watch my back again. It's not gonna be like before, 'cause you were right there."

I point to the courtyard area.

"See right there, just below the steps? I'll be sure to be near the brownstone wall so you can see me. Have my number at the ready so you can text if you see something suspicious. If something breaks, call nine one one. The Third District is right down the street. You good with that?"

"Yeah, but why can't I go with you?"

"Darling knows I work alone. She sees you there, she might decide to roll out."

"Your call, man," he says, like he doesn't believe me.

"I'm not bullshitting you. That's the only reason I don't want you there."

"I believe ya."

"We're early, but keep your eyes peeled. This ain't the girl I used to know."

"Yeah, that's 'cause she got the taste of money and the power that come with it."

That's one wise boy there.

I grab the bottle of Jameson out of my pack, take a healthy swig. Hate being a bad influence, but I hand it over to Calvin.

"Naw thanks. Rather have a couple hits of a blunt."

I reach into my pack again, find my sandwich baggie with a couple of joints in it. I pull one out and give it to him.

"Not the size of one of your blunts, but it's good shit."

"You kiddin' me?" he says. "You used to be a cop."

"Helps me relax. So go on, we're forty-five minutes early. Crack the window and smoke it up, but keep your eyes on."

"Don't have to worry 'bout that. This shit wakes me up."

He takes a disposable lighter out of his jacket pocket and lights it up. I watch him through the rearview mirror. His eyes widen after he holds it for a while, then exhales.

"This some good shit here."

An hour passes, along with most of my bottle and the joint Calvin smoked up. She's late.

"She gonna show?"

"I don't know anymore. These things always go like this when it comes to drug shit, but never has with her. Let's give it some more time."

A few minutes later Calvin says, "That her?"

I turn around. She's walking south on the east side of 16th, same side we're going to meet. With the big man again.

"Yeah, that's her."

"That dude's big, man."

"Bad knees, though," I say, and open the door. "Keep your eyes peeled all directions, all right? Stay low."

"I got it."

I step out, feel for the grip of my gun out of habit, and then the stun gun secured to my belt on the other side.

I walk across the street, hit the corner almost the same time as they do. They stop when they see me. Big man looks ready to take my head off.

There's steady traffic in both directions on 16th. That's a good thing.

I notice a young couple walking our way on W, but on the other side. They stop at the corner like they want to cross but decide not to. They turn and walk south on 16th.

I walk up to the small courtyard area, my back facing W and, I hope, Calvin. They follow, stop a couple of feet from me.

"You had me worried when you wouldn't answer your cell," I say.

"My gun. Give it up," big man says.

"Oh yeah, things have changed. Nothing about this gauze around my head, huh?"

"I figure you're walkin' so you're okay. And I already heard about everything that happened on Queen Street," Tamie says.

"So what about my gun?" he asks again.

"Unfortunately, no."

He looks at Tamie, obviously flustered.

"Police took it from me after that scuffle with Rule."

"Scuffle?" he blurts, like that's an understatement.

"Was it registered to you?"

"Of course it wasn't," Tamie says.

"Then your man here'll be all right. I cleaned it up after I got it in my car. No prints."

"Fuck you," he says.

"Thought we weren't going to go there, Tamie?"

"We ain't."

"You got a name I can call you?" I say to the big man.

"You can call me sir."

"You can call him Eman," Tamie says.

He doesn't react. Guess he's holding a grudge.

"Can you trust what I have to talk about in front of Eman?"

"Yes. Everything."

"Everything?"

"He knows I was playing both sides, but for our advantage."

Shit, she is good. Maybe the best I ever met.

"All right, then. But first, tell me who Jonas Rule is to you."

"So he's still alive?" she says.

"Last I heard."

"He a little big man trying to work his way up the wrong way," Eman says.

"Like I told you before, Tamie, I don't give a rat's ass what you're working now and how you got there. I'm actually happy you're doing well."

"Fuck you, Frankie."

Getting a lot of that from women.

"It's the truth. I'm not going to tell Al what I know or the cops. You leave Al alone, stay away from me, too, and I won't have to take your little kingdom down."

Eman laughs. It's a funny sort of laugh. Almost makes me laugh. Sort of childlike.

"I take it you don't know much about me, Eman?"

"I know enough."

"I don't know if you do, but all the same, I'm going to stop all this alpha shit. You already know you're burned, Tamie, and you said you can trust Eman here, because you'll need his protection. What about the other boys? Specifically, Marlon. Little T."

"I know they run or ran with Rule and know what he was up to. They don't know I know. Ty knows about me now, because of what you said happened at Queen Street, and I'm assuming he heard it."

"You can still get to him, then? Ty, I mean."

"Of course I can." She smiles. "Oh, you mean for you?"

"Yes."

"Why would I want to do that?"

"Because I believe you don't know anything about why Arthur Taylor was at the lot when Al shot him, but I think Ty does, Marlon too. I want him and his cell phone or phones. For all you know, he was there because he knew you were there. You were probably followed."

"Who do you think you are?" Eman says.

"Just trying to help someone out who I thought was our mutual friend," I say to Tamie, because she knows I mean Al. "Maybe help you, too. I know Al took advantage. Hell, so did I. Never tried to get you help when you needed it, because we needed you the way you were. I ain't proud of that shit. You gotta believe me. You know we would've—still would—do anything to protect you."

"She don't need your protection."

"That's enough, Eman, and, Frankie, don't try to sweet-talk me no more. Ty ain't smart enough to try to run things. He's just a little boy. Ain't nothin' without Rule. Neither was Marlon. If they were there with that Taylor boy, it's because Rule wanted them there. Now that they don't have Rule, they're gonna come to Mama."

Eman laughs again.

"Rule's a dipper-smoking little shit. That make him dangerous," she says.

I knew he had to be on that shit.

"Frankie, we don't need to tell you nothing. But Rule was making his play. Cordell had his interests, and I had my interests. And you took care of Rule for us."

"Then you owe me," I say.

"Fuck this," Eman says. "Let me wreck this fool, Mama."

And before waiting for an answer, he lunges forward, connecting with his fist hard, on the left side of my face. That fucking side of my face again, but nothing like the tap Calvin gave me.

It almost drops me. Makes me think how many times am I gonna allow myself to get hit on that side of my face. I feel a trickle of blood. He broke the skin, but not by much. I regain myself quickly, ready to go to blows with this guy, take out that knee. Again.

Instead, I straighten myself up. Face Tamie. He's ready, but Tamie holds him back with her hand, like he's as light as a feather. I don't acknowledge him. Make like it never happened. That can be harder on him than retaliation. It's like it meant nothing. He means nothing.

"You owe me, Frankie. You owe me about ten years of my life," she says.

I wipe the bit of blood from my cheek, but I don't want to soil my suit, so I keep the blood on my hand.

"Bullshit, Tamie. You got what you wanted out of us."

A couple pedestrians walk down 16th. We wait until they cross W.

"I'm askin', Tamie. We can still be helpful to each other in the future."

That gets her brain working.

"I'll get you what you want, Frank Marr, and you'll get me what I want someday. I'll call you tomorrow."

"What time?"

"Just answer when I call," she says, mocking me.

SEVENTY-SIX

W e'll see what happens," I tell Calvin after I get in the car and close the door.

"What—"

"Hold on." I cut him off.

I start the car, pull out quickly, and drive toward 15th.

"Go on," I say.

"What she say, then?"

"What we already know. Cordell. Everything. Rule found out she was an informant but didn't know she was playing both sides. She also knew Rule and his little crew of boys—Ty and Marlon—were out to get her."

"So now what?"

"Drive around a bit. Make sure we're not being tailed."

"I mean after that."

"Wait, and hope she calls me and gives up Ty like she said she would."

"But she knows nothin' about that boy Taylor getting shot?"

"Claims she doesn't, but who knows."

I give Calvin another joint.

"Shit, thanks," he says, and lights it up right away.

"Smoke it up. I'm going to drive a bit before I take you home."

"No problem there."

SEVENTY-SEVEN

I wake up early. It's light out, so not that early. I go into the up-stairs bathroom to change the gauze on my head and clean the wound. I have to peel off the square patch of gauze over my wound because it's stuck to my dried-up blood like glue. I pull some hair out with it. I position the medicine-cabinet mirror so I can see the back of my head in the mirror above my sink. Doesn't look so bad, I think. I clean it with hydrogen peroxide and rub the scabbed-up gash with antibiotic cream. I grab fresh gauze wrap and a patch just in case it starts bleeding again.

I put on my good suit, with a fresh white shirt and my favorite tie. I grab a box of .38 ammo out of my nightstand drawer and put that, along with the gauze and patch, in my backpack. I go downstairs and grab an unopened bottle of Jameson and shove it in there, too.

I pick up Calvin, have him sit in the back again with the binos, and we start with canvassing the 1400 block of Fairmont first, then go from there. I can't wait on Darling. Don't even feel like she's go-ing to call.

My blood gets flowing when my cell rings. I look at the screen. It's Rattan.

"Marr," I answer.

"Can we meet? I have a photo array I need to show you and Calvin, if he's with you."

"He is, and no problem. When and where?"

"I'm not comfortable with the lot anymore. How about the vacant church lot off Fifth, the one the FOP used to use? I can be there in ten minutes."

"Give us twenty."

"See you then," Rattan says.

"That was Detective Rattan," I tell Calvin. "She has more photos to show us."

"Who?"

"She didn't say."

Back in the day, the old church allowed cops to park in the lot for court because parking was such a pain in the ass. It was mostly used for taking naps in cars, though. Rattan is toward the back, facing the entrance. I pull up to her like I did before and open my window.

"I need to show you guys the array separately," she says.

"I know that."

"Didn't mean—"

"You didn't hurt my feelings. Who do you want first?"

"It doesn't matter."

I turn to Calvin. "I'll be right back."

He nods.

I step out, walk around to the passenger side of her unmarked cruiser, and get in.

"These photos might contain a photo of the individual who was using the iPhone when you got into the shooting. Do I have to go through the rest of this speech?"

"No. Just show me the photos."

She hands me a sheet of paper with nine photos printed on it. It doesn't take me more than a second to point to Ty's image.

"Him. He was the one with the phone and the subject I know as Ty, or Little T."

I hand it back to her.

"Thanks for your time," she says.

"Be sure to give Calvin the speech," I say.

She smiles.

I step out, walk to the car. Calvin gets out.

"Your turn, partner," I say.

He looks at me, and I can barely make out a smile on his face. I get in the car and light up a smoke. Not even five minutes pass and Calvin steps out. He gets in the back.

"I'm not supposed to talk to you about it," he says.

"I know, man."

I roll down the front passenger window, and Rattan rolls down her window.

"Let me know how it goes," I say. "And if you get a search warrant for anybody, make sure to include all cell phones and smart-phones."

"Be safe, Marr," she says, and drives away.

"You picked Ty, right?" I say.

"Told you I'm not supposed to say."

"Just testing," I joke.

Seventy-Eight

B ack on Fairmont. A little bit of action, but not much, and no sign of Ty or Marlon. We head to 17th again, drive around the area before trying to park.

"Man, this whole neighborhood be changing. All these fucking rich folks comin' in."

"This the first time you notice that?" I say.

"Naw, just the first time I said it out loud."

"Yeah, well, I grew up in DC. Nothing like it was when I was a young teenager in the eighties."

"No shit, you that old?"

"Fuck you. Forties ain't old. And trust me, you'll get there soon enough. Time has a way of eating you like that."

"Never thought I'd make it to thirty."

"You almost didn't."

"That ain't funny."

"I meant your past thuggish ways when you were runnin' with people like Cordell and Little Monster."

"No you weren't. You talkin' about that time at the river."

321

"I don't know what the hell you're talking about."

"Go on, now. Ancient history for me. Fucking weird thing is, you kinda saved my life, too."

I look back at him briefly but don't have words.

We get to the corner of 17th and Kalorama and park illegally.

"I don't know. I think we're wasting our time. Leave it up to Rattan and her crew. They'll get a warrant. Eventually find him."

"What about your boy Luna? He gonna get fucked in that shooting."

"Only so much you can do, partner."

"You keep calling me partner, so I guess I got a say in things. And I say we keep looking for that little mofo."

I light a smoke. "All right, then."

"You got another one of them joints?"

"Rolled-up fresh."

I grab the sandwich baggie with five in it and toss the whole thing back to him. "Not all at once. Might have to run."

"I got a bum knee, remember."

"Then if I have to run, you take the wheel."

I hear him light one up and smell it after. Stinky as shit, but nice.

SEVENTY-NINE

I check my phone. We've been here more than two hours. I have a couple swigs of Jameson, and before I can screw the cap back on, I see an SUV driving the wrong way down the one-way street from Euclid.

"SUV coming."

"Fucking one-way street."

"Hell, we used to always do that," Calvin says.

It double-parks in front of the house we've been watching. Tamie steps out of the front passenger seat.

"That looks like that big man from the other night, behind the wheel," Calvin says.

"Yeah, and that's our girl."

"Your girl."

She walks up the steps to the front door and enters.

The SUV waits a couple of seconds and then drives toward us. I tuck down.

"Which way is it going?" I say.

"Just took that right onto Kalorama."

I sit back up, take another good swig out of the bottle, and tighten the cap on. I wedge it behind my pack.

"Least we know where she be."

"Yeah, if we don't hear from her today, that'll be a good thing."

"You call the police?"

"Fuck no."

"I'm good with that."

My cell rings.

"Fucking Tamie," I say, more to myself.

"No shit."

"Didn't think you'd call, sweetie," I answer.

"You should know better than that, Frankie."

"Give me some good news, please."

"Meet me at our old spot."

"Kenyon?"

"C'mon, baby, where it all began."

"You sure about that?"

"Sure as I like pumpkin pie in November. I can be there in about an hour."

"I'll be there."

She disconnects.

"We're on for the meet, but I don't trust her."

"What you wanna do?"

"Go meet her. It's not for an hour. Let's sit here. I'll show you how to properly tail someone."

"But your car burned."

"Yep. That's why you gotta do it right."

Thirty minutes pass, and the SUV drives up Kalorama from Ontario, makes a left onto 17th. I'm already leaning back.

"He look at us?"

"Not that I can tell."

"Not really worried. There's a lot of cars like mine in this neighborhood."

Tamie opens the door and walks down the steps before the car pulls up. She doesn't walk around to the front. She steps in the back seat, behind Eman. He drives.

I let them get to Euclid and turn right before I start the car and pull out.

"Hard to do with one car," I say. "Even harder if the car's burned. That's why we're going to stay as far back as we can, and you keep the binos on them."

"Okay."

Euclid's a long block to 16th, unless they made that left turn on Mozart. I ease out to Euclid before I turn.

"They be hittin' Sixteenth Street. Looks like they gonna make a right."

That's another long block to W, and the corner where we met last night. That house is more than likely where they came from.

When they turn, I speed up to 16th, pull out as much as I can with all the traffic going south.

"You see them?"

"Hold on. Yeah, in front of that cab."

I pull out, turn right, get a couple of angry horn honks behind me from an oncoming car.

"They passin' W."

By the time I get to W, they're at U and waiting on a red light. I get in the left lane.

"What are you doin'?" Calvin says. "They gonna make that left on U."

"Letting a couple cars get ahead of me so we can stay behind."

"That makes sense."

"Just have to make that light on V."

Fuck, it turns yellow. The first car, in front of the car ahead of me, crosses. I check my right and cut in front of the car in the next lane and hit it, running the red.

"Shit, man, 3D right down the road."

I get behind that car in the left lane again. The light at U is still red. We're about four cars behind them now. They make the turn when the traffic light's green, and a couple seconds later so do we.

We follow a few blocks. Traffic is jammed, so they make the light at 11th before we can.

"Keep eyes on them."

"They at the light at Tenth. Left-turn blinker on."

"Looks like they decided to take the long way."

By the time we turn on 10th, they're all the way up, turning right onto Barry. I feel better now, unless Eman originally dropped her off to go pick up some other boys.

We lose them when we get to Barry.

"I can't see the car," Calvin says.

"No worries. I'll take the left on Sherman, drive past the construction."

"Oh, I gotcha."

We pass the lot. I can see their car backed in between two trailers.

I keep going and make the right on Euclid and then the next right on 9th. I pass the back of the fire station and double-park before passing the lot.

"The car is parked in the lot there, on the right, between two construction trailers. I can barely see it. Can you get eyes on it?"

He's leaning over the passenger seat, peering through the front windshield with the binos.

"I got it."

"Can you make out who is in it?"

"I can see the big man, and behind him someone who looks like Tamie D."

"Look hard. Any other movement?"

"Can't tell. Don't know for sure."

"Okay. You drive. I'll take the passenger side."

He doesn't question it. Gets out of the car when I do, and we switch up.

"Drive all the way around to the front entrance of the lot and turn in."

We get around the block, back to Sherman, and Calvin turns in.

"Don't pass them. Turn here, and back up so you have an easy out of the front gate."

"You gonna walk out to meet them?"

"Yeah. Keep the car running and get your iPhone out. If something happens to me, just take off and call nine one one."

"Fuck that."

"I ain't joking, Calvin. If something is out of the ordinary, you'll see me hoof it back to the car and we'll both take off. If you hear gunshots that don't come from me, you get the fuck out."

"How am I gonna know if they come from you?"

"'Cause I'll still be standing, shooting my gun. Enough said."

I step out, scan the area before I walk. I take my .38 out and put it in the front pocket of my overcoat, keep my hand on the grip.

EIGHTY

I walk past the trailer where their car is parked. Eman steps out first, and then Tamie. Like regular gangland shit.

He has his right hand on the grip of a gun holstered at his right side.

"Is this all good, Tamie?"

"Course it is, hon."

Still doesn't make me feel comfortable.

She taps Eman's right shoulder as she passes him. He takes his hand away from the gun. I keep mine where it is. I can see she's carrying a phone.

She walks up to me, turns to see my car.

"You got yourself a driver now?"

"Student driver."

She hands me the cell phone.

"You might want to pay special attention to everything recorded on there, not just your shit, but what's recorded before it."

"Where's Ty?"

"You don't have to worry about him, or Marlon."

"I still need to talk to him about the shooting Al got in."

"No you don't. You got this. It'll speak for him."

"All the same—"

"Frankie, those boys be in the wind. Cops won't find them and neither will you. This one was about me more than you and Al. It's taken care of. Code to get into that phone is 1400TY. You need to write that down?"

"I got it."

I type it in to make sure. It opens up to the icons. I look at Darling, then back to the screen and tap the icon for photos. He has more than two thousand photos on here and more than three hundred videos. I tap one of the videos. It reveals him tilting the phone up to my car.

Fuckin' A.

"You be good, Frankie," she says.

"And you stay safe in your new job, Darling."

She turns and walks back to the car. Eman waits for her to get in the front passenger seat, and then he gets in. It's all good. She doesn't know that I know where to find her.

I continue watching the video, but step back to let her car pass me. I watch Eman drive slowly by my car and out of the lot.

Those boys aren't in the fucking wind. They're in the river's current.

I pause the recording and walk back to the car.

I turn it back on when I get in, and Calvin and I watch the whole event unfold, but in real time.

We keep watching, and when I hear Calvin in the background of the recording yelling something inaudible to Rule, the camera is still focused on me as I try to get myself off the ground, like he wanted a good angle when Rule shoots me at close range. That's when I hear Ty clearly, saying, *We need to roll out, Rule.* It's mostly inaudible, but you can hear Rule off camera saying something about calling him out.

Calvin's voice is heard in the background, yelling something hard to understand. Ty is too far away. That's when the camera goes blurry, like Ty is moving it too fast, and then all we see is pavement.

Darkness after that, but with sound, like he shoved it in a pocket, and then only the sound of him running, and then it stops recording.

"That's the shit," I say.

"That what you all mean by 'the shit'?"

"Oh yeah. This clears the fuck outta us, brother."

I give Calvin a slap on the back. He smiles a big smile.

I tap on the video before this one. It shows a close-up of Rule, face all bright, and I realize it's because it's from a marked cruiser's spotlight bouncing off the interior rearview mirror.

"Stay cool, y'all. Stay cool. You get all this, Marlon? You get all this shit?" Rule asks, keeping his eyes focused on the exterior mirror, probably watching the officers approach.

I stop the video.

"Why you do that?"

"'Cause this ain't for our eyes. I've seen enough of this kinda shit in the academy. It's different now."

"I should watch it, though," he says, like he is reverting back to who he was.

"This is real, not some staged YouTube shit. You feel me?"

"Yeah," he says, like he's embarrassed.

I scroll the screen, getting a quick look at all the images, until I land on one that looks like the side of a trailer. I tap it, then press Play.

It shows the scene in front of whoever is walking, like a hand-held, gravel on the ground, construction trailers in the foreground. It's the lot, and I'm afraid to watch, but this one we have to.

"This looks like this place. In fact, right over there," Calvin says, pointing to a trailer about twenty yards to the side of the two trailers Tamie was parked between, and where we used to always park.

The camera pans left, shows Marlon and Ty walking side by side. Ty smiles at the camera.

"We gonna catch this shit now, Taytay. Be some good action," Ty says to the camera.

"Play it smart, boy," Marlon says. "This is business now. So shut the fuck up."

Camera pans back as they get to the trailer. It's focused on the back tire of the large trailer.

"They parked on the other side of that one there," a voice that sounds like Marlon says.

The camera pans up, and whoever is holding it steps out to show the other trailer.

"You move on up, real stealthlike, get them both in the car. That's fucking all we need."

"I got it," an unfamiliar younger voice says.

"So fucking do it," I think Ty says.

Calvin and I are glued. Silent. He can't be feeling what I'm feeling, though.

The one holding the camera turns, gets another shot of Ty and Marlon, as they're leaning down, looking under the trailer toward the other one.

Forward again, as he steps closer.

Fuck. We can make out the rear of what appears to be Luna's cruiser.

Moving a little closer, and there's Luna with a cigar. He turns, the kid still stepping forward, like he's trying to get a better angle.

Al draws his weapon, yelling several commands to drop the gun. The stupid kid walks forward a couple more steps, says, "This ain't no gun."

Al yells again, then several flashes from the muzzle of his weapon. Camera falls, still recording.

"Fuck, man," Calvin blurts out. "Fuck. He ain't have no gun. Fuck."

"Shut the fuck up," I say.

"Get the fucking phone!" one of the boys yells. Someone scooting along the gravel, and a hand scoops up the phone and it goes blank.

EIGHTY-ONE

A l pours Leslie a couple shots of scotch.
"That's too much," she says.

He ignores her.

Leslie's not smiling. She looks distraught, almost like she's been crying. What the fuck? She just saw what we saw, and now we have to show it to Al.

He turns to me and Calvin sitting on the sofa, both of us at either end again. He pours me a nice double. Offers some to Calvin.

"No, man. I can't get used to that stuff. Sorry," he says.

"We'll convert you soon enough. Want some lemonade, then?"

"That's all right."

"Joking. I don't have lemonade."

Al sits in the armchair.

"So, you got something?"

I don't respond.

"What's the matter, Frankie? You okay?" he asks.

"Tired."

"They recovered some evidence, Al."

"For the shooting?"

"Yes," she says. "The shooting was recorded on a smartphone."

"Well, that's fucking good news. That means there were some of his boys there, and they took the gun from the scene."

"No, Al," she says calmly. "There were two of his boys on the scene, but all they were there for was to capture a recording of you with your CI. She was burned, and they were part of a fucking bad crew she was working with, and they wanted to get the both of you together."

"I don't understand."

"The boy had a cell phone, not a gun."

"Fuck you all. He had a gun. Show it to me."

I look at Leslie. She nods. I take the phone out, open it to the video, and show him, holding it in the palm of my hand close enough so he can see.

He watches intently, holding his glass of scotch and taking an occasional sip. When it comes to that moment in the recording, his face drops, along with the glass. It hits the floor, but doesn't break, only spills the contents.

Al drops his head between his knees. "No. That can't be. It was a fucking gun."

"Listen to me, Al. These were some crazy motherfuckers. We got them recording the shooting of those officers on Twelfth and the other officer who was flat-out executed in his car."

"I shot a fucking little kid holding a cell phone. Why didn't he fucking drop it? I told him to drop it."

"Al, you might be okay on this," Leslie says.

"Okay? How the fuck am I gonna be okay?"

"There are several similar cases, and the officers didn't go to jail," Leslie says.

"It's all about your level of fear," I say. "In your head it was a gun. It was more than twenty yards away. The phone was black."

"It was a fucking cell phone. Clear as day on that video."

"We'll fight this, Al."

"No. Just get rid of the phone, and then we'll fight it."

"We can't do that," Leslie says. "This also involves those officers who were shot, two of them murdered."

"Leslie's right, Al. And I don't think you'll go to jail on this," I say.

"How the fuck do you know?"

"Remember the officer who shot the old man when he pulled out his wallet too fast?"

"Am I supposed to laugh?"

"You have Leslie. You're going to fight this. You're a good cop, a great detective with a perfect record. It probably won't even make it past the grand jury, after they see what Calvin and I saw on there. I couldn't even watch. Can you imagine how that's going to affect those civilians on the grand jury? Listen, I'm going to drop Calvin off and come back and stay here with you, brother."

"I don't need you to stay here."

Fucking worried he's gonna kill himself.

"You stay here with him, Leslie, all right? I have to get Calvin home."

"I'll wait for you."

Al doesn't say anything. He keeps his head tucked between his knees. I think he's sobbing.

I take Calvin home.

"I seen a lot of bad shootings on the TV," Calvin says in the car. "Lot of those cops get off."

"There are bad shootings. There are also justified shootings. I told you that before. Unless you walk in their shoes when it happens, you don't know shit."

"I didn't mean it like that."

"I'm not mad at you, man. We have a job, and you did good on this one."

"Working tomorrow, then?"

"I'll be here by eleven a.m."

He grabs his pack and steps out. He limps along the sidewalk. Must've been all that sitting.

Eighty-Two

I release the phone to Leslie so she can turn it over to Detective Rattan.

Al's reclined in the armchair, sleeping. Leslie put a blanket over him. I walk her to the door to let her out.

"He'll be okay."

"I know. He's got you." She wraps her arms around me, and I hug her back. She lets go.

"I'll be back tomorrow morning," she says.

"Okay. Good night."

"Good night."

I step out to the porch, watch her walk to her car parked across the street, get in, and start it. She waves, then pulls out and drives.

I shut the door and lock it behind me. Double-check to make sure.

I head to the living room, undress to my boxer shorts, T-shirt, and socks, sit on the sofa to finish my scotch.

I don't wake up to drool on the cushion and the side of my face, because I didn't sleep. Someone knocks on the door. I check the time.

Fucking 8:00 a.m.

Al's still sleeping. Snoring. I grab my pants, put them on and walk to the door, and look out the peephole. It's Leslie.

I unlock the door and let her in.

"It's like you just left," I say.

"That's how it works when you get older."

"I ain't old."

She takes her coat off, wraps it over a wooden chair.

"You call Detective Rattan?" I ask.

"Yes. I'm driving Al to VCU."

"I don't think it's called VCU anymore."

"I'm driving him there and giving her this phone. I will tell her it was turned over to you by a source, right?"

"Yeah, and I'm fucking gonna get that source to talk."

"That would work to your benefit. Wouldn't want them to think you got it some other way."

"I didn't, Leslie. That's the truth."

"I'm going to make coffee. You want some?"

"No. I'll get some on the way home. I need to change. Call me after you meet. Let me know."

"I will."

She goes into the kitchen to make coffee. I look at Al, still sleeping. Hope she lets him sleep for a while longer.

When I get home, I shower, shave, even brush my teeth. I dress in an older suit and finish my second cup of coffee, which doesn't do anything to perk me up.

When it's time, I make my way to pick up Calvin, double-park like I always do. He's not out like he usually is, though. I check the time. It's after eleven. I'll give him a few and then knock on his door.

A few minutes later his door opens, and Calvin steps out.

"Shit," I say to myself.

He's dressed in what looks like a tailored navy-blue suit, white shirt, dark-blue tie, and black overcoat. He's shouldering his pack.

He hustles to the car and gets in.

"Look at you. Fuck. You're the man."

"I ain't the man. I just got a good job and want to look the part."

"Well, that you do, partner."

He sits down.

"When did you get that?"

"Couple days ago. Just didn't feel comfortable wearing it for some reason, until now."

"You look damn good in it."

"I don't roll that way, so don't go thinking anything."

"Never crossed my mind."

"What do we got today?"

"Finish this job."

"Thought it was finished."

"No. Cordell sure as fuck ain't finished, and I don't know, but I'm thinking your pops might be okay with that."

"Hell, I know I'm good with that. Now more than ever."

We roll out. I slide down the window, get some of the cold winter air to slap my face. See if that works.

ACKNOWLEDGMENTS

Big thank-you to all the bookstores and libraries that have been there for me. There are too many to list, but I would like to give a special shout-out to my friends Eileen McGervey, Terry Nebeker, and Lelia Nebeker at One More Page Books in Arlington, Virginia, who were there from the start; Laurie Gillman at East City Bookshop, Washington, DC; everyone at Politics and Prose, Washington, DC; Kelly Justice at Fountain Bookstore, Richmond, Virginia; Otto Penzler and my rum buddy, Thomas Wickersham, at Mysterious Bookshop, New York City; my compadre in music, Patrick Millikin, at Poison Pen Bookstore, Scottsdale, Arizona; the man of mystery Scott Montgomery at Book People–Mystery People, Austin, Texas; Mystery Mike Bursaw and Virginia and John at VJ Books, on the Web.

A special thanks to my friend Jacques Filippi, who brought it all together for me in Quebec City, when Frank Marr was just an idea and I made it through my first panel; Bill Stankey, for all his encouragement throughout the years and for introducing me to Hunter S. Thompson; my Mulholland writing family, especially Chris (Cordell) Holm, Owen Laukkanen, Joe Ide, and William Shaw.

Thank you, Peggy Freudenthal, production editor at Litt Brown/Hachette Book Group, for cleaning up the books and viding such great copy editors.

Acknowledgments

For my brothers and sisters at the Metropolitan Police Department, Washington, DC, both active and retired. Stay safe and fight the good fight.

The Frank Marr trilogy would not exist if it were not for my incredible agents, Deborah Schneider and Jane Gelfman, and my equally incredible editor, Josh Kendall, at Mulholland Books, who knows Frank Marr as well as I do.

ABOUT THE AUTHOR

David Swinson is a retired police detective, having served sixteen years with the Washington, DC, Metropolitan Police Department. Before joining the DC police, Swinson was a record store owner in Seal Beach, California, a punk rock–alternative concert promoter in Long Beach, California, and a music video producer and independent filmmaker in Los Angeles. Swinson lives in northern Virginia with his wife, daughter, bullmastiff, and Staffordshire terrier.

You've turned the last page.

But it doesn't have to end there . . .